RAVEN SECURITIES
BOOK ONE

AIMEE NICOLE WALKER

www.aimeenicolewalker.com

Cover photo © Wander Aguiar – www.wanderaguiar.com
Cover design © Natasha Snow – www.natahashsnow.com
Interior design and formatting provided by Stacey Ryan Blake of Champagne Book Design – www.champagnebookdesign.com
Developmental edits provided by Charity VanHuss – vanhuss.charity@gmail.com
Copy edits provided by Sandra Dee of One Love Editing: www.oneloveediting.com
Proofreading provided by Lori Parks - lp.nerdproblems@gmail.com

STAND AND DELIVER

CHAPTER 1

ATTICUS

"I'M OFF," I SAID AS I BREEZED THROUGH THE KITCHEN. *OFF TO MEET A man and get fucked.*

And it was about damn time.

I made it as far as the exterior door in the utility room before I had to stop and retrace my steps. The parking situation was just one of many obstacles we'd had to overcome since I moved back in with my parents five months ago. We were always blocking one another since there was limited room in our driveway, and parking on the street was against the homeowner's association rules for our neighborhood. There went my simple escape.

Poking my head into the kitchen, I said, "Mom, could I ask you to move your car?"

She stood at the kitchen sink, staring out the window while she scrubbed a skillet she'd used to make dinner. And though her profile was to me, I recognized her dreamy smile and faraway expression. She might've been standing in the kitchen, but the audiobook she was listening to had transported her to another time and place. Everyone had their form of escapism, and the English lit teacher who raised me dove headfirst into her books.

My chosen escape for the evening hopefully involved a hunk of a man bending me over and railing me within an inch of my life, not that I would share that detail with my mother. And I was going to be late if I didn't get my squeaky-clean and smooth ass on the road.

"Mom," I said a little louder as I approached.

The scrubbing brush in her hand circled around and around, cleaning the same spot, as her grin grew broader and her cheeks turned pinker. Ahh, it was one of those types of books. Someone's bodice was ripping, and someone's codpiece was coming off. God, when had I even learned those terms, and how quickly could I forget them?

"Mom." She still hadn't heard me by the time I reached her side, so I gently touched her forearm to get her attention.

Big mistake.

Mom yelped in alarm as she dropped the scrubbing brush into the sink and swung that fucking skillet like a weapon. Unfortunately for me, she'd been cleaning the ancient cast-iron one she'd inherited from her grandmother. I ducked in the nick of time, and the heavy skillet swung over my head, close enough to ruffle my hair. The heavy bastard smashed into the front of the farmhouse sink with a reverberating *clang*.

My ears rang, and I labored to catch my breath as I slowly stood up, hands out in front of me in surrender. "I'm sorry," I said. "I didn't mean to scare you."

Mom winced as she placed the skillet on the counter, but I couldn't tell if it was because her ears were ringing like mine or if I'd yelled my apology because of temporary hearing loss. Mom pressed a hand to her chest, heaving a sigh, and that's when one of her AirPods flew from her ear and landed in the dirty water.

"Fuck a duck!" Mom yelled. "That's the second AirPod I've lost this week." Growling, she reached down into the water and fished it out. "At least these new ones are water-resistant. No harm, no foul. But the other poor bastard fell into the garbage disposal while I was using it."

Temporarily stunned, I could only stare at my mother in shock.

She arched a brow and asked, "What? You act as if you've never heard me cuss."

"I've never heard you say 'fuck' before," I replied. "And I've certainly never heard you make a bestiality reference." Cocking my head to the side, I added, "But I think I finally have an answer to a lifelong question."

Mom crossed her arms over her chest and grinned. "And what's that?"

"My chaotic clumsiness comes from your side of the family."

Her mouth popped open in outrage, but no denial passed her lips. The longer I thought about it, the more I knew I was onto something. My mother was the epitome of ladylike grace until something or someone startled her, hence my deeply ingrained muscle memory that had prevented a concussion or worse. Mom must've realized how close I'd come to getting injured, too, because she slapped a hand over her mouth and cried out. Hazel-brown eyes, so much like my own, widened in regret as tears filled them.

"I'm so sorry," she said, the words muffled by her hand.

Wrapping her in a hug, I kissed Mom's cheek. "I'm the one who's sorry. I know better than to interrupt your one-on-one time with a book. That must be some story you're listening to. You blushed, you swooned, and you nearly brained your only son."

She snorted, and we both laughed at the ridiculousness of the situation. This was the lightest my soul had felt since moving back home with my heart in tatters and my tail tucked between my legs.

Mom inhaled to catch her breath and patted my chest. "What did you want to ask me?"

"When I so rudely interrupted your book, you mean?" Shaking my head, I dropped my arms and stepped back. "I bet the Braves will call you up any minute, Slugger. You'd make a great pinch hitter."

"Oh, hush." Mom turned back to cleaning the skillet. "Seriously, what did you need?"

Shit! I'd nearly forgotten in all the excitement. "Can you move your car? I want to head out for a bit."

Mom looked at me with a raised eyebrow. "Are you meeting someone?" The hopefulness in her voice was unmistakable, and I needed to frame my response carefully.

"I am, but it's not for a date."

And it wasn't a lie. I'd met a hot guy named Ray on the newest gay hookup app called Randy, and he was very clear about his intentions. He wanted to fuck. A one and done. That's what I wanted too, but I didn't want to share that with the woman who raised me.

"Oh, darn. You deserve happiness, Kit," Mom said, her eyes going soft and dreamy. "Someone who will treat you right. An epic romance."

Yep, Valerie Livengood was still fully entrenched in the fictional world I'd rudely crashed. While she had hearts in her eyes, imagining a fairy-tale romance for her baby boy, I wanted Ray to plow my ass until I came hard enough to see stars. But again, that was TMI for my sweet mother. She was my biggest ally and supporter, but that didn't mean she wanted to know how gay sex worked or what I preferred from a sex partner.

"Thanks, Mom."

"Just take my car. I don't need it tonight."

The offer was sweet and shocking. The sleek, sporty sedan with more horsepower than one person needed was the first thing she'd ever bought just for herself. Dad had teased that he was the one who was supposed to go out and buy a fast car during a midlife crisis, and she'd called the purchase an empty-nest gift to herself. Hell, she'd seldom let Dad drive her precious baby, but Mom offered it to me without hesitation. Me, the chaotic klutz. Was this an act of pity for her dateless, twenty-six-year-old son? Did I want to stand around and ponder the reason, or did I want to accept her kind offer and get on the road? *Asshole to Atticus, we want fucked?* The latter, definitely.

"Thanks, I'll drive carefully." I bussed a kiss across her cheek before darting out of the kitchen.

Our key chains hung from an organizer in the shape of a wooden key by the utility room door, and I grabbed Mom's fob on my way out. "Sorry, Sadie," I called out to my fifteen-year-old, once-silver Subaru hatchback parked in front of my mother's black beauty. Sadie had once belonged to Mom during her sensible, family-car days. She'd bought a new Subaru hatchback and had given her old one to me when I got my license. I've adored Sadie ever since, and the two of us had seen some shit over the past ten years. I paused at the driver's-side door of the sleek black ride. "It's nothing personal, sweetheart. I'll never love this car like I love you."

Sliding behind the wheel, I pressed the button to start the engine, and it roared to life with a throaty purr. Loud music immediately assaulted my ears, and I reached for the volume before my brain could figure out what radio station my mom had been listening to when she'd last driven. It was a song from one of the rock-and-roll hair bands of the eighties where the gravel-throated singer belted out a ballad about unrequited love. As I reached for the gearshift to reverse out of the driveway, the car radio connected to my mom's phone, and a man's husky voice came through the speakers.

"I sank my dick into the sweetest, tightest ass I'd ever known."

My eyes nearly popped out of my head when a new voice, also male, moaned as if he would happily die on the dick splitting him open.

Then the first guy spoke again. "*'That's right, baby. Take it. Take all of me like a good little—'*"

The rock ballad blared through the speakers again, making me flinch. What the hell had just happened? Was my mom listening to a gay romance? Too stunned to move, I stared into space long enough for her to poke her head out of the utility room door and mouth "sorry" at me. I waved her away and eased my foot off the brake, carefully reversing out of the driveway and onto the street after checking both directions twice.

Still shook from what I'd overheard, my heart pounded as the narrator's growly voice echoed through my skull. Take all of him like a good little… what? My mind spun with possibilities as I shifted my foot from the brake to the gas pedal. Mom's car shot forward as if blasted from a cannon, and I eased up on the accelerator. Whoops! Sadie required a much heavier foot to go half as fast. Must've experienced those twin turbos Mom kept talking about when she'd bought the car. I stopped at the next intersection to get my racing heart and hormones under control. The only thing I wanted to wreck was my ass, definitely not my mom's pride and joy.

Get it together, Atticus.

I paused at the intersection at the end of the street to blast the air-conditioning, though my heated skin had little to do with the weather. Spring was my favorite time of year in Georgia. The mid-April sun was warm, even flirting with hot on some days, but the humidity had yet to grip the city by the short and curlies. Anticipation was what rode me hard and made me sweat, just like I hoped Ray would after we got the preliminaries out of the way. He'd suggested we meet in public to make sure I felt safe, which I appreciated, but I didn't want to stay there long. I had big ideas prompted by the few photos he'd uploaded to the Randy app. The images showcased a gorgeous man with brown hair, a neatly trimmed goatee-mustache combo, and the most beautiful blue eyes I'd ever seen.

Not light, not dark, but a medium blue that made me think of vintage blue jeans. His irises had captivated me so much that I'd immediately paused my perusal to look up the shades of denim to find one that matched. Lobelia. And then I'd returned to his photos and forced myself to notice something else about the man, since fixating on his eye color wasn't something you did with a random hookup. It was better to focus on the parts of Ray that mattered most, but he didn't include *those* photos. Not even a shot of himself in tight underwear that showed off a hint of his cum gutters. Hell, Ray wore a simple black tank top and a pair of jeans in a boring shade of blue in every photo. But he was still the hottest guy I'd ever seen, and I nearly sprained my finger when I swiped to match him.

The way he filled out his tank top and jeans should be criminal. Ray's body was impressively large, likely everywhere, and what skin he'd revealed featured lots of sexy tattoos. I hadn't known ink was my kink until I couldn't stop staring at the work of art he'd made of his body. I wanted to take my time to study each piece, but that wasn't what either of us agreed to, so I vowed to be cool once I got him naked. Christ, was I really going to go through with this? Meet a total stranger and present my ass to him like it was no big deal?

Hell-fucking-yes, I was.

Vibrating with excitement, I took a deep breath to calm down before lightly pressing the accelerator again. I zipped through the intersection and forced myself to concentrate on the short drive from my parents' house in Kirkwood to the trendy uptown section of Columbus. Ray had suggested we meet at the Uptown Tap, a trendy new bar near the Chattahoochee RiverWalk. Even though it wasn't a date, Ray had been sure to remind me, he thought it would be a good way to break the ice. Ray gave me the impression he was a little rusty with hookups, which suited me fine since I'd never had one. My first-timer status became painfully obvious in the first message I sent after we matched, asking, *So, how does this work?*

Ray's response had been swift and blunt. *Don't know. I think we meet somewhere and fuck.*

We then traded some messages about where and when to meet, always reiterating that it wasn't a date, and that we wouldn't hook up more than once. The entire exchange had seemed like a lot of drawn-out work to me. Random hookups by definition implied something that happened quickly and without a lot of planning, but Ray and I had taken three weeks to work out the logistics. Was he married and looking for some action? Did he travel for work? Was he a fish out of water like me? Couldn't be. I'd seen his picture. There was no way in hell people weren't launching themselves at him everywhere he went. I nearly jumped the curb when I thought about his thick thighs and that delicious bulge at his crotch. Oh, the things I wanted Ray to do to me.

It was at that unfortunate moment that my brain replayed the snippet from my mom's audiobook, and I imagined presenting my ass to Ray, who would growl, *"That's right, baby. Take it. Take all of me like a good little—"*

Slut. I'd be a total slut for Ray.

A police siren sounded behind me, and I checked the rearview mirror.

Sure enough, a cruiser was directly behind me with its red and blue lights flashing. Fuck. Me. A glance at the clock told me I had ten minutes until I was supposed to meet Ray. How long would a traffic stop take? Should I message Ray and let him know I was running behind? I reached for my phone but thought better of it. Would the officer walk up to my window and think I'd been texting and driving? It was better to be late for my hookup than end up with a steeper fine.

A knock sounded on my window, and I turned my head to smile at the officer. The scowl on her face said this encounter wouldn't be fast or cheap.

Fuck a duck.

The Uptown Tap was in full swing when I walked in. I scanned the crowd but didn't find anyone matching Ray's photos or an empty table. A hostess approached the podium and greeted me with warm eyes and a friendly smile.

"Meeting someone?" she asked.

"Um, yeah, but I don't see him yet."

Hell, I was only seven minutes late. Surely, Ray hadn't given up already and left. Damn it. I should've messaged him while I was waiting for the officer to run my license.

"It's practically standing room only in here. I'm Hannah, by the way."

"Atticus," I replied.

"As in Finch?"

I suppressed both a groan and surprise that she knew the reference, since *To Kill a Mockingbird* topped the list of books people wanted to ban in schools, much to my mother's chagrin. And it was never fun for me to share the same name as a fictional character that some people revered and others loathed. Luckily, I had a hundred and one nicknames that usually spared me from having this conversation. Too bad I hadn't used one of them.

Smiling, I said, "My mom is an English lit teacher who loves the classics. I have an older sister named Tess."

"Ah, Durbeyfield."

"Wow. I can't believe you know the reference." Hannah was probably a few years younger than me, and I didn't know many college-aged people who could name Atticus Finch, let alone Tess Durbeyfield.

"I'm majoring in English lit too, but I want to be a writer instead of a teacher," Hannah said.

"I should get you to sign something for me so I'll have it when you become famous."

Hannah smiled brightly and shook her head. "As if."

A small group in the far-right corner of the bar slid from a booth and headed our way. "Can I have their table?" The spot had the perfect view of the entrance, and I could sit and drink something cool while I waited for Ray to arrive.

"Sure," Hannah said. "Let me go wipe it down really quick."

I checked my phone to see if there was a new notification from the Randy app, but there wasn't. Wait. Had I turned on the notifications for the app? I thought I had, but maybe I'd accidentally turned them off? I tapped the unassuming *R* icon and pulled up the message thread I'd had with Ray. Nothing new from him, so maybe he was just running late too. But I couldn't ignore the tingling sensation in my scalp, a Spidey sense that my evening might not turn out the way I'd hoped.

Wait. That was it? I was just going to give up?

I typed out a quick message, letting Ray know I'd arrived and grabbed a table for us. Then I sent a follow-up message letting him know where our table was. And then I reached out again to let him know that Hannah, the hostess and future best-selling author, knew where to find me. What was wrong with me? That was two, maybe three messages too many, and why would Ray care about Hannah's career ambitions? But once I started, I couldn't seem to stop myself. I typed, *looking forward to seeing you.*

Jesus. Desperate much? Yes! Yes, I was. But if I were Ray, I'd tuck tail and run.

Closing out of the app, I tucked my phone away in time to see Hannah waving me back to the table. I took a deep breath and willed my nerves away. This was a big—huge—step for me after a devastating breakup that upended my world, and I was just nervous. Everything would be okay. Ten minutes later, I repeated the little mantra when Ray still hadn't shown up or responded to my messages. I reread every word we'd exchanged to make sure I had the date and time correct, then did an internet search to see if there were any other bars with similar names. There weren't. I was where we'd agreed to be when we were supposed to meet. I waited another thirty minutes before forcing myself to accept reality.

Ray wasn't coming.

The truth echoed in my brain, and disappointment flooded my system. Then I somehow heard the soft chime over the pounding of my bruised heart and the din of rowdy conversations all around me. I had a new notification. I knew what it was, or rather *who* it was, just as I knew what the message would say. But I checked the screen anyway. Yep. There was a new message waiting for me in the Randy app. Disappointment twisted my gut as I read the words Ray had written.

Sorry. Had an emergency at work and won't be able to make it.

Ray hadn't suggested we meet at a different time, so I didn't either. In fact, I didn't respond to him at all. I held up my hand to flag a server, then placed an order for smoked brisket nachos. Might as well get some pleasure out of the night.

CHAPTER 2

RAYDEN

"An old folks' home isn't what I had in mind when we started our security company." Archer's Texas roots became more prominent whenever his emotions soared high or his energy sank low, so that Monday morning, he sounded closer to Matthew McConaughey than Glen Powell on the scale of Texan twang.

I glanced over at the passenger seat, where my best friend and one of my four business partners flipped through the dossier I'd memorized weeks before our first day on the job. "Silver Maple isn't an old folks' home," I replied. "It's—"

"Premier living for the wealthiest retirees, not only in Green Island Hills, or even Georgia, but the entire country. I can read too, Hawk," Archer replied dryly. He was really annoyed if he'd reverted to using the call sign I'd earned during our Army Ranger days.

"Never said you couldn't, buddy."

"Sorry." Archer heaved a sigh. "I'm just tired."

Resisting a snort, I said, "Yeah, I ran into your latest conquest in the hallway when he left your apartment this morning." The handsome brunet guy with dark brown bedroom eyes had been all dreamy smiles in the elevator.

"Shit," Archer grumbled. "He asked if he could see me again before he left."

I grimaced and sucked air through my teeth. "Did you forget to give him 'the speech' before sex or—"

"You know damn well I didn't forget." Archer's snappish reply had enough bite to leave a bruise. "I always make sure a guy knows the score before I take them home with me. He seemed down with just hooking up, but I'm not so sure now."

I couldn't resist a snort this time.

Archer slapped my thigh with the folder. "Cut it out. You sound like my mom's pug when she sucks something up her nose."

There were far worse things than being compared to Maggie Mae, the pampered pug, but Archer sounded proud of the insult, so I let it go. Besides, I had something much better to wind him up about. "I think you're going to have trouble avoiding your newest friend. It seems you've made quite an impression on him, and I bet you don't even remember his name."

"Of course I do."

"Okay, what is it, then?" I pressed.

"It's Jason, Jack, or possibly Jared. Definitely a name that starts with a *J*. Mostly, I just said Jesus a lot. Man, the stamina on that guy is something else. He made me feel like I was twenty all over again." Then Archer yawned like someone much older than our thirty-five years.

Biting my bottom lip to keep from laughing, I turned onto Silver Maple's tree-lined drive. The vibrant pink blooms and paver tiles stretched ahead of me for as far as the eye could see, offering a glimpse of the expansive, lush green lawn beyond the colorful border.

"Sure is pretty back here," I said. "Are these silver maple trees?"

"Not even close," replied Archer, who came from a long line of landscapers and arborists. "These are crape myrtles. You can't imagine the amount of work that goes into maintaining a driveway to this standard, and a person could retire on the amount of money spent on the pavers used in this driveway. Slow down and look at the intricate pattern."

I'd already dropped my speed to twenty miles per hour, but I eased off the gas even more.

"See that?" Archer asked. "They used four different shades of gray to give it richer texture and dimension. Only people with expendable money care about details like this."

"It's nice."

"Nice?" Archer sounded appalled and annoyed by my blasé response.

"Look, I appreciate the craftsmanship that went into this installation," I said. "Just not as much as you. Where I come from, people use gravel, asphalt, or concrete for their driveways. We don't care about parking our vehicles on texture and dimension."

"You're such a basic Florida bitch," Archer said, his twang now sounding more cunty than country.

"Texan snob," I shot back. "And his name is Bobby."

Archer's head snapped in my direction. "Who?"

"Your hookup from last night. He introduced himself to me this morning." I didn't bother hiding my glee when I grinned at Archer. "I introduced myself as your best friend, and sweet Bobby said he looked forward to getting to know me better."

"Fuck. Fuck. Fuck."

"Yeah, I think that's what got you into this problem," I said. "Your hookups rarely stick around until sunrise, so you must've shown Bobby some extra attention."

"I already mentioned his stamina, but I didn't tell you about his incredible hands. Oh, and he does this thing with his mouth. I—"

Raising my hand to cut him off, I said, "Don't want to hear the details."

"Prude."

"Not even close," I said.

"Okay, you've turned into a monk, then."

The accusation hit closer to home than I liked, so I leveled Archer with a dark glower. My best friend had the good grace to look sorry. He knew damn well why I'd chosen celibacy, even if he didn't agree with me. Archer thought it was beyond time for me to put myself out there again, and so did our other friends.

"I'm sorry, Hawk." Archer's voice jolted me back to reality, and I was relieved to see I hadn't veered off the driveway. "You'll be ready when you're ready."

And the thing was, I'd tried.

Almost two months ago, I signed up for that stupid Randy app—who named this shit—and had even matched with Atticus, a gorgeous man who made me feel things I'd thought were impossible. It took me three weeks to stop jerking off to his pictures long enough to arrange for a meetup. I'd been very explicit about not looking for a date, and Atticus had claimed to feel the same way. I'd gotten the impression that he was newly single or possibly a virgin because Atticus had seemed as clueless as I'd been about how these things were supposed to go down.

Go down. Mmmm. Atticus had the prettiest mouth I'd ever seen, with a well-defined cupid's bow and a full lower lip made for nibbling. I'd really wanted to see my cock sliding through his parted—

"Do you forgive me?"

Archer's question jolted me out of my fantasy, and I jerked my head in his direction. His soulful green eyes could get Archer out of trouble nearly as fast as he found it. I was no more immune to his puppy-dog expression now than I was when we met at ranger school thirteen years ago, so I let him believe I would someday be whole enough and brave enough to risk my heart again. Hell, I'd reached the point in grieving where I needed to believe there was more for me too. I just wasn't ready to say it out loud, not after I fucked things up with Atticus.

It had been a month since I lied to him about having a work emergency. I'd been sitting in my truck when Atticus had whipped a shiny sedan into the parking deck closest to the Uptown Tap. I watched him park, check his teeth in the rearview mirror, and test his breath. I couldn't tear my eyes off Atticus when he climbed out of the car and hurried toward the bar, nearly colliding with someone in his haste to meet me. I'd wanted to get out of my truck and follow him, but fear had a death grip on my heart. I couldn't move and barely breathed as my mind replayed all the reasons why it wasn't a good idea for me to ever love someone again. No matter how many times I told myself it was only a hookup, my heart didn't believe it. I just wasn't built that way. So, I tried my damnedest not to picture his face when I finally freed myself from the crippling fear long enough to tell Atticus I wasn't coming.

I'd spent the past thirty days dreading my choice and not knowing how to fix it. I'd pulled up the Randy app the next morning, intending to apologize and probably to jack off to his thirst traps, but our chat was gone. Atticus had deleted his profile altogether, and that had made me feel even worse. Guilt and remorse had been my constant companions, and I was sick of their company. But what could I do? I'd only communicated with Atticus through the app, so I didn't have his phone number or email.

Yes, I had access to one hell of a search engine through the security company I co-owned. I could learn just about anything I wanted about

Atticus, but tracking him down that way felt like predatory behavior. If Atticus had wanted me to have his personal information, he would've given it to me. Fuck, I just wanted to apologize and maybe explain what had happened so he would know it had nothing to do with him. And I really wanted to know the color of his eyes. They looked brown in some photos and green in others. Did he wear colored contacts? Or maybe his irises changed depending on his mood, the lighting, or the color of clothes he wore. I nearly snorted. Atticus had worn very little in the photos he uploaded to Randy, so I discounted that. I'd heard of mood rings, but I'd never heard of mood irises. I nearly dismissed that too, but decided to look it up later. Color contacts seemed like the logical answer, but what was his true color? Brown or green?

"Hawk?" Archer prompted. "Are we good?"

"Of course. Sorry, I zoned out on you. My mind has already shifted to work stuff." The lie rolled too easily off my tongue, but Archer would never ease up if he knew I was obsessing over a near hookup. "The Silver Maple account is the biggest thing to ever happen to us, and I really want to get it right."

"And we will."

Archer assessed me with an eagle-like intensity, like maybe he wanted to say more, but we'd reached the elaborate wrought-iron gates and the fancy guard shack that one of their employees from RAVEN Securities would assume responsibilities for within the hour. They just needed to have the official change-of-guard meeting with the executive director. I rolled down my window and showed my badge to the ruddy-faced security guard with frosty blue eyes.

"Rayden James and Archer Stone from RAVEN Securities to meet with Caitlyn Juniper."

The guy made a big production of scanning the list as if he didn't know this was his last morning at this location. "Ah, here it is," he said, returning my badge. "You're listed as the soul-crushing bastards who are ruining my life."

I'd expected the outgoing security team to be pissed, but his vehemence caught me off guard. It sounded like he was losing his job, not just getting relocated. While I empathized with his situation, I wasn't about to engage with the man and blow our opportunity. "Open the gates," I snarled.

"Not until I have my say," the guard said, leaning out the window and jabbing a finger in my direction. "I'm out of a job after today because of you. I have two kids in college, with no idea how I'm going to continue paying for their tuition. My wife has cried herself to sleep every night for the past week. Maybe you two aren't personally responsible for ruining our lives, but someone needs to hear it."

He was out of a job because his company did a piss-poor job of providing the most basic security services to Silver Maple, and the board and management team were fed up with it. Telling the guard that wouldn't get them anywhere fast, so I bit my tongue.

But Archer leaned forward to lock gazes with the guard, and I braced myself for whatever might come out of his mouth. Loose cannon was too mild a descriptor. "If I were you, I'd open that gate. Or my friend can storm the booth and open the motherfucking thing himself. Look at his size. He makes the Terminator seem puny. Go ahead, make his day, asshole."

The security guard's gaze swung back to me, and he assessed me with an audible gulp. My size alone usually intimidated most people, but I'd perfected a scowl that deterred even the bravest souls. Realizing my sunglasses shielded him from the full effect, I pushed the shades down my nose and put three years of frustration and misery into an icy glare. "Make the right choice," I said, keeping my voice low, deadly, and cold.

With a nod, the security guard pushed the button to open the gates. "I had my say, and that's all I wanted."

I rolled up my window and hit the gas. From my periphery, I saw Archer fish out his phone and text rapidly.

"Are you letting Vaughn know about our frosty reception?" I asked. "Tell him I'm going to do a thorough inspection to ensure these guys didn't sabotage any of the equipment out of spite."

"Maybe I'm arranging my next hookup," Archer teased.

"Oh, please. You still haven't wiped the grin off your face from last night," I replied. "Bobby might've made you feel twenty-five, but you're not. You'll probably need three nights of rest before you seduce your next conquest."

Archer sighed and stowed his phone away. "I can't help but feel a little sorry for that security guard, but people pay a fuck ton of money to live here, and they deserve good security. Did you see the six-figure amount the residents paid to reserve a spot at Silver Maple?"

"Yep. I memorized every word in the dossier." My shoulders had tightened during the confrontation with the security guard, and I rolled them to loosen the muscles.

"What's wrong?" Archer asked.

"Something is making me feel edgy," I admitted.

"A disturbance in the Force?" Archer had meant the question as a joke, but it was spot-on.

"Yeah, but I can't put my finger on it."

My friend snorted. "Pretty sure you wrap four fingers and a thumb on your problem multiple times a week."

Groaning, I killed the engine and opened the car door. "Shut up."

"Seriously," Archer said as he scrambled after me. "I know you're not ready for a relationship yet, man, but you really need to get laid. The hand shandy only gets you so far. Sometimes you need someone else to touch your dick."

"I'll think about it." But I wouldn't. The tragic end of my last relationship still haunted me, and I wasn't ready to risk my heart again.

"Really?" Archer's footsteps grew louder as he hastened to catch up to me. "No-strings sex could give you a new lease on life. It doesn't have to be with a different rando each time. I know that's never been your style."

And it never would be.

"What about friends with benefits?" Archer asked. "You could meet someone you like spending time with who also gets your blood pumping."

"That sounds like a relationship to me."

"Not if both parties set clear boundaries," Archer replied.

I was just about to remind him how well that had worked out for him the previous evening when a tall, auburn-haired woman in an ivory pantsuit stepped out of the administration building. Her glossy pink lips curved into a welcoming smile as she extended her hand to me.

"Good morning, I'm Caitlyn Juniper, the executive director at Silver Maple."

"Rayden James," I said, "and this is Archer Stone."

She shifted her attention to my friend and nearly swooned from the dazzling smile he gave her. Caitlyn held Archer's hand longer than was polite, then blushed hotly when she realized it. Releasing him, she cleared her throat. "We're happy to have you both here," Caitlyn said. "Can I interest either of you in coffee or pastries before we get started?"

I said "no" at the same time Archer replied "yes."

My friend unleashed his trademark puppy-dog expression on me, and I capitulated without a fight.

"I brought over a nice selection from the dining room for you to enjoy," Caitlyn said as she gestured toward the admin building. "And afterward, I'll give you a tour of the facility and grounds."

"Sounds perfect," Archer said as he followed Caitlyn. He looked over his shoulder at me and whispered, "We'll continue our conversation later."

The hell we would.

CHAPTER 3

ATTICUS

I AM NOT A FUCKUP. I AM NOT A FUCKUP. I AM NOT A FUCKUP.

I repeated the mantra as I left my childhood bedroom and headed downstairs. I'd almost convinced myself it was true as I neared the first floor. Was I quirky? Yes. Chaotic with a chance of klutzy? Abso-fucking-lutely. Which was why I needed to pay closer attention to my foot placement on the stairs to avoid an unfortunate accident. *Especially on this day, of all days.* People were counting on me to be at my best, specifically my Aunt Ronni, who'd stuck her neck out to land me a job when everyone else viewed me as a bad risk. And could I blame them?

Not even a little.

Things had ended abruptly and messily at my previous job, thanks to a broken heart and poor impulse control. But that was then. My new job as Silver Maple's activities coordinator was the fresh start I needed, and I intended to give it my all. Because I was not a fuckup. My heart was almost always in the right place, even when things went a little…sideways. *But not today.* I would make my aunt proud. No, I would make myself proud as I took bold steps toward true independence. And while I was envisioning a better future, maybe I could manifest a sexy man who wouldn't stand me up at a bar.

Damn you, Ray.

I'd deleted the stupid Randy app, but I hadn't been able to forget the man. Why? We'd barely chatted while planning the hookup he'd so easily blown off a month ago. What was it about Ray that had captured my attention so thoroughly? Just thinking about him made me miss the next step, and the room swayed as I pitched forward. Luckily, I caught myself on the handrail before I tumbled the rest of the way down the staircase. Phew! That was close. I stopped to catch my breath and get my racing heart under control before I took the final few steps. My near fall wasn't an omen for how the rest of my day would turn out. Huh-uh. I just needed coffee, and everything would be fine.

I registered the hum of low voices as I reached the first floor and realized my parents hadn't left for work yet. I stepped into the kitchen with a cheery "Good morn—"

"Atticus!" Mom shrieked. She'd had her back turned toward me but still snapped her robe closed. The thin fabric did nothing to hide the fact that my dad's hands were still gripping her ass.

"Good morning, son." Dad slowly retracted his arms from beneath Mom's robe, but I noticed he kept her body in front of him. I didn't want to think too hard about what Mom shielded from my view. "What are you doing here?"

"I moved back in six months ago," I reminded him. "I arrived on your doorstep, jobless and homeless. Ring a bell?" There were other adjectives ending in *-less*, but there was no need to pile on and feel even lower than I already did.

Dad huffed and rolled his eyes. "I'd thought you left for work already. You're usually gone before I come downstairs."

"I completed my training, so I don't need to go in as early now."

Mom whirled around and greeted me with a forced smile as she clutched the top of her robe with one hand and tidied her mussed hair with the other. The beard burns on her pale neck from Dad's morning scruff were impossible to miss. She'd need to wear concealer to work unless she wanted the high school kids to eat her alive. "Today's the big day," Mom said. "Are you excited?"

"Yes, but I'm a little nervous too."

Crossing the room, Dad ruffled my hair like I was a little boy again. "You're going to do great."

"Thank you," I said.

Dad checked his watch and sighed. "Guess I'd best get ready for work too."

My parents exchanged soft words and a lip-smacking kiss before Dad padded out of the room, whistling as he went. I looked through the coffee selection, settling on crème brûlée. I popped the pod into the coffeepot and started the brew before turning to the refrigerator to get the half-and-half. But once I opened the door, I just kind of zoned out. What was it I needed? Not breakfast. My stomach was way too nervous for that. I wasn't sure if it was the splattering liquid or my mother's sharp inhale that made me realize I hadn't set a cup in the tray to catch the drip.

Spinning around, I jabbed my finger into the power button to cut off the stream of coffee. "I am such a fuckup."

Mom was immediately beside me with a wad of paper towels. "Honey, take a few deep breaths. There's no crying over a little spilled coffee."

I took the paper towels and had begun to mop up my mess when the coffeepot belched a puff of steam and dribbled hot liquid on my hand. I hissed and jerked back, more irritated than hurt.

"Let me see," Mom said, reaching for my hand.

"It's fine," I told her.

"You better run it under cold water to be safe."

I'd taken weeks of first-aid training to qualify for my activity's coordinator certification, and I knew my slightly pink skin wouldn't even classify as a burn. I still did as Mom suggested while she assumed cleanup duties.

"At least I didn't get coffee all over my pressed polo shirt."

Silver Maple had provided T-shirts for me to wear during training but had upgraded my wardrobe now that it was time for me to assume the role of coordinator from Cammy, who'd just started six months of maternity leave. The polos had smelled funny when I'd taken them out of the plastic, so I'd run them through the washer and dryer with the rest of my clothes. Big mistake. It had taken me a ridiculously long time to iron one shirt, so I hadn't started on the others yet. Thank goodness I wouldn't have to wear one of the wrinkled polos.

"Do you have tips on how I can minimize the wrinkles to make ironing time faster?" I asked.

"My first piece of advice is to use my fancy steamer system instead of the ironing board and iron."

I turned off the water and dried my hands. "Now you tell me."

She huffed out a short laugh. "I'm an avid reader, Atticus, but that doesn't include minds. You could've asked me for tips before you ironed your shirt. I'm guessing you don't have a backup?"

"No," I admitted ruefully. Wrinkle-free clothes weren't the only thing I'd failed to plan for, hence the reason I stood in my parents' kitchen, feeling like a kid who'd waited until the last minute to complete an important school assignment. I reminded myself to focus on one catastrophe at a time. The wrinkled clothes were something I could fix relatively easily, or so my mother had implied. Scraping together the funds to get my own place? Not so much. "Can you show me how to use your steamer tonight?"

"Of course."

"We have that dinner party at the Masons' house," Dad reminded her as he returned to the kitchen, looking handsome in pale gray slacks, a white dress shirt, and a blue tie. "The school board members will be there, and I'd like to gauge their temperature on naming me as the superintendent of schools."

"You're the perfect candidate for the job, Steven," my mother said.

And he was, but my dad had made himself irreplaceable as a principal. Under his leadership, the high school faculty had won nearly every type of achievement they could receive, including prestigious national math and science recognitions. Every graduation class under his tenure had earned millions in scholarship prizes for college. Why would the board mess with that kind of success? They wouldn't, but Dad hadn't accepted that very real truth.

Mom turned to me. "The steamer is in my arts and crafts room." Aka Tess's former bedroom. My sister had barely finished college and moved into her own place before Mom reclaimed the room as her own. Why hadn't she done the same with my old bedroom? Had a part of her known my ass would be back? "I'll get out the owner's manual for you, and I'm sure you can find YouTube videos if you run into trouble."

"Good thing you moved back home when you did," Dad teased with a grin. "I'd had big ideas for your old bedroom, and it wasn't the home library your mom wanted." He waggled his eyebrows suggestively at my mom, and she giggled as she swatted his arm.

"Behave, Steven."

What had gotten into them? I couldn't remember my parents acting this frisky when I was younger, or perhaps I'd just been too innocent to recognize the signs. I'd have to wear my earbuds around the house to block out the innuendo, though that wouldn't protect my eyes from seeing things no child should, no matter their age. Fighting off a shudder, I pulled out a mug from the cabinet and gave the coffee thing another go.

"Hope you both have a great day," Dad called over his shoulder on his way out the door.

Mom leaned against the counter and looked at me. "He didn't mean it, Atticus."

Exhaling my frustration, I gave her a crooked smile. "He doesn't want me to have a good day?"

"Don't be silly," she said. "Neither one of us had designs on your old bedroom, unless it was to make it a more generic space for guests. Not sure the leftover Zac Efron and Harry Styles posters from your teen years are the aesthetics we'd want for our visitors." She winked and kissed my cheek. "We're happy to have you home again. We didn't get to see much of you after you moved in with…" Her voice had trailed off because she didn't like saying my ex-boyfriend's name.

"Chad's not a demon you will summon just by saying his name, Mom."

She snorted and rolled her eyes. "Are you so sure about that? He's been just as destructive to your life as a demon possession would be. That asshole called the house for you over the weekend while you were out."

"What did he want?"

She shrugged. "For you to unblock his number and call him back. I told him to go fuck himself and to lose our number too."

I laughed and pulled her into a tight hug. "You're the best." Having my parents' support meant the world to me, but I had to be honest with myself and them if I hoped to put the shattered pieces of my life back together. "While it's true Chad wrecked our relationship by cheating on me, the disastrous professional fallout that came afterward was all my fault. I could've handled things…"

Differently? Better? Maturely? By not having a meltdown that involved every single person at the cyber engineering firm where we worked? By not ruining my reputation and getting blackballed from even the most menial positions in my field?

"Smarter," I finally said. "But this opportunity at Silver Maple feels like the chance I need to get myself back on the right track."

"I have to admit I was a little concerned when Aunt Ronni pitched the idea," Mom said. Her doubt dimmed my excitement, and I tried to hide my frown by taking a sip of coffee, but an eagle-eyed teacher doesn't miss much.

"I just don't think you know what you're getting yourself into," she said with a slow shake of her head. "Those residents are going to take advantage of you just like schoolkids do with their substitute teachers."

That was the last thing I expected her to say. "I've been training two months for this position." I'd attended classes for a month to get certified and shadowed Cammy for four weeks while she showed me the ropes. "The residents have been very respectful and welcoming."

"Because you've never tried to instruct them by yourself." She narrowed her eyes and said, "Are you responsible for taking them on day trips too?"

I swallowed hard to dislodge the ball of dread stuck in my throat. "Sometimes, but there's nothing on the schedule for a while."

"You're going to need lots of volunteers to ensure no one runs off. You'll wish you had eyes in the back of your head."

My pulse accelerated like a racehorse thundering down the track. "Mom, you're freaking me out."

"Sorry," she said, shaking her head. "I was having flashbacks to my early days of teaching when sub work was all I could find."

"That was almost thirty years ago."

She held up a finger and said, "One, never remind me how old I am." Then she raised a second finger. "Be wary that I still get triggered when talking about my days in the trenches after all this time."

Had I bitten off more than I could chew? Could I manage the interests and activities for the extensive Silver Maple community? The largest and rowdiest focus group were the active seniors from the independent-living villas, but I also needed to enrich the lives of those residing in the assisted-care buildings. Then there was the state-of-the-art memory care unit where activity and stimulation was a necessity, not just a luxury. And I'd be doing it by myself as of today. Alarm bells went off in my head. *Danger! Danger! Danger!*

"Oh, honey." Mom gripped my biceps, and the pressure jerked me out of my panic. I realized the beeping was the alarm on her watch. She patted my cheek and smiled. "You're going to do great." She turned off the alarm with a resigned sigh. "Summer vacation can't get here fast enough." Mom pulled me into a quick hug and kissed my cheek. "Knock 'em dead, honey." Then she cringed. "Oh, that's wildly inappropriate. Um, break a leg doesn't sound good either."

I waved her off with a laugh. "I appreciate the sentiment."

Lingering around the house would lead to distractions that would make me late for work, so I transferred my coffee to a travel mug and headed out the door to my sweet ole Sadie. Time had taken a toll on Sadie's paint job, so I'd spiffed her up with bumper stickers when I was in high school. The look had been cute when I was a kid, but it would not help me get laid as a grown-ass adult. My girl was reliable, and that meant more to me than looks. I turned the key in the ignition, but nothing happened. Groaning, I thumped my head against the steering wheel.

"Sadie, no. Not you too after all we've been through together. Come on, sweetheart. I need you today more than ever. I can't be late to work."

Holding my breath, I cranked the engine again. This time, Sadie roared to life. Relief surged through my body, but I didn't dare melt against the seat. I patted the dashboard and praised her loyalty, then backed out of the driveway before my luck could turn.

Sadie jolted to a sudden stop with a sickening *crunch*. I looked into my rearview mirror to see that I'd backed into a car someone had illegally parked on the street directly across from my parents' driveway. *Christ, I am such a fuckup.*

CHAPTER 4

RAYDEN

I JERKED TO A HALT IN THE DOORWAY OF OUR SMALL SECURITY OFFICE because Archer had an unexpected visitor, and he didn't look remotely happy about it. Me? I was fucking ecstatic to see the brunet with the dark brown bedroom eyes again. Archer's latest conquest had changed his clothes since the last time I saw him, swapping sexy club clothes and stacked boots for navy blue scrubs and tennis shoes. I didn't bother trying to hide my delight from Archer, whose dark scowl warned of retribution if I dared. And, oh, I damn well did.

"Bobby!" My enthusiasm was over-the-top for someone I'd just met that morning, especially since our only interaction was a singular, awkward elevator ride. "I didn't know you worked at Silver Maple."

"Neither did I," Archer replied, with just a hint of annoyance creeping into his voice.

Bobby didn't seem to pick up on the tension. Maybe reading a room wasn't his thing. Hell, the guy didn't even look pissed that Archer hadn't paid the least bit of attention to what he'd said the previous night. If anything, Bobby looked smug, and when he responded, I knew why. "I told you twice, but I guess you were a little…preoccupied." The poor guy thought Archer's inability to recall anything he'd said was a compliment.

My best friend squirmed like a worm on a hook, and I was willing to bet Archer was less impressed with Bobby's skills in the light of day.

"Sounds like it," I said to ease the tension. "Are you a nurse?"

"Massage therapist," Bobby replied. "I'm very skilled with my hands and know all the good pressure points. The wait list for my services is very long."

"Mmhmm. I bet," I said, doing my best to fight off a smile as Archer scowled down into a coffee cup. Deciding to take pity on my friend, I stepped into the room, leaving a path open to the door since my size freaked some people out. "Hate to break up this reunion, but I really need to talk to Archer about some important business. We want to make a good impression on our first day."

Bobby turned his attention back to Archer and smiled with an affection that seemed too potent for someone he'd just met. "Of course. I don't mean to be a distraction. Um, do you want to grab lunch? The employee cafeteria offers delicious food."

The hopefulness in Bobby's voice made my chest tighten. Archer was going to crush this guy's spirit, and I didn't want to be around to see it.

Archer tilted his head to the side as if considering the offer. "I can't make any promises since I'm still getting my bearings. This place is much larger than I expected." Then he held up the dossier he was supposed to have memorized before our first day on the job. Winking, Archer added, "And someone distracted me from my homework last night."

Bobby blushed, and freckles popped out on his skin like tiny cinnamon kisses. "I've worked here for five years and know the ins and outs of the place. I can include a private tour of the campus."

I waited for Archer's refusal, but it never came. He stared at Bobby long enough to make me extremely uncomfortable before he relented with a nod.

"Does noon work for you?" Archer asked.

Bobby pulled out his phone and scrolled down the screen. "Perfect. I finish with my last morning client at eleven forty-five. Do you know where the cafeteria is?"

"I will by then," Archer promised. "I'll meet you there."

"It's a date." Bobby blew him a kiss and practically floated out of the office.

Shaking my head, I moved to the door and closed it. "Are you fucking crazy? Arch, come on, man. Getting involved with that guy is a disaster waiting to happen. Did you see the way he looked at you?"

"Jealous?" Archer teased.

"No," I replied honestly. "He's completely…besotted."

"Besotted? What have you been watching or reading?" Archer asked.

I rolled my eyes hard enough to strain something. "Okay, Bobby's infatuated, then, and stop trying to deflect from my very valid point."

Archer heaved a sigh and ran both hands through his hair, leaving the strands in a wild disarray that only made him look hotter. The fucker. "You're right," Archer said. "I know you are, and I will handle this."

"Today," I insisted.

"Give me this one lunch with him, and that's it. I'll let Billy down easily."

"Bobby," I growled. "We have so much riding on this job."

"I know," Archer said.

"We're starting to turn a real profit now, and this job could—"

"Enough, Hawk. I got your point." Archer placed his elbows on the desk, leaned forward, and held my gaze. "I won't fuck this up for us."

And I knew how much he wanted that to be true, but follow-through wasn't Archer's strong suit, and a handsome face distracted him more than it should. But it hadn't always been like that. Archer had developed his playboy, devil-may-care persona as a trauma response to a situation we'd barely survived. His stalwart green gaze reminded me of the rock-steady man I'd met in ranger school thirteen years ago. Sometimes I missed that side of him, just as I ached for the more carefree version of myself, but I trusted Archer with my life then, and I would rely on him now.

Forcing my shoulders to relax, I gave him the easiest smile I could muster. "I know you won't."

Archer's lips turned up at the corners, and he squinted. "What the hell is going on with your face?" He pointed to his mouth for emphasis. "Are you trying to smile, or do you need to take a massive shit?"

"Fuck off," I growled.

Archer leaned back in his chair and laughed, reveling in my annoyance. "Seriously, you don't have to worry about me screwing the staff." Archer cocked his head to the side and pursed his lips. "Although if I were tempted to carry out a lunchtime tryst, it would be with the adorable guy who power walked by our office just before…" His words trailed off as he searched for his latest hookup's name.

"Bobby," I supplied for him.

"Yes, Bobby with the good tongue." Archer grinned at my frown and kept flapping his gums. "Back to the guy I saw just before Bobby arrived." Narrowing his eyes, Archer studied me in a way that made me very uncomfortable. Where was our conversation going? "The hottie rushed past my office, looking frazzled and distraught."

"*Your* office?"

Archer waved me off. "The guy gave off dude-in-distress vibes." Dark eyebrows waggled at me, but I ignored them. "And you know what dudes in distress need?"

"A phone to call nine-one-one," I deadpanned.

Archer snorted. "They need a hero. A hot, muscular man to save the day."

"Says absolutely no one," I told him.

"One with a big heart and an even bigger—"

"Knock it off," I growled.

Archer shrugged and grinned like the Joker. "There's no modesty in the military, Hawk. I know what you're packing."

Heat bloomed in my chest, spreading upward to my neck and face. "This office, *our* office, isn't big enough for the two of us." With the door shut, the walls had seemed to close in even more, adding to my agitation. I needed to stretch my legs, get out in the open air, and avoid running into the hot dude in distress. "I've given our team their assignments, so I'll just check in at each station to make sure they have what they need."

Archer's mouth quirked up on one side, letting me know he saw right through my excuse. "Sounds like a good idea. It's best to make sure the ousted guards didn't sabotage equipment."

I knew when someone was mocking my diligence. Turning on my heels, I growled, "Fuck you, Arch."

"Be sure to use that voice for when you rescue your—"

I slammed the door on his suggestion—figuratively and literally. The wood rattled in the frame, triggering an unhinged fit of laughter from Archer on the other side. My actions startled a young brunette woman walking toward me in the hallway. *Way to go, dumbass.* She stopped and pressed her hand to her chest, as if to hold in the heart I could practically hear pounding from five feet away. My size alone was enough to scare people, and Archer's teasing had likely triggered a dark scowl.

I forced the tension from my body and slowly held up my hands. "I'm so sorry I scared you." Curling my mouth upward, I hoped like hell this smile landed. "I don't know my own strength sometimes."

But she relaxed and took a deep breath. "Maybe I'm just jealous because I really want to slam doors around here sometimes too. Is it as satisfying as it looked?"

Archer's laughter had ratcheted up to cartoon-villain level, making me want to open the door and slam it again.

"Not really."

We shared a laugh, and then she approached with her hand out to shake mine. "Hi, I'm Gabrielle Brady, but everyone around here calls me Gabby."

My large hand dwarfed hers, so I kept my grip light. "Rayden James with RAVEN Securities, but most people call me Ray. It's nice to meet you."

Gabby dropped her gaze to the logo printed on my black T-shirt, which included a raven. "You're a big fan of the bird?"

"It's an acronym made from our first names," I explained.

"Ah. That's really cool. Are you settling in okay?" Gabby looked at the door I'd slammed and had to notice the laughter it barely muffled. "And do you have some kind of madman contained inside there?"

The question made me chortle. "That's just my partner Archer. He's having a good laugh at my expense."

Her brow rose. "There's a good story there, I bet."

"Not nearly as entertaining as you'd think," I replied.

Gabby's wry smile said she didn't believe me for a second, but she let it go. "Who are the other three people who make up RAVEN?"

"Vaughn, Ethan, and Nico. You'll likely meet them all since we rotate between jobs."

"Looking forward to it," she said. "It was nice to meet you."

"Likewise."

I exited the building without further incident and headed to the small garage that housed the golf carts provided for management and security personnel. I entered the security code into the digital keypad, and the red light above it turned green. The door unlocked with a whir, and I pushed it open. The exterior of the building was as grandiose as the rest of the structures on the campus, but I expected the inside to resemble a typical garage. Instead of oil-stained concrete floors and cheap metal shelves lining the walls, Silver Maple's service garage was a gleaming showpiece. The contractor had painted the concrete floors a warm beige color with decorative flakes in multiple hues of gray. The sunlight streaming through east-facing windows made the silvery chips look like glittering diamonds. I stopped in the center of the room and studied the cedar shelves lining the walls. They weren't random pieces of wood haphazardly screwed together and shoved into place. Someone had put a lot of care into their construction and finished them with a clear varnish to show off the natural color of the wood. The shelving was better suited for a living room instead of a garage.

"Hell, these are nicer than the bookshelves in my loft," I mumbled.

Tidier too. Someone had arranged everything by size and purpose, with not a single dirty shop rag in sight. I might've bet my next paycheck that the shelves would pass a white-glove test if someone had been there to accept the challenge. I took in the rows of shiny golf carts and acknowledged I had truly stepped into another world. That was nothing new for a soldier, especially one from an elite force, but somehow, getting dropped into the middle of a war felt more natural than stepping into Silver Maple's fancy garage. And what that said about my personality was disturbing, but I shook it off and pushed the button to open the rolling garage door. I climbed aboard the first golf cart and turned the key in the ignition. The electric engine fired right up, but I noticed the battery was only charged halfway.

"Great."

Climbing off, I located the charger and connected it to the port before moving on to the next cart in the row. Second verse, same as the first. That battery had less than a quarter of juice. I plugged it in to charge and moved on down the line. Again and again, each time finding that no one had bothered to charge any of the golf carts. If the employees at Silver Maple polished the wooden shelves in the garage, they likely took excellent care of everything else.

"Sabotage," I groused. "I knew it."

I texted the intel to Archer and received laughing and eye-rolling emojis in return.

Archer: I'm sure it was just an oversight. No need to call out the National Guard.

Me: Fuck you.

Archer: Buddy, I'm all game if you think it will help you out. Just know I don't do repeats and I don't catch feelings.

Me: Better save this speech for Bobby later.

Archer: Fuck you right back.

We could've gone on like this for hours, so I tucked my phone away and chose the golf cart with the most juice. I didn't have to be out long, so surely it would do. Caitlyn's tour had been brief, mostly consisting of the administrative and community buildings. I just wanted to get a feel for the layout of the entire campus and check on our team to make sure they had everything they needed. Sure, I could've just called them on our walkie-talkies or phones, but I liked the personal touch. And I fucking needed fresh air. What was I supposed to do all day in that building? Take turns at the desk with Archer? Hell to the no.

I drove the golf cart out of the garage, parked it long enough to lock everything back up, and then headed out to explore. The fancy driveway material continued throughout the campus, winding around the multilevel buildings that housed apartments for the residents in assisted living, and through the mini subdivisions of cottage-style housing for the independent residents. A woman stepped out onto the front porch of a villa and waved me down.

"Yoo-hoo," she yelled over the hum of the golf cart.

Slowing, I turned into the driveway and cut the engine. The woman stepped off the shaded porch and into the sunlight, smiling at me like we were old friends. She wore her hair parted down the middle, with one side completely white and the other black. It reminded me of a Disney cartoon character, but I couldn't remember which one. She had to be at least five ten in her flat shoes and carried herself with ramrod, almost military precision. It was hard to gauge her age. I knew from Silver Maple's bylaws that she had to be at least sixty to live there, but she looked at least ten years younger.

"Good morning, ma'am," I said, meeting her at the top of the driveway. "Did you need help with something?"

"I'm Veronica Poole, one of the Silver Maple board members." She extended her hand, which I promptly shook, noting the strength in her grip. "Are you one of RAVEN Securities' owners?"

"Yes, ma'am," I said, then introduced myself.

"It's nice to meet you, Ray."

"Likewise. We're certainly grateful for the opportunity to provide security services to the residents."

"Thank you," Veronica said. "That's lovely to hear, but you don't have to be so formal. I'm just being nosy, and you should probably get used to it. All the residents will be curious about the new crew." Her eyes swept over me again, this time a little slower.

"Are all *A*-through-*N* guys just as handsome as you are?"

"More so," I replied.

She laughed and shook her head. "Doubt that. I don't want to keep you from your tasks. I just wanted to introduce myself. My friends call me Ronni, by the way." She leaned forward and lowered her voice as if paparazzi were loitering in the flowering bushes along her porch. "You'd make my day if you called me Ronni in front of all the other residents."

I shrugged. "Okay."

"Great. Now, be on your way. I need to make a call that will trigger the gossip chain. When the phone rings around here, you know it's going to be a prayer request or juicy gossip." She made shooing motions with her hands, and I complied with a chuckle.

"See you around, Ronni."

"If I weren't old enough to be your grandmother, I'd swoon right here on the spot. Say," she said, perking up, "I'd love to introduce you to one of my single nieces or nephews."

I lifted a brow at her open-mindedness. "I'll just be going now."

She laughed and took a few steps backward. "He plays it close to the vest. I like it."

Shaking my head, I wheeled the golf cart around in the driveway and headed out onto the street. I passed the rehab facility, the residents' fancy dining hall and banquet center, and a large community recreation space that was supposed to have a state-of-the-art gym, including an indoor and outdoor pool with spa areas for both recreation and therapy. The campus was beautiful, and I understood why someone would want to live out the last decades of their lives at Silver Maple. There was a parking area near the community recreation area, which sat toward the far edge of the campus. A tall stone fence provided privacy from people driving down the nearby public road, but the rows of trees on the other side were a vulnerable entry spot for someone who didn't belong there. The pool had to be a temptation for punk-ass kids who could easily climb the trees to jump the stone wall.

The unexpected sound of metal crashing against metal caused me to lift my foot from the pedal to hear better. What was that, and where was it coming from? The noise got louder, helping me identify the direction, and I smashed my foot against the accelerator. Archer liked to joke about my sensitivity to energy, but my alarm bells were ringing. Something was wrong. There was no reason for metal to be crashing against metal. I'd checked the maintenance schedule, and there was no planned activity that would account for the sound.

Clang, clang, clang! Crunch!

The last noise sounded like glass shattering. My pulse escalated, and I pressed the accelerator all the way down. "Come on, come on." The little golf cart bucked but then lunged forward.

The clanging and crunching continued, and I wondered why no one had run out of the recreation building to see what the hell was going on. Okay, running might've been a stretch in a senior living community, but at least someone could power walk to check out the disturbance. As I drew nearer, I understood why the building occupants hadn't heard the noise. Music blared from the rear of the building, probably the outdoor pool area.

Clang, clang, clang. Crash!

Rounding the side of the building, I saw a hooded figure wailing away on a grayish hatchback car with a crowbar. He'd already knocked out one of the windows on the side I could see and had likely knocked out one on the opposite side too. I ripped my walkie-talkie off the belt and radioed for help as I willed the stupid golf cart to go faster.

"Are you fucking kidding me?" came Archer's tinny reply.

"No, damn it. I need backup at the community recreational building. Call the police."

"Police? What's going on?"

"Just get here." Thinking of the sabotaged batteries, I added, "Better drive our SUV." As if to prove my point, the electric motor sputtered and whined. "Shit."

Clang, clang, clang. Crash!

The assailant was too busy bashing the rear quarter panel and window on the poor car to notice my approach. I wanted to keep it that way.

"What's that noise?" Archer demanded.

"An assault on a vehicle. Get here."

"I'm already on my way. Almost to the SUV. Should you approach this perp alone?"

"So far, the assailant has only brandished a crowbar. I can survive that."

The electric golf cart battery died, and I bit back another curse. The hooded assailant jerked his head up, noticing me for the first time.

Launching myself out of the cart, I commanded, "Don't move."

The assailant froze like a deer in headlights for all of two seconds before he turned and ran. I pumped my arms and legs fast in pursuit, smiling to myself because I had done my homework, and his chosen path only led to trouble. Sure enough, I rounded the building and saw that the perp had trapped himself between the building on the right, an eight-foot stone wall on the left, and a six-foot privacy fence in front of him that surrounded the outdoor pool, where the occupants jammed to seventies' disco music. The only real escape was for this asshole to get past me, and that would not happen.

"Together. Spread 'em. Together. Spread 'em," called out a man on the other side of the fence.

The assailant raised his crowbar as if he might charge me, then launched it over the pool's privacy fence instead. He took two steps back to get a run, then leaped toward the top of the fence, landing in the middle with an awkward splat. The guy somehow held on to the top of the fence and dug his toes into the wood to climb the rest of the way. His slow progress allowed me to hit the fence directly behind him. My lead foot landed in the middle of the board, and I used the momentum to propel me up high enough to see over the top. Gripping the fence, I flung my body over the boards, eyes scanning the surroundings to see where the man with the crowbar had gone. My gaze landed on a bare-chested, hot guy balanced on the edge of a chair with his toned legs extending in front of him. He was stuck in the spread 'em position as he gaped at me, which sent my mind to places it had no business going under the circumstances.

Awareness sparked and sizzled in my brain as familiar eyes locked on me and widened in surprise. I still couldn't tell if they were green or brown. The world around us faded away, and my descent seemed to slow. Keeping my attention on Atticus was stupid and dangerous. I needed to survey the rest of the area, but I couldn't tear my gaze away from him, not even when I landed on the concrete with a jarring thud.

That momentary distraction allowed the assailant to take a swing at me with the crowbar. I felt the air move and ducked just in the nick of time, so the blow glanced off my shoulder instead of hitting me in the head. I lowered my shoulders and rammed them into his gut, lunging forward with more strength than was necessary to make the tackle. One minute, my feet were on solid ground, and the next, I was falling through air and splashing into the water. My attacker squirmed in my grip, but I wasn't about to let go. I wanted to take the fucker down to the bottom of the pool and alligator roll him until he stopped moving. But a cooler head prevailed, and I dragged the assailant to the surface of the pool.

"Over here, Hawk," Archer called out. "Christ, are you hurt? I told you to wait for me."

"I'm fine. Quit your nagging." I hauled the perp to the edge of the pool, and Archer grabbed him by the scruff of his hoodie and roughly dragged him onto the concrete. I placed my hands on the edge of the pool and pushed myself out of the water to several cheers and a smattering of applause.

Atticus pushed to his feet and ran over to me. His eyes studied me with concern, and I had the answer to my question about his eye color. Hazel-brown with green striations and tiny gold flecks. I needed to assess the situation, but I couldn't force myself to look away from Atticus. Damn, he was even more beautiful in person than in his photos. His messy, dark hair made me think of lazy Sunday mornings in bed, and I got hit with a pang of longing so fierce that I doubled over. Something unwelcome and terrifying stirred in my chest and caused my lungs to freeze. Fuck, I couldn't breathe.

A hand landed between my shoulders, and I knew it didn't belong to Archer. Atticus was touching me, and I wanted to press into it instead of pulling away. There was so much I wanted to say to Atticus. I owed him an apology for flaking out on him and then lying about it. But after less than five minutes with Atticus, I knew I'd been right to cancel our hookup. He made me feel too much.

"Are you okay?" Atticus asked, his voice soft with worry.

I lifted my head and looked at him. Big mistake. Long, dark lashes framed his eyes, and a smattering of freckles dotted his cheeks and nose. I commanded myself to avert my gaze and pull away from his touch, but I did neither.

"Where do you hurt?" Atticus moved his hand over to caress my shoulder. "There's a hard lump forming here already? Do you think he broke your shoulder?"

I shook my head because words were impossible. I sucked in a deep breath and closed my eyes. Exhaling slowly, I repeated the process until I pulled myself together and gradually straightened to my full height. Atticus dropped his hand as he rose with me, and I missed his touch immediately.

"I'm fine," I replied, taking a few steps backward. "Everything just happened so fast."

The squawk of walkie-talkies caught my attention as more of our security team arrived on the scene.

"Cops are on the way," Archer said as he secured the squirming assailant's hands behind his back with zip ties. "What the hell happened here?"

"I caught this asshole bashing the hell out of a car in the parking lot. I commanded him not to move, but he ran instead."

"He took a swing at your head too," Atticus said. "Thankfully, he missed."

Archer gave his full attention to Atticus and grinned. "Well, hello," he said, deepening his voice because he couldn't seem to turn off the charm when a sexy man was near. Atticus was off-limits, and I'd make sure Archer knew it. Not because I wanted him for myself, but to remind Archer that getting involved with the Silver Maple staff was bad for business. "We haven't met yet, though I saw you rush by my office this morning." Archer caught my gaze and smirked. "You looked a little distressed."

Atticus glanced in Archer's direction but didn't react to the flirty tone. He couldn't seem to tear his gaze away from mine, and I liked it far too much. "It was a terrible morning," Atticus said with a frown. "And it seems like my day won't get better anytime soon because my car was the only one parked in the lot when I arrived. Let me guess. This guy beat the hell out of an ancient Subaru?"

"That's the one," I replied.

Archer leaned over and dramatically yanked the guy's hoodie off his head like it was a Scooby-Doo villain reveal. "Know him?"

"Unfortunately." Atticus sighed as if he carried the weight of the world. "He's my ex-boyfriend."

CHAPTER 5

ATTICUS

I'D NEVER FELT AN URGE TO KICK ANOTHER HUMAN BEING AS I DID JUST then, not even when I'd discovered Chad had been cheating with our boss. It was bad enough I had to force my gaze away from Ray to confirm Chad's identity, but—

Holy shit!

A wild surge of emotions seized my body and took me on the wildest roller-coaster ride of my life. I couldn't tell if it was fury, shock, or arousal that caused a flood of adrenaline to short-circuit my system. My hands shook, and my legs trembled with restless energy as if an army of ants marched under my skin. Should I flee, fight, or fuck? I stole a glance in Ray's direction to confirm I hadn't imagined his presence. Yep, he was still standing beside me, rocking the bluest eyes to ever blue.

Nope. Not going there.

Not when the other jerk who'd rejected my affection showed up at my job and attacked my beloved Sadie. And that was the moment the executive-functioning part of my brain decided on which emotion to latch onto and the appropriate physical response. I drew my leg back to deliver a powerful kick, but Ray's big hand landed on my forearm and gently squeezed, pulling my attention back to him. Vintage-blue-jean eyes made my heart do cartwheels and tripped my brain from fight mode into fuck.

My gaze dropped to the wet shirt clinging to Ray's powerful body. Too bad the fabric was black and not white. As shitty as my day was, I could use a wet T-shirt contest to boost my mood. Ray's pecs were stunning enough without his sexy nipples winking at me. And damn. Was that an eight-pack? Six wasn't good enough for this guy? The urge to throw myself into Ray's arms and rub against him like a cat in heat was overwhelming.

"You don't want to do that," Ray said, his voice gruff and deliciously bossy. The combo did nothing to cool my arousal.

"Oh, but I really, really do." Whose husky voice was that? Not mine. Clearing my throat, just in case, I added, "It's been an awful day, and it would make me feel better." But I no longer meant kicking Chad.

Ray's dark eyebrow shot up, and something sparked in his blue depths. Arousal? Encouragement? "He's not worth it."

Ugh, we were back to Chad. I took a deep breath and exhaled my frustration. "Fine. I won't kick him, but you owe me."

Ray's lips curved into a smile, and it looked like he was going to respond, until my idiot ex chose that moment to insert himself into our conversation.

"Damn, Kit, you're even more pathetic than I realized if you're slumming it with this meathead," Chad jeered.

Fury obliterated my infatuation haze, and I turned a hostile glare on Chad. I didn't give a shit what he thought about me, but how dare he degrade Ray. "You're not in any position to insult or judge anyone. And I do mean literally," I said, gesturing to where he lay on his stomach with his hands zip-tied behind his back. "You wanted my attention, asshole, and now you've got it."

Chad scoffed. "Don't flatter yourself."

I could've pointed out that he'd called my parents' house looking for me, so he had indeed wanted my attention, but airing our dirty laundry in front of the residents and Ray wasn't high on my list. "How'd you even know I worked here?" I'd blocked him on all my social media accounts and made them private. No one in my family would've told him where I worked, and we no longer shared a friend circle. Chad pinched his lips together so tightly they turned white, but the answer came to me without his help. "You fucking followed me here!" I blurted.

Chad rolled his eyes, and I thought he was going to deny it, until his lips curved into an ugly sneer. "Still not very observant, are you? I used your cluelessness to my advantage. *Again.*"

Reminding me of how I'd blindly trusted Chad while he'd carried out a long-term affair wasn't the wisest thing to do while trussed up and defenseless. Ray tightened his grip and stepped closer, as if prepared to physically restrain me if necessary. I wasn't going to kick my ex-loser boyfriend, but Chad didn't know that. My chest swelled with pride as Chad's expression morphed into worry as he realized he'd gone too far.

Leaning in, Ray lowered his voice and said, "He's still not worth it." Warm breath tickled my ear and sent a shiver down my spine, making it hard to focus on the rest of the words that followed. "I caught the guy vandalizing your car, and he just admitted to stalking you in front of witnesses. Cops are on the way. Let the law handle him."

I had every intention of doing just that, but why not have a little fun on such a shitty day? I turned to Ray, loving how close he stood to me. Hell, our chests almost touched. "You'll owe me twice," I teased.

A pink blush bloomed across Ray's cheeks, and he'd just opened his mouth to respond when an authoritative male voice interrupted and demanded someone turn off the music. That was probably my job, but it would've required me to pull my arm free from Ray's grip when that was the last thing I wanted. Luckily, someone else obeyed the command, and the only thumping on the silent pool deck came from my heart.

"Can someone tell me what the hell happened here?" *Ugh. The bossy voice again.* "Who's in charge?"

Couldn't he see I was busy doing...what? Making a fool of myself? That thought was the bucket of ice water my dazed brain needed to seize control of the situation. Retracting my arm, I turned and addressed the stern-faced officer scanning the small crowd.

"I'm your huckleberry." It was the worst time to recite my favorite Val Kilmer quote, so that's of course what rolled off my tongue.

An amused snort came from someone behind me, and I suspected it was the flirty security guard who'd arrived second on the scene. *Second on the scene?* I'd have to remember that phrasing when I wrote up an incident report for management.

"Actually, in this instance, I believe I'm your point of contact." Ray's voice was low but assertive, maybe something he used in the bedroom when instructing a lover to—

"And you are?" asked the officer.

"Rayden James with RAVEN Securities," he replied before gesturing to the flirty security guard. "This is my partner Archer Stone."

There was another round of handshakes before the men continued talking. The cop likely gave his name, but damned if I heard anything after learning Ray's full name. Rayden James. It sure sounded like someone who would chase down a crowbar-wielding maniac after catching him in the act of vandalism.

"This is all Kit's fault!" Chad yelled. "He ruined my life."

"No one asked for your input yet," the cop said.

I really should've paid attention when he gave his name. I dropped my gaze to the shiny metal nameplate pinned on his chest. "Thank you, Officer Romero."

The cop turned his dark gaze on me, though his expression was a tad kinder when he said, "Not you yet either. I'll get a victim's statement in just a moment."

"Victim?" Chad sneered. "Kit's got that role down to an art."

Ray, my super-sexy hero, crouched down in front of Chad and leveled him with the deadliest look I'd ever seen. Even Wild West gunslingers would quake when facing off against him. "Not a damn word out of you until Officer Romero asks for your input. Got it?" Ray pitched his voice low and menacing to match his deadly glower.

Chad was many things, reckless and stupid topping the list, but his cockroach-level survival instincts kicked in to save him once again. He clamped his mouth shut and nodded.

Romero's stern, unsmiling mouth briefly twitched at the corners before he resumed control. Removing a small notebook and pen from his pocket, the officer said, "Mr. James, we'll start with your observations since you witnessed the crime in the act."

Ray stood up but kept his gaze on Chad as he relayed the incident in a concise, authoritative voice while using tactical phrases to describe what he witnessed. The impersonal jargon made me forget Ray was talking about me until he described the damage inflicted on my sweet Sadie. She didn't deserve to go out like that. "Then the perpetrator fled the scene to evade capture, and I gave chase."

"And you got assaulted with a crowbar," I said before I could stop myself.

Hattie, one of the ladies from my water aerobics class, stepped forward.

"It's true." Her dark scowl stood out in stark contrast to the sunny yellow swim cap she wore on her head. It was the retro style with three-dimensional flowers all over it, and they shook with mirroring outrage when Hattie pointed a finger at Chad. "He aimed for the hunk's head but missed." Then she smiled charmingly at Ray. "Those are some quick reflexes you have there."

"Thank you, ma'am."

Mr. Murphy, a retired seaman, stepped forward and saluted. "We all saw it, Captain."

Officer Romero glanced up from taking notes and scanned the cluster of residents in their various stages of dress. The modest participants had donned their swim cover-ups or put on T-shirts, but the bolder among the crowd hadn't bothered. Some really leaned into letting it all hang out, and I loved them all the more for their zero-fucks attitude.

"And you'll all give statements to what you witnessed?" Romero asked them.

A chorus of "yes, sir" and "absolutely" answered him.

Romero nodded and scanned the surrounding area. "Do you mind hanging out at the patio tables until I wrap up here? Then I'll collect your statements."

Most of the residents complied easily, but there were a few reluctant stragglers who moved much slower than I knew they could.

"Make sure you hydrate," I called out. "Just because we worked out in water doesn't mean you didn't sweat." We'd started the class early so we could enjoy the benefits of working outdoors before it got too hot.

"Aye, Captain," Mr. Murphy said with a jaunty salute, but made no attempt to move faster. He was the nosiest of the bunch and disguised it poorly.

Romero chuckled under his breath as he turned his attention back to us. "Which one of you is Kit?"

I raised my hand like a dutiful kindergartner during attendance. "That's me."

Romero's pen paused, and he glanced up. "Is that short for something?"

"Kitty cat, I bet," Archer said with a soft purr in his voice.

Ray snapped his head in his partner's direction. "Maybe you should go sit with the water aerobics class. You weren't here to witness any of the events."

"That's not a bad idea," Romero said. "I'll get your statement later as well."

Instead of getting annoyed, Archer's mouth curved into a delighted smile. "No problem." He gestured for the rest of the security staff to follow him too.

The female residents, and even a few of the males, straightened in their seats and preened as the security team approached.

"Okay," Romero said. "Where were we again?"

"Kit is my nickname. It's short for Atticus."

"Ah, got it," Romero said. "Can I have your full name for the report?"

"Atticus Livengood."

Romero met my gaze again. "Livengood?"

"Yeah, but you can't tell it by the way my day is going," I teased. When my gaze connected with Ray's, I realized that maybe things weren't all bad.

"Can you spell your last name for me?"

"*L* as in loser," Chad said. "*I* as in idiot." But that was as far as he got before Ray leveled him with a death stare.

Arousal spiked my blood and made me tremble. I'd hoped it was a delicate, imperceptible reaction, but Romero noticed and asked if I was in shock. That got Ray's attention, but I ducked my head before our gazes connected again.

"No," I said with a dismissive snort. "Just coming down off an adrenaline spike."

Ray stepped closer and lifted my chin, forcing me to look at him. Dark eyebrows knitted together, and worried eyes searched mine. "Do you need juice or something?"

I would've shaken my head, but I liked the feel of his thumb and forefinger on my chin too much. "I'm fine. This was just a tremendous shock." And I didn't just mean the shit with Chad. Ray was here. At Silver Maple. What were the odds? Of all the retirement villages in all the world, he walked—

"I don't know why you're shocked," Chad said. "You've had this coming for six months."

Ray withdrew his hand and turned to deal with Chad, but Romero stepped between them. The officer signaled for two of Ray's security team to come over, then instructed them to move Chad to the opposite side of the pool deck and drop him in a chair to wait.

"I can't let you assault a man whose arms are tied behind his back," Romero said.

"Then cut him loose."

Romero's lips twitched at the corners, but he refrained from smiling. "You don't mean that."

Ray rolled his shoulders and winced. I moved closer to inspect his injury, but he shook his head. "I'm fine." He looked at Romero and nodded. "And you're right. I didn't mean it."

"So, is this a domestic dispute that's spilled over to your workplace?" Romero asked me.

The question caught me off guard and stiffened my spine. "No. This is the first time I've laid eyes on Chad or even spoken to him in six months," I explained.

"And the question is irrelevant," Ray told Romero. "It wouldn't change the fact that Mr.—" He looked to me for help.

"Clark."

"Thank you," Ray said to me before addressing Romero again. "It wouldn't change the fact that Mr. Clark broke the law by vandalizing Mr. Livengood's car, no matter his reasoning."

I didn't like how Ray referred to me so impersonally, especially when the choice to do so felt very personal. I wanted to believe "Mr. Livengood" was his way of maintaining professionalism by not drawing attention to the fact that we'd almost met up to fuck. No. Those words, Mr. Livengood, were two bricks in the wall Ray was building between us.

"You're right," Romero conceded before shifting his attention to me. "I didn't mean to sound like I was victim blaming. That wasn't my intention."

"I appreciate it," I said.

Romero asked us both a few more follow-up questions before moving on to speak to Chad. I wanted so badly to be included in the conversation so I could do damage control, but Romero wouldn't let me. I had to watch from the opposite side of the patio, but luckily, it seemed like the officer cut Chad off anytime he wanted to veer off topic.

"Ex-boyfriend, huh?"

Ray's voice was much closer than I'd expected. I let out a mouselike "*eep*" and whipped around to look at him, stubbing my bare big toe on the tip of his boots. I would've hissed and maybe sworn a blue streak if I weren't almost nose to nipple with his right pectoral muscle. God, the urge to lean forward and nip that hard bud was overwhelming.

"Sorry." Ray's hands landed on my hips to settle me, and I forgot to breathe when he left them there.

Don't look up. Don't look up. Of course, I didn't listen. I lifted my chin up to stare into his denim-blue eyes. I rarely knew what the hell would come out of my mouth, but I shocked even myself when I blurted, "Lobelia."

Dark eyebrows knitted again as Ray closely scrutinized me from head to toe. His gaze met mine once he finished, and Ray looked moderately relieved not to have found obvious signs of distress or illness. "I don't know what that means."

"Um, it's a shade of blue," I said. "Like vintage, medium-wash jeans." I gestured to my own eyes like an idiot and further damned myself by adding, "It matches your irises. I know because I actively searched for a name to describe the prettiest blue eyes I'd ever seen."

Ray blinked a few times, maybe in astonishment or perhaps to signal a rescue. *Clink, clink* went the bricks as Ray stacked them higher. "Um, I've only thought of my eyes as blue."

"That descriptor is too pedestrian. They're so pretty."

A dark blush bloomed across Ray's chiseled cheekbones. I averted my gaze before I blurted weird adjectives to define their jagged masculinity. But then Ray surprised me when he said, "I spent a lot of time trying to figure out if your eyes are brown or green."

I snapped my head up and locked my hopeful gaze on his. "They're hazel-brown."

"Yeah, I see that." The word was a soft whisper that caressed my spine and made me shiver. Ray's fingers pressed harder against my hips, as if he wanted to pull me closer. "With tiny gold flecks around the pupils."

I blinked rapidly, much like Ray had, but it was definitely from surprise. I didn't need rescued. I searched my surroundings, suddenly afraid someone had misinterpreted my gesture, and locked eyes with Archer. He watched us with a wicked smile on his face and an impish gleam in his eyes.

"Um, is your friend okay?" I asked. "He looks maniacal."

Groaning, Ray dropped his hands from my hips and stepped back without so much as looking in Archer's direction. "Ignore him. He's harmless, I swear."

"If you say so."

Rubbing the back of his neck, Ray looked everywhere except at me. "I, um..." he said, gesturing across the patio to where Archer and the rest of his security staff watched us with unabashed curiosity. "Need to talk to my team."

"Of course. I'll see you around, yeah?"

Ray turned then, giving me his full attention. Blue eyes trailed down my chest at a glacial pace, and that's when I remembered I'd only worn a pair of thin swim shorts to class. I begged the universe to show me kindness for once and not let me spring wood right there in front of him and our audience. Ray's gaze grew hotter with each passing second, and I could almost feel my skin sizzle by the time he reached my belly button. *Oh no. Oh no. Don't get hard. Don't get hard.*

"Everything okay over there, Hawk?" Archer yelled from across the patio.

Ray jolted and stepped back, his gaze snapping up to meet mine for a few moments. He looked dazed, confused, and more than a little turned on. That made two of us, pal. "Um, yeah."

"What?" Had I asked him a question?

"You'll see me around." Ray's words came out thick and rough, like the texture of the new bricks he added to the wall.

CHAPTER 6

RAYDEN

"NOT A GODDAMN WORD OUT OF YOU," I GROWLED AS I GOT BEHIND the wheel of our SUV.

Archer stood at the open passenger door but didn't make a move to enter the vehicle. His lips twitched, so he pressed them together to keep from laughing or saying something I'd make him regret. Archer angled his body so I could see the abandoned golf cart beyond him, then gestured dramatically at it with his hands.

Shaking my head, I started the engine. "You look like a deranged game show presenter, only no one wants the prize you're giving away."

Archer pulled a sad clown face, then pointed to the steering wheel and mimed driving. I shook my head. He knew damn well I never rode as a passenger in a vehicle unless I couldn't avoid it. This was just Archer's attempt to wind me up. I revved the engine, so he knew I meant business, then remembered we weren't alone. The residents, aka the witnesses, were crossing the parking lot and not bothering to hide their curiosity. I smiled and waved as they passed. A few of the ladies giggled and leaned their heads together to talk while one of the men saluted me.

"Get in," I said through clenched teeth. "We're causing a show."

Archer's brows went up, and he pointed at his chest.

"Fucking clown." Proving I meant business, I shifted the SUV into Drive and eased my foot off the gas pedal, rolling forward just the tiniest bit.

"Fine," Archer huffed and climbed inside.

"I told you not a word."

He slapped a hand over his mouth in mock apology and pleaded for forgiveness with his green eyes, also mockingly.

"Shut the door, asshole. We're drawing too much attention."

I eased from the parking spot as soon as he complied, waving at the group of residents as I slowly drove by them. There was enough energy pulsing through my body to power Silver Maple's campus and well beyond, but it was important that I kept it contained and under control. I could burn it off later in the privacy of our gym or alone in the shower in my apartment. The silent acknowledgment reminded me of what had amped me up so much, and it had nothing to do with pursuing the hooded vandal or getting clipped in the shoulder with a crowbar.

Atticus. What were the fucking odds of running into him at Silver Maple? Christ, Archer would never shut up if he ever found out about the almost hookup I had with Atticus. He'd find every excuse to push us together if he detected a hint of the energy thrumming under my skin. I had to get my shit together, but damn, those eyes were really something. Hazel-brown didn't accurately describe their beauty. And his body? All that golden-brown skin and that lean muscle on display. He'd worn less in the thirst traps he'd posted on Randy, usually tight underwear that left nothing to the imagination, but those images hadn't prepared me for the full effect of his sexiness.

Wheezing noises came from the passenger seat, and I realized I wasn't the only one in the vehicle who was bursting at the seams with energy. Archer sounded like he was choking on his own elation. There was no way to contain him forever, so it was better to turn him loose in the privacy of the vehicle than in front of witnesses.

"Fucking get it out of your system, Arch."

Laughter blasted from his chest as if it shot from a cannon, followed by hearty bellows that rattled the windows.

"Yuck it up now before we get back to the office. Then it's time to act like a professional."

"I'll try," Archer wheezed. "But drive slower because I have a lot of immaturity to burn through yet."

"I'm only driving fifteen miles per hour. Maybe you should walk back."

Archer cleared his throat a few times and tried to get himself under control, but I made the mistake of glancing over at him and making eye contact. Whatever he saw in my expression triggered another bout of laughter. "You are so fucked, Hawk."

"I don't know what you're talking about."

"He's got messy brown hair, pretty hazel eyes, and a rocking body," Archer said.

"Shut up."

Archer hummed instead. "Bet he spends a lot of time honing that lean muscle. What do you think: Pilates or yoga? And that ass. I'm surprised he didn't give someone a heart attack in his shorty shorts."

"They weren't that short."

"Oh! So you noticed."

"Of course I did." And I would take the memory home and replay it on repeat as I fucked my fist. "As I already stated, I am not a monk."

"Yeah, that much was obvious. I could smell the pheromones you were giving off across from the pool. I wasn't the only one. Your little kitty cat looked like he was seconds away from rubbing his face against your chest and purring."

Damn, what I wouldn't give to experience that. No. Huh-uh. I hadn't been ready to hook up with Atticus last month when we were strangers, so I sure as hell wouldn't fuck him now that we worked at the same place. "He's not my kitty cat, and stop calling him that. His name is Atticus."

"Everyone else seems to call him Kit," Archer countered. "The residents had a lot to say about him. Would you like to hear their thoughts?"

I tightened my grip on the steering wheel. "No."

"You're the absolute worst liar," Archer said. "Fine. I'll keep the juicy tidbits to myself until you're ready to hear them. I won't even make you beg. All you have to do is ask."

"I won't."

"You will."

There was no point in arguing with Archer when he was in such a smug mood. It would only rile me up to an unhealthy level, and I needed to decompress before I did something really stupid like give Atticus my phone number or drag him into the nearest janitor's closet and kiss that luscious mouth. Just the mere thought was enough to send my blood rushing south.

Archer slapped a hand against his leg and burst into laughter again, this time sounding downright giddy. "You've morphed from a wet blanket into a wet cat, but not a cute little kitten in need of rescue. You're the hissing and spitting kind."

"Are you done?"

Archer paused for a moment before chortling at his own wit.

"Glad one of us thinks you're funny," I said.

"I'm hilarious, and we both know it." Archer nudged me with my elbow. "And I'm right."

Now that he'd mentioned the state of my damp clothes, I couldn't think about anything else. I'd dried considerably by the time Officer Romero finished his interviews and hauled the angry ex-boyfriend to jail for booking, but my clothes stuck to my body, and my boots squeaked when I walked. And what the hell was the deal with that Chad Clark guy, anyway? I wondered what Archer had picked up from gossiping with the residents, but I wasn't about to ask. I shouldn't have cared, but Atticus Livengood had me all twisted up.

Archer was still chuckling when I pulled back into our parking spot at the administrative building. "Since you have a contingency plan for every occasion, it's safe to assume you have a change of clothes in here somewhere."

"I do."

"Great, now what's your plan for your kit—"

I cut Archer off with a glare before he could finish the nickname he'd given Atticus. *But damn if it didn't fit.* I wanted to stroke Atticus until he purred. "Since you have so much unharnessed energy, you get to be in charge of the cleanup duties," I said. "That parking lot needs to be restored to its former pristine glory. You'll need to get the golf cart back to the garage and charge the rest of the fleet."

Archer answered me with a curt salute before ruining his obedience with a giggle.

The blinking cursor on the blank page mocked me, and I sighed. "Not feeling so smug now, are you?"

Knuckles rapped against the open office door, and I jerked my head up to see who'd caught me muttering under my breath. *Please don't let it be Atticus,* was my first thought, quickly followed by, *Who the hell cares if it is?*

There was absolutely nothing happening between us, and there never would be. That wasn't a spark of poolside arousal I'd felt, only adrenaline from the chase playing tricks on my nervous system. *Thy name is denial,* said some tragic Shakespearean character. Probably.

Caitlyn stood in the open doorway, her countenance not as friendly as before, not that I blamed her. We'd only been on Silver Maple's campus for a few hours before the trouble started. "Got a minute?"

"Absolutely. Just trying to peck out an incident report."

She approached the desk but didn't sit in the vacant chair. Caitlyn's choice to stand gave her a height advantage that felt strategic, though she didn't technically loom over me. "I won't take up much of your time since I can see you're busy." The corners of her mouth twitched a little, and the tension around her eyes softened. "The writing isn't going well, huh?"

Chuckling, I shook my head. "My partners tease me a lot for the tactical verbiage I use and the writing style I deploy. I want to make a good impression on the board so they won't regret hiring our company."

Furrowing her brow, Caitlyn tilted her head slightly. "Sounds like your partners aren't always nice."

"Neither is my writing."

Caitlyn grinned and said, "Now I can't wait to read that report."

I dropped my head into my hands and groaned for a few seconds before meeting her gaze again. "What can I do for you? I assume you'd like a verbal preview of what happened this morning."

"Yes, but now it feels like asking for spoilers. It will take the joy out of reading your report later." Caitlyn sighed and sat in the vacant chair. "Gossip travels faster than the speed of light around here, and the board members who live at Silver Maple will have already heard about the incident. I anticipate a phone call requesting a meeting at any minute."

"That sounds frustrating."

"Sometimes." Caitlyn rubbed her hands against her thighs and said, "Enough of my whining. Tell me what happened this morning at the recreational center."

I ran through the highlights and gave myself a proverbial pat on the back for not using a single military phrase. Caitlyn's mouth parted in a shocked gasp when I told her about the assailant hitting me with the crowbar. I'd left out the part where I'd failed to properly assess my surroundings because my gaze had gotten snagged on a certain person's assets.

"Oh my god! Are you hurt? Do you want one of our nurses or physical therapists to examine your shoulder?"

I rotated my arm to show I was just fine. "I'll probably just have muscle soreness and a bruise."

Caitlyn was frowning again, but I didn't think her concern was all for my benefit. "Poor Kit. Is he okay? I cannot believe something like this happened to him."

"He wasn't physically injured, but I'm sure the incident was a big shock to his system." It wasn't my business, but I couldn't resist asking, "Kit won't get in trouble for this, will he?" No matter his history with that douchebag Chad, he hadn't invited that kind of trouble to Silver Maple.

"Not with me. Kit's not responsible for someone else's crazy actions. He's the sweetest guy, and the residents adore him. I'll track Kit down soon to make sure he's doing okay." Caitlyn's phone chimed with an incoming text, and she checked the screen with a snort. "Right on cue. A group of board members have demanded a meeting in my office at my earliest convenience. That means they're on their way now."

"I hope it goes well."

Caitlyn crossed her fingers and stood up. "Good luck with the report. Maybe don't fret about the language. Write it up however you like, and let the board and your partners deal with it."

"Thanks."

After Caitlyn left, I took her advice and tackled the report, providing a detailed account of the vandalism and chase without fretting about word choices. A text appeared in our RAVEN group chat not even two minutes after I emailed the report.

> Vaughn: Seriously, Hawk? You couldn't make it until lunchtime on our first day without tackling a perp into the pool?
>
> Archer: Our boy's just gifted like that. Wait until you hear about the new friend he made.
>
> Ethan: Let me guess. It was the one the cops hauled off in handcuffs.
>
> Nico: I knew Ray Ray secretly liked trouble.

I tucked my phone back into my pocket without responding. I'd learned it was just best to ignore their fuckery because engaging only added fuel to their fire. They'd eventually wear themselves out and find something else to do or someone else to harass. I couldn't help snorting as I grabbed my lunch bag and headed for the door. *Liked trouble.*

"Hardly."

But the memory of hazel-brown eyes fringed with dark lashes taunted me. "Okay, maybe I like trouble sometimes." But I had no intention of acting on it. Atticus was off-limits.

CHAPTER 7

ATTICUS

THE LOW HUM OF AN APPROACHING GOLF CART MADE ME GLANCE UP from the clipboard in my hands. Aunt Ronni was headed in my direction, which meant she'd already heard about the incident with Chad. *Fuck me running.* I scrawled my signature at the bottom of the authorization form to have my sweet Sadie hauled to my family's preferred body shop, not that there was much hope for her.

Harland had a reputation for being a wizard with cars, but he wasn't a real magical being who could wave a wand and fix the massive dents and shattered windows. The repairs would cost more than Sadie was worth. To save money, I'd recently cut back coverage on my car insurance policy to liability only, so I'd have to pay for physical damages out of my pitiful savings or sue Chad for damages. While I had a clear case against him, airing our dirty laundry in a courtroom didn't appeal to me.

I handed the clipboard to the driver, whose name tag identified him as Hermie. "Thanks for getting here so fast."

"No problem. I'll get the car loaded onto the trailer and clean up the glass and debris for you," he said.

With that taken care of, I could no longer ignore the woman who'd stopped her golf cart at a respectable distance and waited to speak to me.

Aunt Ronni had pulled her hair into a low bun and wore a visor to shield her face from the sun. As I approached, I noticed she'd dressed for a morning of golf. Her nearly flawless face was a neutral mask, and her dark eyeglasses prevented me from seeing the expression in her light blue eyes. But she couldn't be happy with how my tenure at Silver Maple had started.

"What a clusterfuck," she exclaimed.

Aunt Ronni, my grandmother's much younger sister from her father's second marriage, was closer to my mom's age. In fact, they acted more like sisters than aunt and niece. Her salty language didn't surprise me one bit because I'd grown up hearing my grandmother refer to her as eccentric or a free spirit. It took me a while to realize that Nanna used the term to define every aspect of Ronni's life that she didn't approve of, including but not limited to her radical activism, thumbing her nose at societal norms, and lesbianism. I loved Ronni more than life itself. Hell, I wanted to be just like her when I grew up. I had the gay part down pat, so maybe I was off to a good start.

"I'm so sorry I've disappointed you, Aunt Ronni."

She pulled her sunglasses down low so I could see her blue eyes twinkling with mischief. "Are you kidding me? This is the most excitement we've had around here in ages. First that hot-as-hell security guard, and now this? Tongues will wag for days, maybe weeks."

"I'm still sorry Chad caused a scene," I said. "I don't want to embarrass you and make you regret getting me this job."

Aunt Ronni waved off my concern. "We need to get a few things straight. First, I didn't get you the job. I only got you an interview, where you earned the position on your own merit." Of course she'd say that to spare my feelings, but the twinkling expression in her eyes turned steely, shutting down further discussion on the issue. "And second, you're not responsible for that asshole's actions." Ronni pursed her lips together tightly. "I never liked that Chad. Not even when you guys dated in high school."

"He didn't like you either."

"Of course not. I could see right through his bullshit." Ronni pinned me with those shrewd blue eyes. "Demand better for yourself, Atticus."

"Yes, ma'am."

Another vehicle approached, and my heart lurched when the RAVEN Securities SUV came into view.

Ronni perked up too. "I wonder if it's the hottie I met this morning."

The bright sunshine created a glare on the windshield, blocking our view of the driver. "What was his name? Hayden? Holden?"

"Rayden," I replied absently. "He goes by Ray."

"Ah, so he's the one who went into the pool?"

"Uh-huh."

"Bet he looked amazing wet," Ronni said. "His clothes clinging to that body."

"Yeah." I turned and looked at her. "Since when do you get worked up over a man?"

She swatted playfully at my arm. "Not for me, dear. I have your best interests at heart. The best way to get over that dickhead Chad is to get under a hunk like Ray."

I wanted to scream, "I tried," but I kept my mouth shut. The last thing I needed was Aunt Ronni playing matchmaker when Ray couldn't construct that brick wall fast enough to keep me out.

The SUV got close enough for us to see the driver, and we both sighed our disappointment that it wasn't Ray.

"He's smoking hot too," Ronni said under her breath. "Is that like a prerequisite to get hired at the company?"

I looked over at her. "Smoking hot?"

"Isn't that what the kids say these days?" Ronni asked.

"I hear smoke show more often, but it means the same thing."

"Hello again, Kit." Archer smiled as he approached, but it lacked the flirty punch from earlier. "I'm sorry about your car."

"Hi, Archer. And thank you. I'm going to miss this old girl. We've been through a lot together."

"A few wars, it seems," Ronni said, injecting a bit of snobbery into her voice. She stepped forward and extended her hand to Archer, which he politely shook. "I'm Veronica Poole, one of the board members and residents at Silver Maple."

"Archer Stone. It's good to meet you, ma'am."

"I'd heard about the ruckus and wanted to see for myself what happened." She tsked and shook her head. "Things like this rarely happen around here. Thank goodness one of your men was here to prevent things from escalating."

"I'm glad we could assist." Archer turned his attention to me. "Do you need a ride someplace?"

"I, um—"

"I'll give him a lift in my golf cart," Ronni said. "Some of the board members want to meet with the executive director, and they might have questions for Kit about the incident."

And just when I thought my mood couldn't get any lower.

"All right," Archer said. "I'll see you around."

"See you," I said.

Ronni strode to her golf cart like a woman on a mission, and her rigid posture commanded that I follow without delay.

"Hang in there, Kit," Archer said. "It's going to be okay."

I tossed him an appreciative smile as I walked away. Ronni's face was an expressionless mask once again as I boarded the small vehicle, and she accelerated before my ass hit the seat.

"In a hurry for me to go before the firing squad?" I teased.

"Don't be silly," she hissed once we were out of Archer's earshot. "The board is comprised of sensible people who will realize this wasn't your fault. But this needs to be a onetime incident, Kit."

"I don't have any other ex-boyfriends, and no one else hates me enough to cause such a scene." I regretted not calling Chad after he left a message with my mom. Maybe none of this would've happened if he'd been able to vent his frustrations, misguided as they were.

"Of course you don't. You're the sweetest damn kid on the planet." Ronni patted my knee, then veered her golf cart to the right instead of continuing toward the administration building. "You're going to need something to tool around in today since your Sadie is heading out of here on a flatbed truck." She parked next to the property service garage and angled her body toward me. "Sign out a golf cart to use. It's part of the perks that come with your job, so take advantage of them. What are you going to do for transportation to and from work?"

"I'm not sure yet."

"I know you love that car, but I think she's destined for the junkyard," Ronni said.

"Yeah, I'm afraid you're right." Sadness pressed on my shoulders and squeezed my heart. Poor Sadie.

"Kit," Ronni said firmly. "Do you have money to buy something else? If not, I can lend—"

"No." The word blasted from my mouth with more force than I'd intended, and I apologized. "It's time I stood on my own two feet. You already helped me get this job." I held up my hand when Ronni looked like she was going to protest. "You did help, whether you just secured an interview or twisted Caitlyn's arm until she hired me."

Ronni rolled her eyes. "I did no such thing."

"I can't ask for more."

Reaching over to pat my cheek, Ronni said, "You don't ask for enough from the universe, Kit. That's part of the problem. Stop shrinking yourself down to fit into someone else's mold. It's okay to take up space and demand a better life. Manifest more for yourself. Envision what you want, and go after it."

An image of Ray came to mind, his beautiful blue eyes staring into mine. Oh no. Nothing but trouble lay ahead in that direction, and pursuing him wouldn't get me out of my old bedroom. Well, maybe for a night or two if I were lucky, but it would be a temporary reprieve that would lead to more awkwardness at best and heartbreak at worst. Ugh. I'd had one nightmare workplace romance, and I didn't need another.

Aunt Ronni's giggle yanked me back down to reality. "The blush on your cheeks betrays the direction your thoughts had taken."

I shook my head to deny the accusation, but my stupid mouth acted of its own volition, curving into a devious smile. "Ray looked so good soaking wet. Muscle upon muscle." I sighed and shook my head. "But no. It was a fleeting thought." One I'd take home and use as often as I wanted. "A relationship is the last thing I need right now." I held up a hand before Ronni could interject. "And this job is too important for me to risk it with a casual hookup." Even if I were willing to risk that kind of rejection again.

Ronni arched a brow. "Even with that smoke show?"

"Yes. The hotter the man, the deadlier the burn. It's best I keep my distance."

My aunt nodded her approval, as if I'd passed a pop quiz. "Do you want a ride home tonight?"

I shook my head. "I'll phone a friend or order a ride on my app."

Ronni narrowed her eyes. "I really wish you'd let me help."

I climbed out of the golf cart and smiled at her. "You've done enough. Don't worry about me. I'm a survivor."

Ronni sighed and backed out of the parking space. "It's time you become a thriver," she said.

If only it were as easy as she made it sound.

"About your transportation?" Ronni pressed.

Sighing heavily, I prepared to say the hard part out loud. "I'll have to sell Sadie for scrap metal and use that money as a down payment for something affordable."

Ronni didn't like it, but she relented with a nod before driving off toward the admin building.

The next two activities went much smoother than the first, though the residents in both groups were full of questions about the morning's incident, proving how quickly news traveled on campus. Luckily, the wheelchair volleyball attendees were more excited about their session than peppering me with questions about my misfortune, and the advanced yoga attendees were too excited about the drama to notice they were far more advanced in their skills than their instructor. I'd need to double down on my training in my free time and find free courses on YouTube.

My stomach growled like a caged beast when I parked my borrowed golf cart outside the employee cafeteria's double doors. Silver Maple employed the best chefs for the residents, and the perks spilled over to the employees. Our lunch options weren't as grand as those offered in the main dining room, but the quality was second to none. Tilting my head back slightly, I sniffed the air and tried to guess the lunchtime lineup. Definitely something fried, but that could be meat or vegetables. I caught a hint of something smoky like paprika, but that clarified nothing for me. Chef Sofia showed the same passion for seasoning the batter for her green tomatoes, zucchini, and okra as she did for her fried chicken. No plain-Jane salt and pepper for her food. Even those with dietary restrictions received food prepared with the utmost care and flavor. Sofia was pure magic, and I closed my eyes in anticipation.

"Kit! Look out!" Archer called.

I opened my eyes in time to avoid crashing headfirst into a signpost designating the parking space for employees only. Damn, how had I veered so far off the sidewalk in such a short amount of time? I turned to thank my savior with a smile.

"Dude," Archer said, sounding winded. Had he run to save me? "That was close."

Bobby, one of the massage therapists on staff, approached at a slower pace. A scowl marred his handsome face, and he dragged his gaze over my body in an unfriendly manner. So strange. Bobby had been so nice to me since I started working at Silver Maple. "You should really pay closer attention to where you're walking. It was like you were in a trance or something." His tone of voice was as sour as his expression, so I hadn't misread Bobby. He was pissed at me for some unknown reason.

Archer placed a hand on my shoulder and squeezed. "Hey, you've had a rough day. I'm worried about you." In contrast, Archer's voice was gentle and kind.

Bobby's gaze grew chilly as he watched my interaction with Archer. "Maybe you should go home and try again tomorrow."

Offering my most reassuring smile, I eased back a step so Archer would drop his arm. "I just need food, and everything will be fine. I promise."

Archer's brow rose, but he didn't argue. "Do you want to join us for lunch?"

One look at Bobby's arctic expression had me shaking my head. "I appreciate it, but I'm going to find a quiet spot somewhere. You guys enjoy lunch."

"Oh, we will," Bobby purred. "And afterward, I'm taking Archer on a very private tour of the grounds and buildings."

Ahh. I better understood Bobby's anger. He wanted Archer all to himself and saw me as a threat. Nope. Not me, and I'd make sure he knew it. I could not afford, nor did I want, any more drama at work. "See you around, fellas."

I felt their stares as I walked away, and things only got worse when I entered the cafeteria, where at least a dozen people observed my every move. Was this how it felt to be famous? Fuck that. I kept my eyes straight ahead and placed one foot in front of the other until I arrived at the food counter. The delicious aroma that had flirted with my senses and nearly caused head trauma came from a mound of golden-brown fried chicken. My stomach growled with a need that bordered on lust, and I think a soft moan escaped my lips.

Carl, a tall Jamaican American, greeted me with a toothy smile. "That's some day you're having, huh?"

"The worst," I admitted. "But I think you're about to make it better."

The smile got wider, and the gleam in Carl's amber eyes turned wicked. "My wife tells me this all the time."

"I bet," I replied. "I'm going to get my lunch to go today. Can I have a few drumsticks with a serving of potato salad and a piece of cornbread?"

"Coming right up."

Carl packed my order into carryout containers and placed them in a paper bag. I met him at the end of the line, where he placed a packet of freshly baked cookies into the bag. "My treat to turn your day around."

"I appreciate it," I told him as I punched my employee number into the keypad to deduct the cost of my lunch from my paycheck. "Thank you, Carl."

"Chin up, kid," he called out as I walked away.

Following his advice, I noticed how much the small gesture boosted my mood. The pond wasn't far, so I opted to walk instead of motoring there on the golf cart. The midday sun blazed hot above, but a strong breeze made the brief trip almost pleasant. My favorite bench sat under a massive oak tree, so I could enjoy my lunch in peace as long as Matilda and Marty, the resident mallards, behaved. I spotted the happy couple in the middle of the pond, ducking their heads underwater and splashing about as if they didn't have a care in the world. What must that be like?

I was so focused on the lovebirds that I didn't realize someone had already claimed my favorite spot until it was too late to back away without making things more awkward than they already were. Intense blue eyes locked on me, and I froze in place just like a little rabbit before a hungry wolf pounced. Ray didn't growl or gnash his teeth, but he didn't look pleased to see me.

"I wasn't looking for you," I blurted.

"Okay."

"This is just my favorite lunch spot." I held up my bag as evidence. "And this is my lunch."

Ray's mouth quirked up on one side. "It's a beautiful spot." He sniffed the air and narrowed his eyes. "Do I smell fried chicken?"

"Yes," I replied. "It's amazing, but someone who looks like you probably doesn't eat fried chicken. Or fried anything." Oh god. My mouth was on a mission to ruin my life. I flexed my biceps to show my meaning. "Because you're strong. Bet you need a lot of protein to fuel that body." *Oh god. Just shut up, idiot.*

Ray's mouth curved into a wry smirk. "I eat a lot of protein, and sometimes I like it double battered and fried to a golden crisp." He held up half of a wrap and said, "Today, it's a boring turkey club."

"I'd be willing to share my chicken with you," I said. "And I have other goodies too."

Ray looked between his lunch and mine, then patted the bench in invitation.

I didn't skip to him, but my feet barely touched the ground.

CHAPTER 8

RAYDEN

"ARE YOU SURE THIS IS OKAY?" ATTICUS ASKED BEFORE HE SAT DOWN.

No, I wasn't sure. Furthest thing from it, actually. Inviting Atticus to sit and share lunch with me had come out of nowhere. It had to be the enticing aroma of the chicken, not the tempting promise of his company. I held his gaze and said, "I don't say things I don't mean."

Yet Atticus didn't sit. He cocked his head to the side and narrowed his eyes. "But you didn't invite me with words. I interpreted the silent pat as an offer to join you. It could've been a muscle spasm or something."

Staring into his hazel-brown eyes triggered involuntary reactions in my body that made me hunger for so much more than the chicken. Atticus was giving me an out, but I didn't want to take it. "Would you like to join me?" I asked.

Atticus sighed and smiled. "This is the first good thing that's happened to me all day." He sat down on the opposite end of the bench, leaving a two-foot gap between us and making him both too close and too far away. Atticus angled his body toward me slightly and pursed his lips. A sexy combination of citrus, cedar, and vanilla teased my senses. Was it his bodywash? I hadn't noticed earlier, but that was likely from the shock of running into Atticus at work. "Well, maybe this is the second-best thing to happen," he said. "Carl gave me free cookies to compensate for my crappy day."

A kind gesture for someone who deserved it shouldn't stir an uncomfortable feeling in my gut, and it sure as hell shouldn't make me question Carl's motives. "That was nice."

"He's a great guy. I think you'll like him."

I replied with a noncommittal, "Uh-huh."

Atticus smiled nervously and opened his brown bag, letting the smell of fried deliciousness escape. He moaned, or maybe that was me, and shifted the contents for a better look. "Cookies aren't the only goodies in here."

My mouth had salivated at first whiff, and it took great effort not to snatch the bag from Atticus and bury my face in it. Or scoot closer and bury my face in his neck.

"I'll show you mine if you show me yours," Atticus teased.

My mind went straight to the gutter, of course, but Atticus wore a stunned expression that said he hadn't meant his taunt to be a double entendre. I arched a brow and bit my cheek to keep from smiling at the blush creeping across those stunning cheekbones. I had the craziest urge to run my finger over the skin to see if it felt as warm and soft as it looked, but I didn't give in to that desire either.

Taking pity on him, I pulled out the items in my lunch tote. "I have the wrap I told you about, plus a container of watermelon, and a summer salad with strawberries, corn, quinoa, and avocado that I lightly drizzled with balsamic vinaigrette."

His mouth parted in surprise. "Wow. Did you make that?"

I liked the awe in his voice, more than I should, and it made me want to impress him even more. "All of it, including the vinaigrette."

"Wow." Then Atticus shook his head. "I sound like a broken record." He opened his lunch bag and said, "I've already told you about the fried chicken." He placed the container on the bench, and I moved closer, scanning the surrounding area before meeting his curious gaze. Atticus arched a questioning brow.

"With the way your day is going, some loose dog or wild animal is about to descend on this bench and steal our chicken," I told him.

"Our chicken, huh?" Hazel eyes danced with happiness in the same way sunlight shimmered off the pond.

I couldn't resist getting caught up in the moment. It had been so damn long since I let go and experienced joy, and there was this adorable man who beamed it from his pores. I owed Atticus the truth and an apology, but I was afraid he'd leave. And it wasn't the chicken I'd miss most. "You promised to share," I teased.

Atticus agreed with a slight nod. "So I did."

"What else is in there? I smell something buttery." I sniffed the air, and my eyes widened with recognition. "Is that cornbread?"

Atticus grinned broadly and pulled out a large square wrapped in wax paper. "Carl was generous with his portions today."

That guy again. I nodded toward his bag, a silent command for him to keep going so my brain didn't wander too deep into the weeds. Atticus removed a container of potato salad with a single fork taped to the top.

"What else is in there?" I asked. "I believe you mentioned cookies."

Waggling his brows, Atticus said, "There's a paper sleeve overflowing with them. Want to close your eyes and guess the flavors?"

Closing my eyes meant letting down my guard. Did I want to relinquish that kind of control to Atticus? We weren't in a war zone or in hostile territory. Sure, another one of his crazy ex-boyfriends could spring out of nowhere and take another swing at me with the crowbar, but I liked my chances. Closing my eyes, I leaned forward. The paper sleeve rattled when Atticus lifted it from the bag, and I sensed him move toward me more than I heard his body shift on the bench.

Cinnamon was the first thing I smelled, followed by something fruity. "Oatmeal raisin is one," I said. I took another sniff and moaned when my brain registered toasty nuts. "Peanut butter." I picked out chocolate on my next inhale, which was a common ingredient in many cookies. I went with the most obvious and said, "Chocolate chip."

"Yep. There's one more."

"Four cookies?" I asked.

"Mmhmm."

I inhaled deeply one more time, but the flavors had blended into an indiscernible but mouthwatering bouquet. "You stumped me."

"Sugar," Atticus said breathlessly, making the word sound more like an endearment than a cookie flavor.

I opened my eyes to discover Atticus was much closer than I'd realized. His hazel gaze looked greener beneath the shady tree, and the yearning I saw there held me prisoner, until he licked his bottom lip, drawing my attention to its wet and shiny perfection. Kissing had always been my favorite form of foreplay and was the single thing I missed most about intimacy. My body craved the biological release of an orgasm given to me by someone other than myself, but my soul missed the deeper connection I got from kissing. I couldn't—wouldn't—press my mouth against his, but I could pretend I'd acted on the impulse later…in the shower…while fucking my fist. I felt the ache deep in my core, a bottomless yearning I wouldn't appease.

"Carl must like you a lot," I finally said.

"So does his wife, Sofia. She's our main chef."

The relief flooding my system pissed me off enough to scoot a little to the right, setting a boundary Atticus couldn't miss. He straightened and gestured to the food on the bench.

"I just have the one fork."

"Same," I said.

"I don't mind if you get your vinaigrette in my potato salad," Atticus said.

"And I don't mind if you get your potato salad in my summer salad." That was much better than sharing a fork. I pulled out the second half of my wrap and handed it over. "Turkey, bacon, feta cheese, spinach, and a tzatziki-style yogurt sauce."

Both brows shot up, and Atticus smirked. "I'm surprised you didn't include your cooking skills in your Randy bio." His cheeks turned bright pink, and Atticus slapped a hand over his mouth. I could tell by his immediate embarrassment that he hadn't meant to acknowledge our previous acquaintance. "Sorry." The word came out muffled behind his fingers.

It was better for us to lay our cards on the table and put the botched hookup behind us. "Guys on those apps don't really care about my kitchen skills, do they?"

Atticus lowered his hand and grinned sheepishly at me. "You have a point. In case you couldn't tell by our brief messages on the app, I don't know much about hookups." His confession sounded so vulnerable and honest, the least I could do was match his sincerity.

"Me either. You're my first attempt." I should've left it at that, but I couldn't seem to slow the train now that it had left the station. "And the last."

Atticus's beautiful mouth opened, closed, and opened again to let a sigh escape. He had questions but didn't want to ask.

I had answers I didn't want to give, but I still owed him the truth and an apology. I wouldn't get a better chance. "I didn't really have a work emergency on the night we were supposed to meet."

"So, you do say things you don't mean," Atticus said.

"Not normally."

"Then why did you lie?"

Damn, I hated that Atticus thought of me as a liar now. Telling him the truth would probably make things even messier, but he deserved to know what really happened. "I showed up on time, early even, but I couldn't make myself get out of the car." Fuck. I'd made things worse instead of better.

Hazel eyes shimmered with hurt, and Atticus worked his bottom lip between his teeth. When he released the soft flesh, it was wet and so alluring that I nearly lost the thread of our conversation. "It's okay. You were allowed to change your mind. I'm not everyone's cup of tea." Atticus turned his head toward the pond and blinked a few times.

Oh god. I couldn't let this beautiful man think I'd found him lacking. "I wanted you too much, and I panicked."

Atticus snapped his head to meet my gaze, his eyebrows forming angry slashes over expressive eyes. "There's no need to placate me when I've given you an out." He reached for his food as if he meant to go. "Maybe we should just—"

I reached over and wrapped my fingers around his forearm. His skin was warm and so damn inviting. Stroking my thumb over his arm, I fought the urge to close my eyes and memorize the way Atticus felt under my hand. "I know I've fucked this up six ways to Sunday, but please don't go. I promise there's a genuine apology coming."

Atticus held my gaze for several seconds before giving me a subtle nod to continue.

"I wasn't in the right headspace for intimacy, and I haven't been for a while. I thought I was ready. I truly wanted to be, but I wasn't."

Atticus looked down to where I still held his arm. "Wasn't?" The hope in his voice tugged at the loose threads of my patchwork heart.

Forcing myself to release him, I withdrew my hand. "I'm not, and I'm not sure when or if I'll ever be."

Atticus looked at me with so much tenderness that it stole my breath. "You've suffered a devastating loss, haven't you?"

"My life has been one tragedy after another," I replied with an honesty that rocked me. What was it about Atticus, this virtual stranger, that made me open up in ways I couldn't with anyone else, not even my best friends?

"I'm really sorry, Ray."

"No, I'm the one who's sorry. I tried to message you the next day to explain and apologize, but you'd deleted your profile from the Randy app." I cocked my head to the side. "Or did you just block me?"

Atticus laughed. "I deleted my profile and removed the stupid app from my phone. I'm not a hookup guy. My best friend encouraged me to get out there and live a little after my breakup with Chad. And while I'm down to fuck, hooking up with a random guy just isn't my thing."

Down to fuck. I swallowed hard and picked the first thing that sprang to mind that didn't involve getting Atticus naked and under me. "So how do you plan to meet these men you're down to fuck?" What the hell was wrong with me? Imagining Atticus with a different man made me…stabby.

"The old-fashioned way, I guess," Atticus replied with a casual shrug. "I'll go to a bar or club and chat someone up. See how it goes. Maybe I'll stop being stubborn and accept the invitations of well-meaning people who want to introduce me to a friend or relative. What's the worst that will happen? I make new friends?"

"Uh-huh." *Really cool response, man.* There were a ton of things that could go horribly wrong. Atticus could meet a shady dude with bad intentions. He could get his heart broken again, or…he could meet the man of his dreams. Shouldn't I want that for him? The churning acid in my gut said I didn't like that option. And what did I do? Blurted out the worst possible thing. "Or they follow you to your workplace with a crowbar and a shitty attitude."

Atticus widened his eyes in shock, and his pretty pink mouth gaped open to allow a horrified squeak to escape.

Flames of humiliation engulfed my entire body as I scrambled for a way to unfuck the situation. Atticus finally blinked and closed his mouth. He blinked faster, and his lips curved into a devilish smile. Then the laughter started; soft chuckles became deep-belly rumbles that stole his breath. Atticus slapped my arm as he gasped for air and wiped the tears from his cheeks. He circled his hand around his face in a gesture I couldn't decipher.

"What?" I asked, fighting back my own laughter.

"Your expression is priceless," Atticus wheezed when he had enough breath to speak.

"Because my remark was way out of line, and I'm so sorry."

"Well, it's your job to provide security to Silver Maple, so you should know about potential threats to the residents and staff." Atticus tilted his head and narrowed his eyes. "Speaking of crowbar-wielding maniacs, I never thought to ask how Chad got onto the property?"

Atticus had let me off the hook with far more grace than I deserved, and I was happy to solve this mystery for him. "Officer Romero called me about an hour ago and said that Chad had climbed a fence on the far-west side of the property. They recovered his car where he'd parked it on the side of the road. He'd hiked through the woods bordering Silver Maple and climbed the perimeter fence. I rode out there and was surprised to find a typical chain-link fence but then remembered that the residents aren't prisoners. I updated my incident report, and time will tell if the board wants to update the security." Cocking a brow, I asked, "Should they? Are there any other angry ex-boyfriends that might show up here?"

Atticus chuckled and shook his head. "Nope. You've met the only guy I've ever dated."

I choked and sputtered, "W-what? No fucking way."

"Are you making fun of me?"

"Of course not," I said. "I just find it so hard to believe. You're so… so…" I waved a hand in his direction. "You."

Full lips quirked into a teasing grin, and Atticus said, "And you think I've got them lined up down the street to take Chad's place?"

Our conversation suddenly felt like verbal foreplay, and the volleying made my blood hum and rush toward inconvenient places. "Come on. You must know how good-looking you are. I've seen the thirst traps you uploaded to Randy. So, yeah. I think they're lined up down the street to get a single minute of your time."

Atticus averted his gaze as a pretty blush bloomed across his cheeks. "I can't believe I took those photos, let alone uploaded them. But according to my research, those slutty pictures are expected." Atticus licked his lips, and I watched the glide of his tongue. Was he nervous? Aroused? He raised his head, and the glimmer of gratitude in his pretty eyes twisted my guts. "It's been a long time since a man made me feel this good about myself," Atticus said with a wry smile. "Even if I think you're laying it on a little too thick as an apology. But seriously, thank you."

"I meant every word."

"Because you don't say things you don't mean."

"That's right," I replied, pointing at the food. "Better eat."

Atticus sighed heavily and forked a bite of my summer salad, but he didn't bring it to his lips.

Figuring the morning's incident still weighed heavily on his mind, I said the last thing either of us likely expected. "Do you want to talk about the breakup with Chad?"

"It's really simple. Chad and I worked at the same company. We shared a home, a bank account, and a life. I thought we had a great one. But then..." Atticus paused and shoved the bite of salad into his mouth and chewed. The timing felt suspicious to me. Was he buying time to figure out what to say, or was he hungry? And did I care when I got to watch that gorgeous mouth move? He swallowed the food and moaned. "Fuck me. That's so good."

"Thank you." I didn't want to rush him, but my lunch break was almost over, and I hadn't sampled the chicken yet. "But then..." I prompted before biting into a drumstick. The flavor hitting my taste buds made my eyes roll back in my head. "Fuck me."

"Right?" Atticus agreed. "What were we talking about?"

"Chad."

Atticus snarled so adorably. "Right. I caught Chad cheating with the member of senior management that we reported to, which was against company policy."

"The no-fraternization policy didn't apply to you and Chad?"

"No." Atticus squirmed a little on the bench and bit into his half of the turkey wrap. His eyes expressed "fuck me," but he didn't verbalize the request, thank god. He swallowed his bite and said, "We were just low-level worker bees, and they didn't care if we were in a relationship as long as it didn't interfere with our work."

"What did you do?" I asked before digging into the potato salad. The chef had added some herbs I didn't expect. A sprinkling of dill, perhaps. Possibly chives.

"I sent explicit proof of the affair to everyone in the company, including the corporate office in Atlanta, to make sure the lovebirds couldn't keep it quiet."

A chunk of potato went down the wrong pipe, and I coughed until I worked it back out. Atticus groaned and squatted down in front of me.

"Christ, I'm sorry."

I chugged half a bottle of water and cleared my throat. "It's fine. I just didn't expect that level of pettiness from you. How explicit was the proof?"

"Well, I cropped the photos to make them NC-17, but I also included damning screenshots of their explicit text messages, where they admitted to fucking all over the office, including on top of the big boss's desk."

"Fuck."

"Do you think I'm terrible?" His hazel-brown eyes looked enormous and suspiciously wet.

I wanted to run my fingers through his messy brown hair to comfort him. Damn, this was getting out of control. "Hell no. I bow to your diabolical brilliance."

"Really?" His smile was bright enough to outshine the sun.

"Absolutely," I replied.

Atticus pushed to his feet and resumed his seat on the bench. "I guess that's a consolation prize to losing my job."

"That hardly feels fair," I protested. "You weren't the one who broke company policy."

Atticus was quiet for a moment, and I got the feeling he was biding his time again. What didn't he want me to know and why? "My employer decided I was more trouble than I was worth. A liability. People were afraid I'd start spying on them and tattle to corporate." Atticus sighed and shrugged his shoulders. "But that was six months ago, and I'm not sure why Chad waited until now to retaliate. I can only assume things didn't work out for him and Win, and he took it out on me."

"Win? What kind of name is that?"

"Winston Jacob Ellison the third," Atticus said haughtily.

"That name should've died out a couple of generations ago."

"He's every bit as entitled as the name implies," Atticus said. "He had no problem coming into my home and fucking my boyfriend in our bed."

Wincing, I said, "That's brutal."

"Yeah," Atticus sighed heavily. "Enough about my dating disasters. Is there anyone you want to talk about? I'm a good listener."

An image of Javier flashed in my mind, his dark eyes twinkling and lips curled into a devilish smile as I clumsily confessed my feelings for him. It had taken years for that beautiful memory to resurface and replace the one of a smoldering heap of charred metal that had claimed his life. Javi's loss was an ache I still felt deep in my bones, but for the first time in three years, my self-imposed loneliness cut deeper than heartbreak.

And that's when panic kicked in.

Clinging to despair and misery kept Javi's memory alive, and it prevented me from risking my heart again. I wasn't just unlucky in love; I was a walking tragedy, and I couldn't risk inflicting my bad karma on another living soul, especially not one as sweet as Atticus. It was time to nix this—whatever it was—before things got out of hand and someone got hurt.

I shifted my gaze away from his mesmerizing hazel eyes to stare at the pond again. "Um, no, but thank you." Finishing my drumstick, I tossed the bone into my bag. "I need to get back to my office." *Real smooth. Totally convincing. And the Oscar doesn't go to Rayden James.* Gesturing to the food containers, I said. "I'm happy to leave my summer salad and watermelon here for you."

"Oh, um, no," Atticus said, his joy deflating more with every word. "You didn't eat much, and you might get hungry later."

I closed the containers and repacked my bag instead of making sure. The air between us felt tense and awkward again, and I should've been glad. It was what I wanted, yet it felt so wrong. "Thank you for sharing your lunch with me. I'd heard good things about the food, but it exceeded my expectations." And the company was stellar too.

"Thank you for sharing your lunch. Chef Sofia will need to look out if you decide to switch careers."

I chuckled awkwardly as I stood up.

"So, I'll see you around," Atticus said.

"Yes."

Atticus arched a brow. "Often?"

I turned to face him. "No. My partners and I will rotate in and out, probably not on a consistent schedule."

Atticus didn't bother to hide his disappointment. "Oh, I see."

It was time to leave, yet I stood there staring into his expressive eyes. "I saw your car rolling out of here on a flatbed truck. Do you have a ride home tonight?"

Atticus nodded, but it wasn't very convincing.

"Are you sure?" I asked.

He smiled faintly. "Yeah, my friend is coming to pick me up. The body shop owner made an offer to buy Sadie as a derby car. I need to sign some paperwork and pick up the check. It's not a lot of money, but it will make a down payment on something else."

"Okay. I hope the rest of your day gets better."

"Yours too."

Walking away, putting space between myself and this temptation was the right thing to do, even if it felt so damn wrong.

CHAPTER 9

ATTICUS

I CHECKED MY MESSENGER BAG TO MAKE SURE I'D GRABBED THE VITAL stuff. Cell phone? Check. Earbuds? Check. Wallet? Check. Anything else could wait until I returned to work the next day. Turning off my office light, I stepped into the hallway and immediately collided with someone.

Gasping and clutching my chest, I stepped back to offer an apology, but seeing the unbridled fury in Bobby's eyes caused the words to die on my lips. Suddenly, our run-in didn't feel like an accident. Had Bobby been waiting for me in the hallway? And if so, I suspected I knew the reason. Fuck me. Couldn't I get just one break?

"How do you know Archer?" Bobby's voice was as hostile as his expression. "Or should I ask, how well do you know him?"

I sighed. "Well, my answer to both is the same."

Not expanding on my response was a form of antagonism best kept in my arsenal for another day, especially with the borderline manic gaze boring holes in my skull. A muscle in Bobby's cheek spasmed, pulling his mouth up on one side to reveal tightly clenched teeth. I blew out a breath and took pity on him before something erupted or he choked the life out of me.

"I don't know Archer at all. I just met him this morning." I raised both hands up with my palms out in front of me. "I'm no threat to your relationship with him, whatever that is."

"We fucked for hours last night. Barely slept. That's what Archer is to me."

"Okay," I said, slowly backing down the hallway. "It's none of my business, but more power to you. The guy does absolutely nothing for me."

An image of Ray's blissful expression while eating fried chicken sprang to mind. What I wouldn't give to put that look on his face and evoke those moans from his lips. Now, Ray did it for me, and I'd damn near sell my soul for him to do whatever the hell he wanted to me. Distracted by the acknowledgment, I tripped over my own two feet in my typical clumsy fashion. I nearly fell to the ground, which would've given Bobby too much of an advantage. I righted myself physically and emotionally. We weren't starring in a horror film, and Bobby wasn't going to kill me.

"Besides, I'm already seeing someone," I blurted.

Crossing his arms over his chest, Bobby stalked forward as I continued my backward retreat. "Who? I've never heard you mention a boyfriend."

Alarm pulsed through my body, urging me to pivot and run, but I remained calm. Mostly because I needed my job, but I also didn't trust the universe to show me an ounce of kindness, and I didn't want to end up in the ER. "It's t-too new to t-t-talk about," I stammered. Clearing my throat, I searched for something else to say that would ease Bobby's mind. "I don't want to jinx anything or make a bigger fool of myself than I already have."

The last part made Bobby smile, which softened his expression from a potential threat to the snarky massage therapist I'd met on my first day. "You do have an uncanny way about you," Bobby said. "Your kind of chaos would be sweet and endearing to the right person. I thought that person might be me when you first got hired, but it didn't take me long to realize we wouldn't be a good fit."

His words shouldn't have hurt my feelings, considering I'd cast him as the villain in a horror film just moments prior. But they did. Everyone, even this weirdo, found me lacking. When would I ever be enough?

Bobby tipped his head as if reconsidering something, and I worried he'd veered back into jealous territory. Then he smiled brightly and said, "Archer isn't a good match for you either. He'd want someone with a bit more… prowess."

"Definitely," I agreed, clutching that olive branch as if my life depended on it. My phone chimed with an incoming text, and I bit back a sigh of relief.

"That's probably my ride." Fishing the phone out of my messenger bag, I checked the screen.

Emma: Here

"Yep. My best friend is here. Gotta go."

I'd loved Emma Cortez from the moment we met in third grade, when her family moved to Georgia from Puerto Rico. We'd been inseparable ever since, so this wasn't the first time Emma had ridden to my rescue, nor would it likely be the last.

Bobby held my gaze for a few seconds before he nodded. "Don't want to keep them waiting."

"See you tomorrow."

"Bye, Kit."

I pivoted and walked down the corridor as calmly as I could, feeling Bobby's intense stare on my back the entire time. Once I turned the corner, I bolted for the front door and to the safety I'd always found in Emma. She'd parked her sleek, red Mazda 3 Turbo parallel with the curb and had left the engine running, which any smart Georgian would do on a hot day in May. I cast one last glance over my shoulder and sighed in relief when Bobby was nowhere in sight. Reaching the car, I yanked on the door handle, but it was locked. I ducked my head and looked at Emma through the lightly tinted window.

"Open up. Hurry." I pulled on the door handle again to stress the urgency, but Emma just lowered her sunglasses to stare at me as if I had lost my mind. Glancing over my shoulder, I caught Bobby watching us from the doorway. Turning frantic eyes back on my best friend, I smacked my hand against the window and mouthed, "Let me in! Please!"

Emma rolled her dark eyes and hit the switch to unlock the door.

I dove into the passenger seat and shouted for Emma to drive before I'd even shut the door.

"What the—"

"Go! Go! Go!"

Emma hit the gas pedal hard enough to launch her car forward like a rocket. Since my ass wasn't squarely in the seat yet, the momentum threw me backward and sideways, crashing me into the hard console between us and cracking my head on her closed moonroof. "Oh my god. Are you—"

"Keep driving!" I shouted when she eased up on the gas. I righted myself in the seat and yanked the seat belt strap across my chest and buckled myself in. "That was too close."

"What was too close?" Emma asked as she sped toward the guard shack with the dropped arm barrier preventing our escape.

"Slow down," I urged, fearful she intended to plow right through it.

"Which is it? Speed up or slow down?" Emma slammed on the brakes and fishtailed to a stop with the nose of the car just inches from the yellow arm.

The slack-mouthed guard stared at her in disbelief and gestured for her to roll down the window. When Emma complied, he glowered at her and sternly asked, "What seems to be the problem here, ma'am?"

"He is," Emma said, pointing at me. "He came running from the building like Satan himself was on his heels and yelled for me to floor it."

I sank lower in the seat, worrying this guard would report the incident to Archer, Ray, or both. I'd made an absolute fool of myself and had sucked Emma into the vortex of fuckery with me. I had to think fast to come up with an excuse as to why we needed to leave in a hurry. The guard's brow went up, indicating he was waiting for me to answer.

"I have a case of explosive diarrhea!" I blurted. *What the fuck?* I couldn't take it back, so I might as well sell it. Groaning, I covered my stomach and leaned forward as if seized by a vicious stomach cramp. "Must've been something I ate at lunch." I sucked in a sharp breath and moaned pitifully. "Here it comes again."

"Oh man," the guard said. "Been there before, and it sucks." He hit the button inside the shack and raised the barrier. "Hope you feel better." To Emma, he said, "Try to maintain a reasonable speed, okay?"

"Easy for you to say. You're not stuck with Butt Vesuvius. Hold on, mi amor." Emma gunned the car forward as soon as the barrier was high enough. "Okay, what's really going on?"

"It's a long story," I said.

Emma reached over and patted my leg. "I've got nothing but time for you, baby doll."

"Well, you know how my day started…"

"You backed into a car illegally parked across from your driveway, and then dickface showed up at your work and beat sweet Sadie to death with a ball bat," Emma said.

"Close. It was a crowbar."

"Okay, a crowbar," Emma said. "But then some sexy stud muffin tackled him into the pool after dickbreath took a swing at him with said crowbar."

"Yes, and—" I stopped when my brain caught on to what she said. "I never mentioned a sexy stud muffin." I also hadn't told Emma that Ray, today's hero, was also Ray, last month's hookup zero, because I wasn't sure how she would've responded. Emma probably would've come to Silver Maple during her lunch break and given Ray a piece of her mind for hurting my feelings.

Emma tilted her head back and laughed gleefully. "I could tell by the tone of your voice when you called and asked for a ride. You sounded mesmerized and horny."

"Did not."

"Did too," Emma said.

"Maybe a little."

Emma smiled wickedly. "What's his name? Tell me all about him."

So I did, and was careful not to leave out a single detail because my goddess would know it. For her part, Emma stayed quiet until I said, "And that was that. Ray walked away without a backward glance. He said that he'd see me around, but I have a feeling he's going to do everything in his power to avoid me."

"I'm upset that he wasn't honest with you about why he canceled your hookup plans, but at least he didn't ghost you," Emma said. "And he'd wanted to come clean and apologize. That shows good character." She sighed as she covered her heart. "He sounds like a poor, lost lamb."

"No one on Earth would describe Ray in those terms. He's so big, strong, and muscular. Capable and brave." He was all the things I'd never be, that was for sure.

"I'm not talking about his physical appearance, though he sounds smoking hot. I'm talking about here." Emma tapped her chest before returning her hand to the steering wheel. "He sounds like someone who's experienced a great loss and doesn't know what to do with himself." She glanced over at me. "If I had to guess, you got under his skin in unexpected and scary ways."

"You can't possibly know that. You weren't there."

"No, but I'm experiencing it through your words," Emma said.

I snorted so hard it hurt. "I'm the least reliable narrator on the planet, and I'm likely projecting all my unrequited desires onto him."

"You want him bad, huh?" Emma asked.

"In the worst way." I sighed heavily. "It's not to be, and I need to accept it instead of causing myself more grief. Besides, my last workplace romance ended in disaster, and I can't afford that now. I need to focus on getting my feet on solid ground, not trying to rock my world with hot, sweaty—" I swallowed down the rest of what I was going to say. "You know what I mean."

"I do, but it's been so long I can hardly remember."

Emma was one of the most gorgeous women I'd ever seen, so if she was celibate, it was by design. "You're not the only one with horrible taste in men." Emma glanced over and smiled. "We both deserve better."

"Can't argue with you there."

"Now, tell me why you ran out to my car like the hounds of hell were nipping at your heels."

"I'm not sure you're far off the mark." I told her about Bobby's behavior, both at lunchtime and when he confronted me outside my office.

"Okay, that guy definitely gives off a weird vibe," she admitted. "It was smart to make up a boyfriend."

"I just hope he doesn't start pressing me for information about the relationship. I have a hard enough time managing my real life and can't imagine juggling a fake one too, just to keep Bobby off my ass."

"One thing at a time," Emma said. "Finding a replacement vehicle takes precedence."

"We have to swing by Harland's so I can sign Sadie's title over to him and collect my money. Harland has a cousin named Ernie, who owns a buy-here-pay-here lot that offers decent cars at a fair interest rate. I don't need anything too fancy. She just needs to get me to work and back."

"Good things are going to happen for you, baby," Emma said. "I can feel it."

"Maybe you're about to get explosive diarrhea."

Emma gasped in outrage before she burst into laughter. "You'd better not have cursed me just now."

"If I had that kind of power, Bobby would be stuck on the toilet for the rest of the night."

Honest Ernie greeted us when we arrived at his used car lot. He extended a ham hock–sized hand for us to shake and provided cold beverages as we toured the available cars. Ernie offered a bigger selection than I'd expected but with price tags I wasn't willing to consider. Much to Emma's chagrin, I leaned closer to Ernie and asked if he had more affordable options.

"How much cheaper?" Ernie asked.

I named the amount I could put down and a monthly payment I could comfortably swing.

Ernie rubbed his chin between his forefinger and thumb. "I don't have an available car on the lot in that price point." He cocked his head to the side and held up his forefinger as if remembering something. "Well, I have a scooter I won in a poker game. It's not the prettiest thing in the world, but it has character and runs great. I could sell that to you outright, and you'd still have enough money for licensing and tags."

Emma groaned and pulled me to the side. "Baby, no. A scooter? I think it's time you consider drastic measures here."

I shook my head vehemently, knowing what she was going to recommend. "No, Em. Don't go there."

She gripped both my hands in hers. "I think it's time you sold some of your collectibles." And damn, Emma went there.

"I can't. I won't."

"Mi amor, how many ancient gaming systems, games, vinyl records, and DVDs do you need?

"They're priceless classics."

"I know how much you love those things," Emma said, "but selling them and freeing up the money you spend on a temperature-controlled storage unit would change your life. You could likely move out of your parents' house and get your own place." She gestured to the car lot filled with solid vehicle options. "And you could get something safer to drive."

She was right, and we both knew it. But I'd just had to say goodbye to my sweet Sadie, and I wasn't ready to part with the collection I'd cultivated over years of going to yard sales with Emma and her grandmother, Ramona.

"A scooter, Kit? Really?"

In her question, I detected an unspoken accusation. *You're going to drive a scooter? You can barely walk without killing yourself on the best days.*

I had no real defense, so I shrugged. "Shouldn't I at least look at the scooter before deciding?"

"It comes with a custom matching helmet," Ernie said.

Emma threw up her hands. "Well, then, by all means." Her reply was pure sarcasm, but I chose not to see it that way.

"I'll have a look at her," I told Ernie.

He led us toward a small shed on the outer edge of the property.

"It's so rad they have to keep her locked up," I whispered to Emma, who didn't acknowledge my remark with so much as a blink.

Ernie unlocked and opened the double doors, then stood back. Sunlight beamed into the dark interior like a spotlight, and at center stage was a golden beauty that stole my breath.

Emma groaned, "Oh no."

But I nearly tripped over my two feet to get to her. "Oh my," I whispered reverently. "The metallic paint makes her glitter like a diamond."

"A road hazard if I've ever seen one," Emma muttered. "You'll blind someone with that death machine and cause a wreck."

"Will not," I argued as I ran a finger over the scooter's bronze racing stripe.

"Will too." Emma trudged in behind me and picked up the helmet hanging from one handlebar. "Is this the matching helmet?" Her voice rose an octave with each word until she was nearly shouting.

I was so enthralled with the scooter that I hadn't noticed, but she had my full attention now. The helmet was the same gold color as the bike, but someone had painted bronze and black cheetah spots all over it. "Wow."

"Hell no. And I'm putting my foot down," Emma said, then stomped to emphasize her point.

"I'll take her."

"Are you listening to me?" Emma asked. "You don't even know how to drive a scooter."

"I can show him," Ernie said. "There's nothing to it."

Emma spun on her heels and squared off against him. "I need to have a private word with Atticus, please."

Uh-oh. She never first-named me, choosing to call me Kit, KitKat, Atticat, or some other endearment. Ernie looked scared for my safety, so I gave him a reassuring nod.

"Em—"

She shook her head to cut me off. "This is too dangerous. I bet this thing only drives about thirty miles per hour. Someone will run over you."

"It maxes out at about sixty-five miles per hour," Ernie called out from somewhere nearby.

"You're not helping," Emma yelled.

"Sorry," came a mournful reply.

I reached for her hands, and she gripped mine tightly. "Em, this is what I want. Something I can buy free and clear."

"Because you don't want to sell your collectibles?"

I squared my shoulders and took a deep breath. "Because I do not want to surrender another damn piece of my soul to the shittiest year on record."

"I'll lend you the money you need to buy a car from the lot. You can write up a payment plan that works for your budget. Please." Tears filled Emma's eyes. "I can't lose you, KitKat."

"You won't. I promise. Ernie will give me instructions. I'll practice in the lot for a while, and then you can follow me home. I'll drive slow and safe."

"Great. So I get to be the one who runs over you when the scooter topples over? No, thanks."

Her doubt stung, but I knew it came from a place of love. "Let's make a deal. Let me at least try it out before you start planning my funeral. Okay?"

"Fine."

Forty-five minutes later, I was the proud owner of Blanche, the snazziest scooter named after the most glamorous Golden Girl. I was nervous when I pulled out onto the public street for the first time, but knowing Emma was at my back gave me the confidence I needed to zip home without incident. Endorphins and pride were a dizzying combo, and my legs were a little unsteady when I climbed off Blanche after parking her under the carport attached to our garage. I wanted to celebrate what felt like a roaring success when everything else had sucked. I thought of my lunchtime conversation with Ray and realized it hadn't all been bad.

I jogged to Emma's car, and she rolled down the window. "My parents won't be home until late. You want to get dinner?"

"Can't. Gotta get back to the salon. I have a late client tonight." She waggled her eyebrows. "Take advantage of your alone time and bust out the only collection you brought with you to your parents' house."

Heat bloomed in my cheeks. "Only because I was too embarrassed to leave it at the storage unit. What if the property manager had to enter my unit for an emergency and stumbled upon my box of..."

"Dildos in various shapes and sizes?"

"Hush," I said, looking around to see if any of the neighbors were lurking nearby. "I don't want anyone to hear."

"Which is why you've probably lived a very dull life since moving back in with the folks. Seriously, my dude, go relieve some stress in the most epic way. Light a candle, turn on some music, and romance yourself."

I wanted to dismiss her suggestions, but damn if she wasn't right again. "Bye, Emma," I said, backing away from her car. "Thank you for everything."

"I won't be the one you're thanking when your legs are limp noodles later. It'll be Ray."

"No." He might be responsible for the hormones humming in my body, but I refused to think about him while getting off.

"Yes, Ray!" Emma shouted as she backed down the driveway. "Ohhh. Right there, Ray!"

I surely set a world record for unlocking a door and darting inside a house, and not to rip off my clothes and ride a dildo, although the idea was taking on a life of its own. It had been over six months since anything penetrated me besides my own finger during a quick jerk session in the shower. My parents had an en suite bathroom, but I had to use the first-floor bathroom to shower, which was too close to the living room and kitchen for my comfort.

An extended shower would raise too many questions, especially if I carried more than a change of clothes with me. Hiding a dildo and lube in a rolled-up shirt or a pair of pants sounded like no big deal unless Klutz was your middle name. I could just picture myself tripping over my own feet, dropping the dildo, and watching it roll across the floor in slow motion. The damn thing would come to a stop against my dad's foot for sure. Just the thought was enough to make me lose interest in a night of debauched self-pleasure.

No, no, no. *I deserve this, damn it.*

I raced upstairs to the locked trunk I kept hidden under my bed. Key chain still in hand, I found the key I needed to unlock my intimate collection. Emma made it sound like I had dozens of dildos, but I only had a few. They each offered unique features and stimulators, but I went for Fat Bastard with the suction cup behind its big, juicy balls. Just looking at its thick veins made my ass pucker in anticipation. I snatched the lube from the box and hustled down the steps, stopping on the bottom tread to make sure I was still alone. Forget the candles and music. I just needed Ray's thick cock inside me. I nearly ran headlong into the bathroom door when I realized my mistake.

"Fat Bastard," I reminded myself. "Not Ray."

I shut and locked the bathroom door, then turned on the water. Steam filled the room by the time I'd stripped down the rest of the way and carried the lube and Fat Bastard to the shower. Using my body to block the water, I attached the dildo at the perfect height. For once, I didn't care that the showerhead was puny and offered a piddly stream of water. I took my time slicking Fat Bastard up, closing my eyes and allowing my mind to assemble a fictional man to stroke. He'd be tall, with broad shoulders and a powerful chest. My mystery man would have thick thighs and a muscular ass.

"Mmmmm."

My blood flooded south, and my dick plumped as I let my imagination run wild, picturing myself on my knees, learning my guy's scent up close and personal. I loved the smell of a man's arousal, musky and masculine. I'd tease him with my tongue and taste how excited he was for me before working my mouth up and down his shaft, hearing him moan and plead for more. Strong fingers would slide through my hair and grip my head, guiding me up and down his length. Damn, I missed giving head as much as I missed receiving it.

My dick was hard as stone and eager to receive the same treatment I was giving my fictional man. I could almost feel hot breath against my skin, the brush of facial hair against my pelvis or thighs. Perhaps a neatly trimmed goatee framed the luscious mouth parting to suck me in? Facial hair? Since when was that a thing I liked? My fictional man with the broad shoulders, powerful chest, thick thighs, bubble butt, and a massive dick morphed into a very specific image in my head.

"No, no, no. Not Ray." Someone like him. Someone attainable. Yeah.

Aching with need, I turned to face the water and worked lube into my ass, stretching it as much as the weird angle allowed before lining up my hole and pushing back onto the dildo. With one hand braced on the shower wall and the other on the glass door, I set a slow, delicious pace, relishing each rasp of thick veins over sensitive nerve endings. I canted my hips at different angles until I hit the happiest spot on Earth.

"Ahhhhhhhh." My voice sounded loud in the bathroom, but who cared. Nobody was home. I needed this release. I deserved it. That was the moment I gave myself permission to let go, which my brain took as its cue to double down on the Ray fantasy. It was his voice urging me to use him, to fuck harder and faster. It was his hands gripping my hips and holding me in place for the pounding of a lifetime.

"Yes! Yes! Yes!" I chanted as I rode the length of the dildo, squeezing my eyes tighter to hold on to the sexy images as I felt my body surrender to an intense climax. I didn't want it to end, but the pleasure was almost too much to bear, so I fucked faster. The dildo pegged me just right, so I wouldn't need my hands to get off. My cock bounced furiously, slapping against my stomach and making the experience more erotic.

"Oh fuck. Too soon," I moaned as my first jet of release burst from my cock. I kept rocking and thrusting as the pleasure detonated in my balls and rumbled through my body like an earthquake. I came and came until I could barely stand on my noodle legs. I remained there, practically dangling from the dildo, while trying to catch my breath and feeling happier than I'd been in a very long time. It had been a truly shitty day, but thank fuck something had finally gone my way.

CHAPTER 10

RAYDEN

I WOKE BEFORE MY ALARM WENT OFF, HARDER AND HORNIER THAN I'D ever been in my life. But then I'd thought that yesterday and the day before, and the one prior to that too. Hell, I'd thought it every day for the past two weeks I'd avoided Atticus. The evasive maneuvers hadn't been easy to pull off. First, I needed a reasonable excuse for why I'd wanted to take the night shift at Silver Maple, when I was usually the one who disliked working third shift the most. When we'd originally planned a schedule, the five of us rotated between first and third shifts with our staff. We'd never ask our team to do a job we wouldn't do ourselves. That didn't mean we wouldn't grumble about the jobs or shifts we didn't like, and I was the chief whiner about working overnight.

But one of our employees had a newborn at home with some health issues that made nighttime extra hard on his wife. Volunteering had been the right thing to do, shooting down offers from the guys to pick up some of the slack had earned raised eyebrows and too many smirks to count. While their smug, knowing expressions annoyed the hell out of me, it wasn't the hardest part about avoiding Atticus.

I just fucking missed him. It had taken me a week—maybe ten days—of grunts, growls, and terrible moods, resulting in more than one side-eye from the guys, to recognize the truth, which only made me snarlier. Who the hell was Atticus to come along and disrupt my life? The pining, moping, and frustration did nothing to cool my lust. If anything, it made me want him more.

I dreamed of Atticus, waking up with my hard dick in my hand most afternoons. I thought of his lips, his banging body, and his pert ass while fucking my fist. It wasn't enough. I needed more, but I couldn't—wouldn't act on the feelings Atticus stirred. Maybe I could have if I'd only felt lust, but sharing one lunch with Atticus made me crave something more than just a physical release. He was interested too. I saw it in his gorgeous eyes and by the way he leaned toward me as if magnetically drawn. And that was the rub.

I groaned at the thought and blindly reached for the lube I didn't bother returning to my bedside table drawer. If I'd only wanted sex, I would've claimed Atticus. But he made me crave companionship with someone who knew me better than I knew myself. I wanted to experience comfortable silences with him and discover his various reactions to the food I created. I yearned to lose hours just from kissing his mouth. I wanted to share insider jokes with him that only we would understand. Atticus made me want things that scared the fuck out of me. And so I ignored the urge to go into work early and find any excuse to accidentally run into him or take one of the guys up on their offer to swap nights for days, even sporadically. I needed to stay as far away from Atticus as possible for my own good.

But in the privacy of my bedroom, in my dreams, or in my shower...I was all his, and he was all mine. There was no room for fear or remorse. Tired of my hand, I grabbed a silicone sleeve out of the drawer and drizzled some lube inside. It didn't trick me into believing it was Atticus pleasuring me with his ass or mouth, but it was a nice change from my callused fingers. Behind my closed eyelids, Atticus looked up at me from his knees, eyes shimmering with lust as his mouth stretched wide around my cock. It didn't take me long to get off with the steady glide of the toy up and down, the slick friction, and my vivid imagination. I removed the sleeve at the peak of orgasm and finished with my fist, imagining my release painting lush lips and the sexiest cupid's bow. Afterward, I lay there in the center of the bed with my spent dick lying against my stomach and the sheets tangled around my calves. My body felt great with my lust temporarily slaked, but my mind was in a sudden tailspin. I was both overstimulated and underwhelmed, restless and lethargic.

Recognizing the anxiety response, I reached for a tool I'd learned from past therapy sessions, books, and mental health podcasts. Instead of ignoring the emotions, it was better to close my eyes and sort through them, naming each feeling before placing it in an imaginary box. I'd felt downright ridiculous the first few times I tried the container method, even though I'd been alone. Over time, I'd learned to start my sessions by boxing up the traits that resisted a mindfulness practice. Toxic gender and societal norms were the first to go in the containers, giving way to an unexpected type of cleansing, which made it easier for me to relax and lean into healing.

Because I'd wanted better for myself than living in a constant state of numbness. My emotions since meeting Atticus weren't harder to name, but they'd become twisted and tangled around one another like strands of Christmas lights. It seemed impossible to separate lust from fear and loneliness from curiosity. Guilt had become a multistrand beast, wrapping itself around hope, joy, and happiness like a deadly python that choked out what little air I'd allowed them to breathe since Javi died.

My head pounded, and my chest felt impossibly tight. I couldn't just wrap them all up in a tight ball and throw them into one imaginary container or ignore them because that avoidance would only lead to bigger problems. I switched to grounding exercises, focusing on what I could see, touch, hear, and smell. The tightness in my chest eased, and the chaos quieted in my brain. Cycling through a series of breathing techniques eased the remaining tension in my body, and I reached for the gnarly strands of guilt that threatened my peace of mind. But my alarm went off before I could separate the survivor's guilt from the standard variety of shame that came from avoiding my friends and taking the easier road instead of going after what I wanted.

Who I wanted.

Healing my trauma would have to wait. I had work to do. Slamming my hand down on the alarm to shut it up, I eased out of bed so I didn't drip cum everywhere. The discarded towel from my morning shower-and-jerk session was nearby, so I snatched it off the floor to wipe my stomach and hand. Carrying the silicone toy with me to the bathroom, I cleaned it and brushed my teeth while waiting for the water to heat. My days and nights were turned around, but my routine remained the same, no matter the time of day.

Wake, jerk off, eat, work, eat, jerk off, and sleep. The normalcy of the ritual should've given me comfort, but an ever-present agitation softly hummed beneath my skin and wouldn't allow me to find solace in the ordinary. No true peace to be found, no quarters given. Something had to ease up before I did something stupid.

I'd set my alarm early so I could have time to enjoy a nice meal and return the book I'd borrowed from Silver Maple's impressive library before my shift started. The choice between tacos and burgers for dinner and what book to read next were supposed to be the toughest battles I faced on a Friday night. All I had to do was get out of the building without running into any of the guys. The third-floor corridor of our renovated warehouse was funeral-parlor quiet when I stepped outside my apartment, so I assumed my best friends were either in the offices on the first floor or on a jobsite somewhere.

I thought Lady Luck was smiling down on me until I noticed the elevator was stuck on the second floor, the communal space where the five of us gathered as a group to eat, hang out, and watch television. Since it was almost dinnertime, I suspected the other four had gathered there to wait for me since I'd been a no-show more often than not the past two weeks. The four people who meant the world to me got caught up in my selfish coping mechanisms, and it seemed they'd run out of patience with me. Which one of them locked the elevator in place and forced me to use the stairs? And how many of them were waiting to confront me on the second-floor landing?

Most people thought our work-life setup was weird, and some assumed it was kinky. One therapist defined our relationship as trauma bonding, while another labeled it an unhealthy, codependent relationship. We called it surviving and didn't give a fuck what anyone else thought. The five of us healed in the way that worked best for us. And I loved our arrangement ninety-nine percent of the time. This bullshit fell into the rare exception when I wondered if something else might be better for me.

How dare they force a confrontation? I had plenty of opinions about their coping mechanisms, but I kept my thoughts to myself. Maybe not for long. I growled my frustration and headed down the corridor to the emergency stairs, cursing each of my best friends with each step. It was hard to say which chafed more, my guilt or their fucking gall. I expected to hear murmurs or snickers as I approached the second floor because we could easily revert to childhood pranksters, but the only sounds in the stairwell were my footsteps.

The silence felt patient, kind, and resolute, so I knew who was waiting for me before Vaughn's handsome face came into view. He was the one I couldn't easily ignore or shove down the steps. We were all roughly the same age and had contributed the same amount of startup money, but Vaughn was the unofficial leader of the business and a fatherly figure to the group. None of us, especially me, wanted to disappoint him.

Vaughn's blue eyes didn't express anger, frustration, or even disappointment. All I saw was sympathy and understanding, which was why I stepped into his open arms without hesitation. He hugged me tightly and kissed my cheek. "Stop hiding and talk to us, yeah? We love you." Vaughn's voice was gruff with humor and affection.

"I love you guys too." And I did. This brotherly love was the only kind I would permit in my life, and I cherished it more than my next breath. If given the choice between my life and theirs, I'd always choose them.

Vaughn patted my back and pushed me out to arm's length, holding my gaze with his steady one. "Nothing is so big my smoked barbecue ribs can't fix it."

"Not so sure about that."

"It's okay to want, Hawk."

It didn't surprise me that Vaughn knew the reasons I'd kept to myself the past two weeks. Archer had blabbed to everyone about my initial reaction to Atticus, and he'd somehow learned about my shared lunch with him by the pond. Thank god Arch hadn't found out about my failed hookup attempt in April, or he never would've relented. But the secret felt too burdensome to carry alone, which was why I confessed everything to Vaughn, turning the silent stairwell into a confessional.

He listened without judgment, his strong hands bracketing my shoulders and his steady gaze holding mine. Vaughn didn't say anything until I finished, and then he pulled me in for another hug. "I got you, Hawk. Always."

Relief turned my legs to spaghetti noodles, and I sagged in his embrace. Vaughn supported my weight until I was ready to stand on my own once more. When I stepped back, he ruffled my hair and met my gaze.

"Do you think it might be better to act on your attraction to Atticus?" Vaughn asked. "Avoiding it and trying to convince yourself it's wrong or unsafe only seems to make you feel worse."

Swallowing hard to dislodge the sudden lump in my throat, I said, "I can't. I'm not ready."

"Okay," Vaughn replied patiently.

My refusal to move on from Javier's gut-wrenching death had changed over the three years, but the reason for my stubbornness had shifted. Sadness and guilt would always play a big part, but survival had become the name of the game, both mine and whoever had the misfortune to fall in love with me. Daydreaming about what I could have with Atticus always led to nightmares of a rocket-propelled grenade ripping through the lead car in our embassy convoy and knowing the love of my life was trapped inside the vehicle and burning alive.

There'd been nothing I could do to save him, and I would've died trying if not for my guys. They'd gotten me out of Budapest alive; they'd made sure Javi's remains were returned stateside, and they stood beside me when we'd laid him to rest. I would've died a hundred deaths since then if not for Archer, Vaughn, Ethan, and Nico. They deserved better from me, so I pulled myself together.

"Barbecue ribs sound good."

Vaughn searched my gaze, looking for hints of deception, and nodded when he found none. "Good. You've got macaroni and cheese duty. I bought all the ingredients, so you'll just need to combine everything together."

"Doubt it," I teased.

My mom's old recipe called for cheap, individually wrapped American cheese slices, but Vaughn's blue blood wouldn't tolerate something so basic unless it was a dire emergency. He'd likely bought an expensive hunk of cheese from a specialty store, but I'd use it because it made him happy. Didn't mean I wouldn't give him shit about it. It was our weird love language. Vaughn squeezed my shoulders, then nudged me through the stairwell door and followed me into our communal space. The conversation lurched to a halt, and four pairs of eyes assessed me from head to toe.

"He lives!" Ethan exclaimed, his green eyes shimmering with humor. I ruffled his dark brown hair before hugging him. Ethan was the golden retriever of the group, always welcoming us with a huge smile and good-natured energy.

"I live," I agreed.

Nico stepped into my space, silently wrapping me in a hug. He was a solid, quiet presence and the most like me, but Nico's edginess hadn't quite reached my level of standoffishness, and I hoped it never did.

Patting his back, I said, "I'm good, Nic."

Archer appraised me as he spooned something into his mouth, but his twinkling green eyes spoke loud and clear. He thought I was a fool, a cowardly one at that, to walk away from something—someone—so good. If he dared voice his opinion, I'd divert everyone's attention to a discussion about Bobby. Archer saluted me with the spoon before dipping it back into his bowl, but the smirk tugging at his lips promised my reprieve was only temporary. I fucking loved that ornery bastard, so I closed the space between us and hugged him tight.

"Love you too, asshole," Archer grumbled.

I got a whiff of strawberries as I stepped back and peered down into his bowl. "Ice cream?"

"Freshly made in that fancy gadget you gave me for my birthday." Archer spooned a big bite into his mouth and shimmied his shoulders.

"That good, huh?" I asked.

"The best! I've really nailed the process." Archer waggled his eyebrows. "If you're nice, I'll share."

"I'm contributing macaroni and cheese for dinner."

Archer grinned and said, "I am definitely saving ice cream for you."

Vaughn, who'd donned an apron declaring him Smokin' Hot, gestured to the kitchen island with a pair of tongs. "Speaking of the mac, I've laid your ingredients out for you. I'm going to wrap the ribs and let them rest a bit."

"Thanks."

Nico followed me into the kitchen and opened the refrigerator. "I'm putting together the Caesar salad."

And by putting it together, he meant opening the kit from the store and tossing the greens with shredded parmesan cheese, seasoning, and the creamy dressing. Ethan would've grabbed a fruit or veggie tray on the way home, and Archer's contribution was his latest ice cream concoction. My favorite had been the s'mores ice cream with pieces of toasted marshmallow and chunks of graham cracker, but the vibrant smell of strawberries ignited my senses and made me think of Atticus enjoying my summer salad. I squelched the thought before it could morph into other suggestions for his gorgeous mouth.

Nico gave me a soft nudge with his elbow. "If you want us to stop worrying about you, then you'll need to stop staring into space. If you don't want us to mention *his* name, then stop smiling about memories we don't share or thoughts we can't hear."

"Who says we want to hear his thoughts about you know who?" Ethan asked.

Archer raised his spoon. "I do. Every naughty last one."

"Pervert," we all replied collectively.

Archer laughed and shrugged while I gave Nico my attention.

"There are no thoughts or memories to share," I lied.

Nico rolled his eyes and lifted his right leg. "Pull this one, and it plays 'HOT TO GO!' As in, you're hot for—"

I covered his entire face with my hand to shut him up.

Nico laughed as he squirmed free. "Okay," he said. "I'll be good."

Dinner was delicious, though I still thought the macaroni and cheese would've been better made with single slices. There was just something so creamy about Mom's method. Or maybe it was just the pleasure I got from making it the way she used to on special occasions. Most of the time, she'd bought the boxed dinner with the powdered mix because it was cheaper. Using a whole package of sliced cheese for one meal wasn't something a single mom on a shoestring budget could afford. But man, what a treat it was when Mom served it, usually with discounted steaks or fried chicken.

"Who wants ice cream?" Archer asked once we finished.

"I gotta get going. I want to swing by Silver Maple's library to return a book and check out a new one." Books were my favorite way to wind down, and losing myself in a thriller sounded like a perfect way to spend my weekend off. "Thanks for dinner." I saw the protest in their expressions, but none of them asked me to stay longer. "Brunch tomorrow?" I asked.

Vaughn gave me an approving nod. "I'll make my sausage gravy and biscuits."

A cheer rang out behind me as I left.

"How's it going, Clint?" I asked when I pulled up to the guard shack.

"Just settled in, boss, but Jenkins said it's been a quiet day so far." He held up crossed fingers and grinned crookedly. "Hoping it stays that way."

"That makes two of us. Let me know if you need anything."

"Will do."

I drove around to the side of the administrative building, where I noticed a gold scooter parked near the employees' entrance. I'd never seen it before and couldn't imagine who in the hell drove that flashy death trap. Grabbing my bag from the passenger seat, I headed into the building. Atticus was always gone when I arrived for work, and his office door was usually closed. But this time, it hung wide open, and the lights were on inside, making it impossible to miss a gold helmet with cheetah spots sitting in the middle of the desk.

Fuck. That answered my question about who drove the flashy death trap to work. I stopped and stared at the offensive helmet for a long time, imagining all the horrors that could happen to Atticus while riding the scooter. He could get hit and killed. He could lose control on loose gravel and get killed. He could get abducted by evil people and—

Unable to finish that thought, I hastened down the hallway and muttered, "The fuck that death machine belongs to him." I barely slowed down when I approached our security team's office. "I'm here for the night, Miller. Gotta run something down, but you can cut out."

"Thanks, boss," he called out as I continued down the corridor.

Now I just had to figure out where the hell I might find Atticus and demand he stop driving that damn scooter. I pulled out my phone and checked the online activity calendar but didn't see an event planned for the evening. Surely Atticus had something better to do on a Friday night in June. *Or someone.* My stomach pitched at the thought, churning unwelcome acid and jealousy. That realization stopped me dead in my tracks. I had no claims on Atticus, not on his time or how he spent it. Or with whom. Ugh. Damnit. I didn't have any right to demand he stop driving the scooter either, even if it was in his best interest.

I cycled through a few deep breaths when I really wanted to put my fist through a wall. Once I had a better handle on my emotions, I decided to head over to the library to swap the self-help book for a nail-biting thriller. I wouldn't be gone long, and the team could reach me on my phone since I hadn't stopped long enough to grab the walkie-talkie from Miller. The arts and literature building was the next one over, separated by an enchanting garden with meandering pathways and water features. I wished I felt mellow enough to stop and smell the roses, literally, but frenetic energy kept my legs moving because knowing Atticus wasn't my business and accepting it weren't the same things. I still wanted to—

Light from the art room's windows spilled onto the lawn, telling me exactly where I could confront Atticus. No, not confront him. Reason with him. That's all I wanted to do. But I wouldn't. I removed the borrowed book from my messenger bag as a reminder of my true intention for entering the building. Return one book and grab another. But when I reached the art room's open door, I walked through it instead of past it. Damn it. A glance around the space revealed it was empty. Relief—definitely not disappointment—flooded through me when I flipped the switches and pitched the room into darkness, except for a small sliver of light coming from somewhere in the far-left corner. I'd never had a reason to enter the space, but I remembered seeing an L-shaped storage closet on the building specs and blueprints.

Maybe Atticus had left the lights on. Perhaps he was in the closet, putting supplies away. I told myself to forget about it and leave. I didn't pay the light bill, and I didn't need to orchestrate a run-in or confrontation with Atticus over that stupid scooter. Nope. That was the last thing I needed, but it was also the thing I wanted most. Huffing a sigh, I switched the lights back on and casually strode across the room.

I wouldn't raise my voice or issue stupid demands. I'd just make sure everything was okay. When I reached the door, I discovered why only a sliver of light had spilled through it. Someone had stuck a ruler between the door and the doorjamb to keep it open. Setting my stuff on an empty table, I reached for the handle and opened the door. The ruler fell onto the floor, and I reached down to pick it up when off-key singing reached my ears. I knew without looking who it belonged to, and it did weird things to my pulse. Mesmerized, I stepped into the closet and let go of the handle without picking up the ruler or considering why Atticus had placed it where he had. The door slammed shut behind me, making me flinch. I tried the handle, but it didn't budge, not even a centimeter.

Fuck. I'd just locked us inside the closet. The storage area stretched on in front of me, then turned to the left. Atticus wasn't in the main part, so he must've been around the corner. I braced myself for him to dart around the bend to check on the door, but he kept singing off-key. He must've been wearing noise-canceling earphones because I couldn't hear the music, and he'd missed the slamming door. I pictured his lean hips and perky ass swaying in time to the music or likely off rhythm if his dancing skills matched his singing talents. But then I remembered my dilemma. Thank fuck I still had my phone on me, so I called Clint and explained the situation. We only kept a skeleton crew on campus overnight, and I insisted Clint stay in the guard shack.

"I can wait for you to locate Mazy or Kowalski," I told him.

"You got it. We'll have you out in a jiffy."

I could've waited where I was, and Atticus wouldn't have known about my blunder, but his singing lured me closer. Yeah, that was it. I was the sailor, and Atticus was the sexy siren in this Greek mythology reenactment. I rounded the corner, and Atticus let out a bloodcurdling scream that made my ears ring. He reflexively flung something at me. I ducked in the nick of time, and it soared over my head, landing on the concrete floor with a clang. I turned to see a small can of paint rolling away. Atticus leaned against the shelving unit, his eyes going wide with recognition and embarrassment. I was the one who needed to apologize, and I would do so as soon as my ears stopped ringing.

Putting distance between us, I turned and retrieved the can of paint. It was pint-sized but mostly full. It would've hurt like hell if it hit me in the head, though I would've had it coming for scaring him half to death. When I turned back to Atticus, he was in the same spot, breathing hard and clutching his shirt. Wide hazel eyes stared at me unblinkingly, and I felt as low as a human could.

"I'm so sorry," I said.

"What?" Atticus shouted.

I gestured for him to remove his earbuds, and he snorted as he complied.

"Sorry," Atticus said, gesturing to the paint can in my hand. "I've waited my whole life for the fight reflex to kick in. Sorry you were on the receiving end."

I extended the can to him. "Eh, I had it coming for scaring you." Our fingers brushed when Atticus took the paint from me, and that briefest contact triggered sparks I could feel clear down in my toes. Oh hell.

Then we both said, "What are you doing here?"

Atticus snorted and shoved the paint can onto a shelf in front of him. "You first, since organizing art supplies is part of my job duties."

I looked around the closet for the first time and couldn't help but compare the outrageous clutter to the tidiness of the property maintenance garage. The shelf behind Atticus contained every type of paint supply a person could need, but they were haphazardly stored here and there. It seemed that I'd interrupted Atticus while he was attempting to organize the little pint-sized cans by color on a shelf.

"What kind of art do you make with those?" I asked, pointing to the paint. "That looks like samples you buy from the hardware store to see which color you like best on a surface."

Atticus notched his head higher. "I have no idea how they got here or why, I just know I can't take this mess anymore."

"You don't have anything better to do on a Friday night?" I wanted to claw the words back as soon as they left my mouth because they sounded more like an accusation than casual conversation.

Atticus frowned for a moment before responding. "I did have better plans. Much better."

"But…" I prompted.

"You go first. What are you doing in my storage closet?"

"I saw the lights on in the art room," I replied lamely. "So I turned them off and noticed a shaft—"

Atticus snorted and slapped a hand over his mouth. Eyes wide, he uncovered those sexy lips and said, "Sorry. I didn't mean to resort to childish behavior. You said shaft, not penis. I blame my nerves." He swallowed hard, and I watched his Adam's apple move. "Anyway, you saw the shaft of light coming from the art closet and decided to investigate?"

"Yeah." I took in his blown pupils and the wildly beating pulse in his neck. "Why are you nervous?"

Atticus blew out a breath. "I've been thinking about this moment ever since you walked away from me two weeks ago, and I'm screwing it up."

"No, I claimed that honor when I scared you half to death." I cycled through a deep breath and said, "Can we start over?"

"Absolutely."

I racked my brain for a safe conversation starter and had ruled out banal topics, such as work and weather, when my mouth moved of its own volition. "Hi, my name is Ray. I'm thirty-five years old, a Capricorn, and a complete dumbass sometimes."

Atticus grinned from ear to ear. "Hi, my name is Atticus. I'm twenty-five, a Gemini, and a complete klutz all the time." He cocked his head to the side. "Now what?"

"Tell me more about the scenarios you imagined when we ran into each other again."

"No chance," Atticus replied. The pretty pink flush spreading across his cheeks told me his thoughts were likely as filthy as my own.

"Pity," I said with a casual shrug. "I would've reciprocated."

Atticus licked his bottom lip as he searched my gaze. "Are you flirting with me, Ray?"

"Do you want me to be?"

"Yes."

I stepped forward, bracing my hands on the shelf behind Atticus and boxing him in. "Good, because this is my best flirting."

"What if I demonstrate my favorite reunion scenario instead?" Atticus suggested. "Would you still reciprocate?"

It was the worst of ideas; it was the best of ideas. It was the end and the beginning, even if I hadn't known it just then. "Yes."

Atticus fisted my shirt and dragged me closer until our bodies touched. He rose onto his tiptoes and pressed his lips to mine, tentatively at first, and then he boldly licked into my mouth, touching his tongue against mine. A snarly, desperate need detonated in my soul and rumbled through my chest, demanding I take more. Atticus moaned and melted into me. I angled my head and staked a claim on his mouth like it was my fucking right. Atticus slid both hands into my hair and whimpered into my mouth. Nothing had ever tasted so sweet, and I couldn't get enough of him. The urge to reach between our bodies and caress his—

Loud laughter ripped through the storage closet like a shotgun blast, and we jerked apart in shock and confusion. I blinked the world into focus and saw Bobby standing a few feet away.

"Well, well, well," he said, waggling his eyebrows. "What do we have here?"

CHAPTER 11

ATTICUS

YOU'VE GOT TO BE FUCKING KIDDING ME. *THIS GUY AGAIN?*

Maybe I would've spoken my snarly thoughts out loud if my lips weren't still tingling from kissing Ray. That had been the single hottest thing that had ever happened to me. I might've made the first move by grabbing Ray's shirt and pressing my lips to his, but Ray had immediately taken over and plundered my mouth like the greediest pirate. And Bobby had to come along and ruin it. Any minute now, reason would return, and Ray would step back to put distance between us again. I could almost hear those damn bricks clinking together as the wall went back up. *Damn you, Bobby.* Why was he even here? Was everyone obsessed with the lights being on in the art room?

"I was at the guard shack when you called Clint for help." Bobby hooked his thumb over his shoulder, gesturing to the exit he needed to walk through immediately while I stood a chance of reigniting the spark between Ray and me.

Wait. Ray had needed help? I looked at him, but he'd given Bobby his full attention. And he hadn't stepped away from me yet. Why?

Oh. Ohhh. Ohhhhh my god. The answer, thick and long, pressed proudly against my stomach. Ray's arousal almost felt aggressive, and it made me giddy with pride. *I did this to him? Me!*

"I appreciate you opening the door for us," Ray said. "Please tell me you propped it open with something."

The conversation finally penetrated my lust-fogged brain. We'd been stuck? I sucked in a sharp breath, and Ray pressed his fingers into my hips. Was it reflex or comfort?

"Yeah," Bobby said, "there was a ruler on the floor, so I wedged it between the door and the doorjamb."

"That was my bad," Ray said.

Nodding, Bobby said, "Ah, you're new. Everyone else knows the handle doesn't work."

"If everyone knows, then why isn't it fixed?" Ray asked.

"Building maintenance isn't my responsibility. If management doesn't worry about the stupid handle, why should I?" Bobby turned his full attention to me and grinned wickedly. "This sexy hunk must be the new boyfriend you mentioned. Why'd you get so cagey when I pumped you for more information?"

Ray's body tensed against mine. Oh no. This looked really fucking bad. I searched for the right words to diffuse the situation, but my brain misfired like an overloaded circuit board, and I couldn't focus on anything but the magnificent erection pressed against me. I stared at Bobby, who raised an impatient eyebrow.

Ray kissed my temple and nuzzled his nose against my ear. "Breathe," he whispered.

Bobby softened his gaze and smiled sweetly. "Aww, you guys make a cute couple."

"Thanks. Things are still new between us," Ray said. His hands slid lower until his fingertips brushed the upper swells of my ass. What was he doing? "So you can understand why we might be stingy with our time and privacy."

"Yes, I see," Bobby said, though he clearly didn't. Instead of getting the hell out of there, he crossed one foot over the other as if settling in for a long chat. "You're smart to guard your relationship."

Ray's body remained impossibly rigid, and I hated to be the source of his stress. I brushed my hand over his spine, just one long, greedy pass. The caress elicited a slight shiver, and I worried I'd gone too far until Ray relaxed against me. Well, everything went slack except his dick. Pressed so tightly together, there was no way to avoid getting hard too. I knew the moment Ray felt my reaction because he huffed a soft grunt in my ear. My insides quaked, and my asshole throbbed. I bet he'd grunt like that when he shoved that big—

"Kit, I'm sorry about my behavior when I thought you were trying to steal Archer from me," Bobby said. "I should've known better."

Ugh! This guy! Christ, man, read the room.

"It's fine," I said. "We're cool." I slid my hand up Ray's back and left it between his shoulder blades. He gripped my hips tighter, and I decided not to push my luck and used my groping hand to wave off Bobby's concern. "Water under the bridge. Don't give it another thought."

"Thank you."

If Bobby wasn't planning on leaving anytime soon, I needed to change the subject away from dating and relationships. "What are you even doing here on a Friday night?"

The light in Bobby's eyes dimmed to something darker, like irritation. "You know how demanding these rich clients can be." That wasn't my experience with the residents at all, but before I could respond, Bobby said, "They expect me to drop everything and come running whenever the mood hits."

"Even on the weekends?" Ray insisted.

Bobby shrugged. "Not typically, but my best-tipping client injured himself on the golf course and needs extra TLC. I didn't have anything else going on, so why not help the guy out?" He looked at his watch and scowled. "I'd better get going. I don't want to keep my client waiting. Behave, you two."

"Bye," Ray said.

"Don't lock us back in here," I added.

"Seems like you were making the best of it before I so rudely interrupted. Sure you don't want me to lock you in until morning?"

The mere thought caused my heart to race.

"No!" Ray and I yelled in unison.

Bobby's laughter faded as he walked away.

"I'll make sure the door handle gets fixed or replaced immediately," Ray promised as he stepped back. "Boyfriend, huh?"

Groaning, I covered my face. "I don't have a boyfriend."

"Bobby thinks you do, and now he's convinced it's me." Ray chuckled and ran a hand through his hair. "Are you sure I don't owe someone an explanation?"

I tilted my head toward the exit. "Can we have this discussion outside the closet?"

"Of course." Ray stepped back and gestured for me to lead.

I sucked in a lungful of fresh air like a drama king as soon as I stepped inside the art room. Then my gaze landed on a paperback book on a table next to a messenger bag. *Life after Loss: When Just Surviving Isn't Enough.* Reading the title stole my breath and made my heart ache. *Oh, Ray, what happened to you?*

Forcing my gaze away from the revealing book, I turned and faced Ray. "Look, I made up that bullshit lie about a fictional boyfriend to get Bobby off my back. He got weird and possessive every time Archer talked to me or even looked in my direction. I just wanted to avoid drama at work." I tried for a self-deprecating smirk, but it felt more like a sneer. "The last time I got creative, I lost my job. The boyfriend lie felt harmless."

"Oh, okay." Did Ray's shoulders ease just then? "No smoking hot date tonight, then?"

"Not unless you consider plans to get drinks with my best friend a date. Emma had volunteered to be my wingwoman at a gay bar to help me over the…hump? Dry spell?" Ray's lobelia eyes turned a darker shade of blue, almost an indigo. Was that a bit of possessiveness or just wishful thinking? "But I passed on the idea. We were going to check out a local band at their first gig, but Em had a hair emergency." When Ray raised an eyebrow in question, I added, "That's when someone royally screws up their hair during a home treatment and needs a professional to sort it out."

Ray blew out a relieved breath. "Ah, I'm glad."

"That Emma had a hair emergency, or that I decided it would be the perfect night to organize that hot mess in the art supply closet?"

Ray chuckled. "No, I'm glad you don't have a boyfriend."

"You are?" *Settle down. Don't get your hopes up.*

"Sure," Ray said. "I'd hate to disrespect another guy by kissing you the way I did."

No one had ever made me feel as wanted as Ray had, and I refused to regret our kiss. I didn't want him to feel guilty about it either. "There's nothing to worry about, and listen, kissing you was no hardship." Uh-oh. My mouth was slipping its leash and was about to run wild. Desperate to reel it back in, I said the single worst thing I could at that moment. "It was nice."

"*Nice*?" Ray winced and rubbed his sternum. "I've been out of practice for a while, so I knew my skills were rusty, but nice?"

"Your dick's reaction time was impeccable though. You went from zero to a hundred in a flash." *Oh god, oh god, oh god.* I'd just made it ten times worse.

Ray dipped his head and chuckled. "Like I said, it's been a while."

My gaze darted back to the book. "How long?"

When he raised his head to meet my gaze, I thought Ray was going to answer. But he sighed and shook his head. "I should get going. I'm technically on shift."

Hoping my disappointment didn't show in my expression, I said, "I should head out too. I've totally lost the mood to spend another minute in that supply closet until it gets fixed."

Ray shoved his book into his messenger bag, then hoisted the strap over his shoulder. "I'll put in the work order now and will ride someone's ass until the handle gets fixed. I'll keep you posted."

His phrasing reminded me of how his erection felt pressed against my abdomen. Heat bloomed across my cheeks, and I suddenly felt bold, maybe even a little reckless. "Oh, do you plan to email me or use a carrier pigeon to keep me informed?"

Ray frowned. "What?"

"How will you communicate your results when you work night shifts to avoid me?" I'd meant for the question to sound flippant, but it came out bratty instead. "I guess you could leave a note on my desk."

Ray tensed, and those gorgeous blue eyes held me locked in place. I couldn't even breathe as I waited for his response. He blew out a breath and said, "Okay, I have avoided you the past few weeks."

"I'm sorry I made you feel so uncomfortable."

Ray shook his head. "It's not you."

I snorted. "It's always me, and it's okay. I'm not everyone's cup of tea."

Ray closed the distance between us and kept coming until he backed me up against the table. "You don't know how wrong you are."

I tipped my head back to look into his eyes, but they were locked on my mouth again. I'd give almost anything to feel his lips against mine and have his tongue dominate my mouth one more damn time. "How am I wrong?"

"I like you a lot. Too much. But I...I can't. You deserve so much more than I could ever give you."

With anyone else, it would've sounded like a bullshit line to ease my feelings, but Ray laid his agony bare in his expression. I thought of his book, and my heart ached for the beautiful man. I would've done anything, sacrificed everything, to comfort him, even at the expense of my own well-being.

And that's why I choked down my emotions and offered a smile. "What about friendship?"

Ray sighed and rested his forehead against mine. "I think we both know what would happen."

"So arrogant," I teased. "You think I can't resist your charms?"

He lifted his head, and I immediately missed our connection. "I'm worried I won't be able to resist yours." Ray inhaled deeply, then said, "But I really enjoy talking to you. Lunch was a lot of fun."

My laugh came out shaky as I leaned my forehead against his chest. "Then come back to first shift once in a while so we can have more fun lunches. I'll work on being less charming."

"You could try, but I won't hold my breath," Ray said. He seemed on the verge of caving in, and I should've offered some kind of promise to behave. Instead, I did the absolute worst thing.

"Between the lie I told Bobby and the kiss he witnessed, he's going to gossip about us all over campus."

"I don't care what people say about me." Ray's strong hands landed on my hips again. "I'd hate for you to take the brunt of the fallout though."

"So come back. Have lunch with me." I waggled my eyebrows. "We'll give them something to talk about."

Ray chuckled and stepped back. "I don't know about that last part, but lunches at the pond sound great. It might take time to rework my shifts, but I'll be back. I promise."

I wanted so badly to seal his vow with a kiss, but I stuck out my pinky finger instead. Ray hooked his around mine, and we shook.

"God, you're fucking adorable," he said.

Hope had no fucking business planting her little seeds in my heart, but she did it anyway. We turned off all the lights, and then I shut and locked the art room door. I needed to get my stuff from my office, so I walked to the admin building with him.

"I want to talk about your new mode of transportation," Ray said.

"Blanche! Oh my god, I love her so much."

"Too bad. She needs to go."

"Hell no. I bought Blanche free and clear, and she drives like a dream. I've never felt more liberated than when I straddle her."

Ray released a strangled breath, or maybe he wheezed.

"Jealous?"

"Absolutely," he admitted. "But that isn't why Blanche—" Ray stopped suddenly and moved in front of me to block my way. "Why that name?"

"I named her after the most famous Golden Girl. Blanche would absolutely wear a shiny dressing gown in that color."

Ray tilted his head to the side to consider it before meeting my gaze. "Okay, the name makes sense, but risking your life on the scooter doesn't."

"I'm fine."

"It's June. We get a ton of storms," Ray said.

"I pay attention to the forecast and borrow a vehicle from my parents on the days it rains or storms."

"Pop-up storms and showers happen all the time with this humidity," Ray countered.

"I know, but so far, it hasn't been a problem."

Ray's hands went to my hips again, fitting as if they'd been designed to rest there. "So far isn't a solid plan to keep you safe." He closed his eyes for a few seconds before meeting my gaze again. Ray's agonized expression stirred the same devastation as when I saw the title of his book. God, what had he lived through? "I know I'm giving you all kinds of mixed signals, and I'm sorry. I just have a thing about keeping the people I care about safe."

"Me?"

"I need you safe," Ray said. "Please."

Oh god. "I'll try to come up with something else to drive." I held up my hand before Ray could speak. He wasn't the only one with a tumultuous life. "It has to be on terms I can live with and payments I can afford. It might not be tomorrow or even next week, but I will get a safer vehicle."

Ray's relief was a palpable thing. His breath came easier, his tension eased, and he planted a kiss on my forehead. "Thank you."

The hopeful seeds sprouted in my heart, leaving me breathless.

CHAPTER 12

Rayden

A sharp whistle pierced the air when I stepped outside my apartment on Monday morning. I turned from locking my door to find four grinning knuckleheads waiting in the corridor for me. I'd known these men long enough to know which one had sounded like an air-raid siren while objectifying me.

"Nice, Arch," I growled.

Ethan grimaced and wiggled a finger in his ear. "Damn. I bet every dog within a ten-mile radius heard that."

"It's his new mating call," Nico teased.

"Ha," Archer barked. "I sure as hell wouldn't deploy that here. None of you have ever appreciated me the way I deserve."

The four of us groaned, and I pushed off down the hallway toward them. "Let's get this over with," I said.

Archer batted his eyelashes like a Southern belle. "Whatever do you mean?"

Great. His accent was pure sass on the sliding-twang scale, but I was too amped up to come up with Dolly Parton's Texan contemporary. I circled my hand in the air to encompass the four of them standing in the hallway. "Whatever this is."

"We just want to wish you luck," Vaughn said.

Sighing heavily, I stopped in front of them. "Why today, of all days?"

Ethan waggled his eyebrows. "You know why." He circled his finger, gesturing for me to turn around. "Let's do an outfit check."

I leveled my darkest scowl at him. "I'm wearing the same thing I always wear to a jobsite." Pants, a black shirt with our logo on it, and boots.

"You're wearing a nice pair of dark-wash jeans instead of black cargo pants," Nico pointed out. "They're looking pretty snug through the thighs. Let's see how your ass looks."

"No." I raised my arm in the air, but the sea of bodies didn't part. "Come on, guys. I need to go."

Archer stepped forward instead of backward. "Let's do a quick breath check."

I held out my hand and pushed against his chest. "Knock it off. I'm as minty fresh as a Peppermint Patty."

"Fine," Arch said as he circled around to my back. "His ass looks amazing in these jeans. I approve."

I turned to go back to my apartment to change my pants, but Archer stepped into my path.

"I don't think so, Hawk," he said. "You've come this far. Don't turn back." Archer's green gaze held mine, silently pleading with me to be brave.

They'd known what it had cost me to ask for the shift change during Saturday brunch, just as they'd known why I requested it. Gossip traveled just as quickly through RAVEN Securities as it did the Silver Maple community, and Bobby was the common denominator for both. That little shit. I'd expected the guys to tease me and offer some pointers, but they hadn't mentioned the kiss Bobby had interrupted. I might've convinced myself that my secret was safe, if not for the unusual hum of energy that had pulsed in the room and the Joker grins on their handsome faces.

Hell, I'd barely finished asking for *some* first shifts, thinking we'd alternate weeks, when Vaughn had smiled and said, "It's already handled. You're back at Silver Maple on Monday morning."

"For good," Nico had added. "I'm taking over the night shift from now on."

And that was that. Done and dusted.

But since I'd exchanged phone numbers with Atticus, something friends would do, texting him and inviting him to meet me for lunch on

Monday seemed like the logical next step. Friends eat lunch together. No biggie. Atticus had been quick to accept, and I should've left it there. But nope. No chill. I'd texted Atticus to let him know I was bringing the food. And he'd replied with a drooling emoji and said he'd treat me to fried chicken on Tuesday.

I'd spent the rest of the weekend replaying Friday's events and overthinking Saturday's text exchange while preparing mini quiches, roasted pepper hummus and pita chips, orzo salad, and fruit skewers with a whipped cream dip. I hadn't realized the ridiculous scope of my gesture until I had to upgrade from an insulated lunch bag to a small cooler to contain it all.

Archer eyed my lunch vessel with a smirk. "You sure are packing."

"That's what he said," I deadpanned.

That only encouraged Archer's juvenile behavior. "If not yet, he sure will."

"Looks like you've got enough food for two," Nico said.

Ethan stepped up beside me and placed a hand on my shoulder. "Feeding people is your love language."

"Nah, that's Vaughn." But I suspected the golden retriever was closer to the mark than I wanted to admit.

Cooking had started out as a random hobby to get out of my head. I'd tried other things first, but nothing stuck. Sticking to easy recipes helped me gain confidence, and I challenged myself to go bolder with each new skill I mastered. I loved testing new recipes and introducing the guys to different cuisines, but cooking for them had taken on a deeper meaning. The transition hadn't been sudden, but it was undeniable, though I'd just deflected the suggestion.

"Leave him alone," Vaughn said. "You'll make him late."

"Thanks."

But then Vaughn slapped my ass and said, "Go get him, Hawk."

Denial was futile, so I left with a casual wave goodbye. I had much better luck during my drive to Silver Maple. Traffic was minimal, every light was green, and Macy was on duty in the guard shack. She was a no-nonsense person who wouldn't give me any guff about what happened on Friday night, though I noticed an ornery shimmer in her dark eyes when I stopped at the arm barrier. Yeah, she knew all about the closet incident. Fucking Bobby.

"Morning, Macy."

"Morning, boss. Have a great day."

"You too. Call me if you have any problems."

Macy responded with a broad smile and a two-finger salute as I drove past. My body hummed with an energy I didn't want to name when I spotted Atticus's gold scooter near the entrance. *We're just friends who lunch. Nothing more.* Huffing a frustrated sigh, I parked the SUV and grabbed my gear from the passenger seat.

Caitlyn's eyes widened in welcome surprise when I walked into the building. "You're back."

Offering a wry grin, I said, "For the foreseeable future, it seems. Hope that's okay."

"Of course." Her eyes glittered with barely repressed curiosity, and I suspected her enthusiasm might have more to do with a front-row seat to my supposed romance with Atticus than seeing me around campus. I knew I was right when she lowered her voice and said, "So, how are *things*?"

Fucking Bobby.

"Good. And you?"

Caitlyn grinned knowingly. "Things are running smoothly around here for once, and I am eternally grateful for the reprieve."

"Uh-oh," I teased.

Her smile turned into a grimace. "Ugh. I probably just jinxed myself." She checked her watch, then said. "I have a phone conference starting soon, so I'll let you get on with your day."

"Thanks. Hope you have a good one."

"You too," she called out as she walked away.

I flipped on the light switch and stepped inside RAVEN's office. Ethan had taken the time to personalize the space, hanging photos of the five of us on the wall from various places around the world. We wore field fatigues and sunglasses in many of the images, but not in all of them. The not-so-fab five also modeled softball uniforms, beachwear, military dress blues, and even tuxes. There was so much history staring back at me, a reminder that not everyone I dared to love had died. These guys had seen me through my best and worst of times, just as I had for them, and we'd continue to be there for one another, come hell or high water. The tight knot under my sternum eased with my next deep breath. There was nothing to fear. I was just going to have lunch with a new friend.

Atticus was already sitting on the park bench under the oak when I arrived at the pond. He had his phone out to record the mallard couple's latest shenanigans. Marty flapped his wings and splashed the water obnoxiously, while Matilda squawked her displeasure. The louder she protested, the more he splashed around.

"That's right, Matilda. Give him hell!" Atticus called out.

"She's probably pissed because Marty's been avoiding her," I suggested.

Atticus snorted, then tapped the screen to stop the recording. He turned his megawatt smile on me. Then his eyes widened when he saw the size of the cooler. "Well, all Marty needs to do is feed her, and she will forgive him."

I really wanted that to be true. I sat beside Atticus, keeping a few feet of space between us to leave room for the food. "Hope you're hungry."

"Always." Atticus leaned toward me as I unzipped the top of the cooler, and our heads bumped. "Sorry! I'm just a little excited. No one has packed a lunch for me since my days in elementary school. I hope you didn't go to much trouble."

"Not at all. It's just simple food."

"If you made a peanut butter and jelly sandwich, I bet it would be the best I'd ever had."

I desperately wanted to be the best Atticus had ever had, and not just with my culinary skills. Swallowing hard, I forced my mind from the gutter. "The guys were giving me a hard time about the amount of food I made, so maybe I got a little carried away."

"Does that happen often?" Atticus asked.

"Do I get carried away?"

Hazel-brown eyes shimmered with humor, and that smile of his made my stomach do somersaults. "No. Do the guys tease you all the time?"

"Relentlessly and ruthlessly, but I give as good as I get. Vaughn is the voice of reason and prevents us from taking jokes and pranks too far."

"Oh, I haven't met him yet," Atticus said.

"Vaughn is our handsome, charismatic leader. Archer is the sexy playboy, as you've probably guessed after seeing him in action. Ethan is a lovable golden retriever. And Nico is the boyish charmer."

"And how do you see yourself?" Atticus asked.

The question caught me off guard because it sounded like something a therapist might say. "I'm stoic or standoffish and maybe a little rough around the edges."

"I don't think that about you at all," Atticus said before tilting his head and studying me. "Well, maybe at first glance, but there's nothing standoffish or rough about you."

"How do I come across to you, then?" I wanted to take the words back as soon as they left my mouth, and my discomfort grew while Atticus took his sweet time considering his answer.

"I think you're still, not stoic. Everyone knows that still waters run deep." He pointed to the pond, where Matilda and Marty had resumed their peaceful gliding. "Above the water, nothing is moving, but their feet are going wild under the surface. I think you're a lot like that. I bet your brain doesn't rest much."

"Not really."

"And you seem like you're always on alert, as if maybe you're stuck in a permanent protector mode," Atticus said, his voice and expression softening with tenderness. "I think you shoulder the burden for things you shouldn't, and it must get exhausting." He scooted closer but didn't reach for me like I wanted him to. "We're safe right here. There are no threats. No one will bug us."

His perception was so accurate it was scary. Atticus made me feel seen and vulnerable, but in the best ways. I must've held his gaze without responding for a beat too long because his cheeks turned pink.

"Sorry," Atticus said. "I didn't mean to get so philosophical. No wonder I can't make friends."

I snorted. "I don't believe that."

"It's true. The last friend I made was Emma. She showed up as the new girl one day in third grade and claimed me as her best friend. We've been inseparable ever since."

"That's adorable." Everything about Atticus was so damn charming. I shifted my attention to unpacking the cooler before I did something dumb, like drag him into my lap and kiss him breathless.

"Wow," Atticus said once I'd set all the containers on the bench and handed him a fork. "Just simple food, huh?"

"Yep."

"Did you toast your own pita chips?" Atticus asked as he dipped one into the hummus.

Heat spread up the back of my neck. "Okay, so I'm a lot to take sometimes."

"I bet you're a lot to take most of the time," Atticus said, his voice dripping with innuendo. "Sorry. I'll behave." Then he bit into the pita chip and moaned in the most misbehaving way. Fuck, was he that vocal in bed too?

"Uh-huh," I said, looking around to make sure no one was close enough to overhear us. "You might want to tone it down, or there will be rumors about us engaging in sex at the pond." And damn if that didn't sound like the best idea I'd ever heard.

Atticus hunched his shoulders and giggled. "Sorry." Then he nudged the container of hummus closer to me and said, "Have some."

I dipped a chip into the hummus and had to admit it was damn good. "Not bad at all."

Atticus reached over and swiped his thumb over the corner of my mouth to remove hummus remnants. Instead of wiping his hand on a napkin I provided, he stuck the digit in his mouth and sucked it clean. My blood started moving south, and I fought the urge to squirm on the bench. *Think of something to say, dumbass.* But my brain gave me nothing to work with. Traitor.

"I must suck at making friends too," I admitted. "I can't think of a good conversation starter. Weather and baseball are common topics, but what's to talk about? It's fucking hot outside, and the Braves are braving."

Atticus cocked his head to the side as if pondering our awkwardness while he ate quiche. He swallowed, wiped his mouth with a napkin, and held up his forefinger. "I got it. Let's talk about what we did over the weekend."

I'd spent the entire two days thinking about Atticus, planning food for him, and fucking my fist while fantasizing about him. I needed time to come up with alternative activities to discuss, so I blurted, "You go first."

"Aw, I like a man who insists I go first." Atticus winked, and then he launched into a cute summary of going to a neighborhood yard sale event with his best friend, Emma, and her grandmother, Ramona.

He'd diverted the story long enough to tell me that Ramona was Emma's hair emergency on Friday night. Ramona had wanted to give herself layers and bangs, which apparently hadn't gone well. I understood the last one but was clueless about layers. All I knew was that Ramona was my hero. Thanks to her, I got locked in the closet with Atticus and shared one hell of an epic kiss.

"Yard sales, huh? You seem kinda young for that."

"Maybe," Atticus said. "I guess I'm curious about the things people deem unworthy and disposable." There was a hint of sadness in his expression that caught my attention, but he blinked, and it was gone. "Your turn. What did you do this weekend?"

"Well, I slept a lot to prepare for the shift change."

Atticus bit his lower lip. "Thank you."

"I did the laundry and researched new recipes."

Atticus widened his eyes, and his voice came out breathy when he said, "For me?"

Why would that be so surprising? Then I remembered his remark about no one making him lunch since elementary school. Atticus deserved thoughtful gestures all the time. I barely knew him, and yet I understood that. How had no one else? Our gazes met and held. I needed him to see the truth when I said, "Yes, for you."

Atticus swallowed hard. "Thank you."

"You're welcome."

Neither one of us moved, ate, or even blinked. Something big and scary passed in the space between us.

"What's the next topic?" I asked.

Atticus hummed as he considered my question, never taking his eyes off mine. "If you could be anywhere in the world right now, where would it be?"

"Right here." And holy fuck, I meant it.

"With me?"

"Yes."

Atticus inhaled slowly and deeply. "Do you say such sweet things to all your friends?"

This was my chance to backpedal, but I didn't want to take the words back. "No. Just you."

Atticus held my gaze for several heartbeats. Then his lips curved into a beautiful smile. "I'd choose you too."

Damn, we were so bad at this *friendship* thing.

Reaching the oak tree first on Tuesday, I sat down on my side of the bench and watched the pond's surface ripple beneath a soft breeze. I closed my eyes and imagined the wind sweeping all my negative thoughts away. *Goodbye, guilt. Don't let the door hit you in the ass, fear. So long, self-doubt.*

The delicious smell of fried chicken interrupted my nature therapy session a few seconds before I heard Atticus approach. Turning my head, I took in the gorgeous curve of his sunny smile and the joy that radiated from his every pore. *Hello, happiness. It's been a long-ass time, my old friend.*

"Sorry I'm late," Atticus said breathlessly.

"I hope like hell you didn't run all the way here from the cafeteria in this heat."

Atticus dropped onto the bench beside me, and not the two feet we usually kept between us. The urge to move didn't strike, so I stayed put. The desire to touch him hit me with the strength of a bomb, so I did. Placing my hand on the back of his neck, I rubbed away the tension while Atticus closed his eyes and enjoyed the breeze.

"Heaven," he said.

"Or as close as we'll get."

Atticus took a deep breath and sighed. "Okay. It's my turn to feed you, and I pulled out all the stops." He looked over at me, then down at the heavenly smelling bag of food on his lap, as if just realizing how close he'd sat down. "Oops. I didn't leave room for our picnic."

I reluctantly dropped my hand to the back of the bench, and he scooted down. "The tongues would really wag if we started carrying a blanket to the pond with us every day."

Atticus lifted a container from the bag and froze. "Every day, huh?"

"Well, I..."

Biting his lip, Atticus set the carton down. "I'm just teasing." Then he lowered his gaze to the bag once more and added, "But this is one of those times I find it almost impossible to resist you."

My heart leaped into my throat and beat wildly. "Oh yeah? And what would you do?"

"Kiss you, for one thing."

"For one thing? You'd do more than kiss me in front of the residents and fellow employees?" I gestured at the pond and said, "And the ducks?"

Atticus pursed his quivering lips together, but the dam broke easily, spilling magical laughter into the air. "If our kiss on Friday was anything to go by, I'd likely forget where I was and climb onto your lap as soon as our lips touched." He shook his head sadly. "I can't be trusted."

"It's a good thing we're just friends, then," I said with absolute zero conviction. "For the ducks' sake."

Atticus scoffed. "Those sluts canoodle and do whatever ducks do without regard for our feelings."

I looked out at the water, where Marty was shaking his tail feathers for Matilda. "You have a point."

"But, yeah, just friends," Atticus said. "That's what you can give me, and that's what I agreed to accept." He briefly closed his eyes and shook his head. "Yikes, I didn't mean to make it sound like your friendship is a consolation prize for not getting your dick." Eyes widening, Atticus pointed to his mouth. "Uh-oh. It's about to run off again."

I did the only possible thing I could think of to save Atticus and pressed my lips to his. I didn't dare linger, not that I really believed he'd straddle my lap on the bench. When I pulled back, Atticus smiled at me and held up his thumb and forefinger a centimeter apart.

"This close," he said. "I'd lifted one leg off the bench."

"And we better change the subject before we get into trouble."

"Fine," Atticus said, handing me a rectangular carryout container.

"What's in here?"

"Sofia's finest. Chicken, collard greens, black-eyed peas, and cornbread."

Pretty sure I moaned in ecstasy at just the thought of eating the food. "I'll probably be in a food coma in an hour."

"Nah," Atticus said. "You're too disciplined for that. How's your day going so far?"

I opened the container and stared down at the feast until Atticus whacked my leg with a package containing disposable utensils, a napkin, and a wet wipe. "It's been pretty good so far, but it's shaping up to be excellent. How was your morning?"

"Maintenance fixed the door handle on the art room closet," Atticus said.

"Fixed or replaced?" I'd really hoped for the latter, but I suspected they'd go with the cheapest option first.

"Um, I'm not sure. We were working with modeling clay when Gary swung by to fix it. I just know the handle turns."

I made a note to get the paperwork from Gary so I could document and close out the incident report.

"Enough about work," Atticus said as he held a drumstick near his mouth. "I want to talk about your tattoos."

My eyebrow shot up. "What about them?"

Atticus bobbed his head while he chewed, then took a drink from one of the water bottles he'd brought. "I have so many questions. First, why do you cover up your beautiful skin art when you're at work?" He tugged on one of my long sleeves. "Aren't you burning alive in that thing? And also, tell me about some of your tats. I tried to zoom in on the pictures you uploaded to Randy, but that only made them blurrier. Is there a theme to your ink?"

I paused with my fork halfway to my mouth. Damn, he'd given my tats a lot of thought. Dropping my fork into my container, I gave him my full attention. "I haven't purposely planned a theme for my ink. I guess you'd just say they're a representation of places I've been, experiences I've lived, and people I've loved. So, I guess the theme is life."

Not that I'd done much living beyond breathing, eating, and working over the past three years. But I thought I was ready for more, even if I wasn't exactly sure what that meant. Our lunchtime conversations drew me closer to Atticus and left me craving more. I'd made myself vulnerable to him, but was I emotionally strong enough to explore the physical part of intimacy?

"Wow," Atticus said. "That's a gorgeous way to describe your tattoos." He sighed. "Your body is a beautiful canvas, and I think you should flaunt it."

"Thank you. The older generations don't always think highly of people with tattoos, and I don't want to cause any issues here or anywhere. The combination of my height, muscles, and ink is intimidating to many people, and I don't want to make anyone uncomfortable. I wear long sleeves on every job."

"I see where you're coming from," Atticus said, "but it's disappointing you have to hide such beauty. How do you stand wearing that shirt though?"

"It's made from a special material that helps keep the body cool in hot weather," I said. "They use similar technology in the military."

"Well, you don't have to cover up around here because the residents are dying to know what you're rocking under your shirts. One of them glimpsed part of a tattoo under the cuff of your sleeve, and the tongues have been wagging since. The security hunks are a hit with the Silver Maple crowd."

I chuckled. "Is that what they call us?"

"Uh-huh. A particular security hunk is our favorite," Atticus said.

My heart swelled about three sizes. "Our favorite? You live here now?"

"I was encompassing the staff and residents under one Silver Maple umbrella. One hunk makes a *huge* impression." Atticus winked as he took a bite of his lunch and chewed. "And if the Silver Maple crowd discovered the hunky heartthrob can cook too…" He shook his head. "They'd all want to be your lunch buddy, and I'd have to fight them off."

Lunch buddy? The label was much too mundane to describe the way I felt about Atticus, but I wasn't ready to put into words what my heart already knew. So I speared a bite of greens and said, "Do you have any tats?"

Atticus cocked his head to the side. "You've seen me wearing nothing but a pair of swim shorts."

"I haven't seen below the waistband." Suddenly, the moisture-wicking fabric failed to do its job because my body heat soared to a dangerous level.

"No tats, but I sometimes wear a belly button ring."

I choked on a bite of cornbread, and Atticus pushed a bottle of water into my hand. I took a drink and regained my composure. "Why didn't you include that in your thirst traps?"

"It's kind of cliché, right? Chad told me it made me look trashy and immature."

I barely suppressed a growl from hearing that asshole's name. "Do you like wearing it?"

Atticus worked his lower lip for a few seconds. "Maybe I should've outgrown it, but I really do."

"Then wear it for yourself." *Or me. I'd love that.* "Who cares what anyone else thinks?" Funny how I didn't apply that same logic to my tattoos.

Atticus sat taller. "You're right. I totally should. Thank you."

"You're welcome." And then because I was a masochist, I asked, "So, no other piercings beneath the waistband?"

"No. My act of rebellion was pretty tame."

I caught his gaze and held it. "There's nothing tame about you."

Especially not the way he made me feel.

Atticus watched with rapt attention as I unpacked my insulated lunchbox.

"I didn't get carried away this time," I said. "I just brought chicken salad on croissants and fresh fruit. Oh, and Saratoga chips."

"You made the chips, didn't you?"

"Um, it sounds harder than it really is."

"What's your idea of roughing it?" Atticus asked.

An image of me railing him from behind sprang to mind. "Oh god," I wheezed.

Atticus put both hands on my shoulders. "Are you okay? Is it asthma?"

I cleared my throat and offered him a weak smile, hoping none of my dirty thoughts lingered in my expression. "No, um, I just sucked air down funny."

"Uh-huh," Atticus said slowly. "Why don't I believe you? I'm the clumsy one in this friendship." He cocked his head to the side. "Did your thoughts go somewhere unexpected?"

"No," I croaked.

"Uh-huh. Well, I mucked this up, so I need to get our minds out of the gutter."

"Ours?"

"You think my mind didn't go to naughty places before the words had even cleared my mouth?" Atticus shook his head and sighed. "Sorry. I didn't mean to make things worse."

"It's fine." I handed him his wrapped sandwich and a cup of fruit. "What would you rather talk about?"

"I'd prefer to hear about us *roughing it,* but that's not a good idea. So, we'll talk about the nerve and audacity of Chad."

Snorting, I looked up from my sandwich. "That almost sounds like a book title."

"Yeah, well, I hope it reads better than reality," Atticus said. "An envelope came in the mail for me yesterday. It was from Chad, of all people, and it included a letter and a check for five thousand dollars. My dad thinks it's because Chad hopes a judge will go easier on him when his case goes to court if he's already paid me restitution for damages."

"Wow," I said. "Not to belittle your lovely Sadie, but five thousand seems significantly more than her value."

"The dick owes me money for other things. I should've seen the writing on the wall when he stopped contributing his half of the rent money and other household expenses. Five thousand doesn't cover everything, but I'll accept it as his debt repayment if that will get him out of my life for good."

"Did he apologize in his letter?" I asked.

Atticus snorted. "Hell no. Chad was more concerned about justifying his actions than taking responsibility for them. He basically detailed how I'd ruined his life and implied I'd had it coming without saying I'd had it coming."

Even though I knew the answer would only raise my blood pressure, I asked it anyway. "How are you responsible for ruining his life? Explain it to me like I'm five years old."

Atticus slapped my arm. "You have a way with words."

"Said no one ever." I pointed my sandwich at him. "Now, talk." I started to take a bite but stopped. "How likely am I to choke to death on food if I eat while you attempt to explain the audacity of Chad?"

"Highly likely."

I set my food down and gestured for him to continue.

"Well, I didn't do it for him sexually any longer," Atticus replied.

Thank god I hadn't taken a bite of food. And yep, there went my blood pressure. "What? He put that in a letter that might go before a judge?"

"Not in so many words. In the letter, Chad said I'd failed him as a boyfriend, but he'd explained in great detail why he cheated after I found out. I'll spare you what he told me."

"Because it's all bullshit," I blurted.

"You can't possibly know that after one kiss."

"It was one fucking hot kiss, and hell yes, I can."

Atticus reached over and cupped my cheek. "Your face is getting red. Is steam about to come out your ears?"

"Maybe."

"Your lap is looking so damn good right now."

It took every ounce of willpower I had not to pat my thighs. Instead, I turned my face and kissed his palm. Atticus retracted his hand, looked down at it, and folded his fingers protectively around his palm. "You're killing me, Smalls."

Atticus grinned and shook his head. "You already know that I got both of us fired with my stunt."

"Yes, and I still haven't achieved that level of vengeance."

"Stick with me, kid." Atticus winked playfully. "Well, I also got us blackballed from finding jobs in our fields. We both hold a master's in computer engineering, but no one was willing to hire us."

"The troublemaker and the fuckboy?" I teased.

"That almost beats out the audacity of Chad for the best book title." Then Atticus arched a brow. "I'm the troublemaker in this scenario, right?"

"Obviously."

"Chad didn't come right out and say Win had dumped him on his ass, but he referenced that he'd fallen on hard times while I came out smelling like roses. Chad pointed out that I was able to land this cushy job because I'm a nepo baby."

"Come again?"

"My Aunt Ronni sits on Silver Maple's board. She got me an interview for the interim activities coordinator but claims I earned the job on my own merit. And there's nothing cushy about keeping up with these seniors."

"I think I've met your aunt. She has Disney villain hair and a feisty personality, right?"

"That's my gal. Unforgettable." Atticus smiled impishly. "She thinks you're pretty special too."

"Aw, that's nice to hear, but don't distract me from my point." When Atticus held up his palms in surrender, I continued. "Why the hell would you believe anything dipshit Chad thinks, especially when it contradicts what your aunt told you?"

Atticus averted his gaze until I tucked my fingers under his chin and turned his face toward me. "It's so much easier to believe the bad stuff people say, especially when it matches your internal voices."

"If Ronni told you that you earned your job on your own, then you did. Period."

"I never in a million years would've imagined myself working here, but I freaking love my job, and I give it my all. It shouldn't matter how I got hired."

"Would it help you feel better if I told you that Vaughn's grandmother sits on Silver Maple's board too? She might've been the main reason we got the security contracts."

"Aww. We're all nepo babies."

We shared a laugh and took a few bites before I circled back to the conversation. "As for your other self-doubts, I'll battle those assholes one by one until they disappear."

Smiling shyly, Atticus said, "That might take a lot of lunches."

"Good thing there are tons of new recipes waiting for me to try."

Atticus stared into my eyes with so much naked yearning that my heart physically ached from it. "I like you so much."

"I like you more." I pointed to his stash of Saratoga chips. "Now, try one of those. Archer nearly lost a fingertip on the mandoline."

Atticus narrowed his eyes. "You made the chips sound easy to make."

"Oh, they are when someone else risks their digits on the evil slicer."

Shaking his head, Atticus said, "What am I going to do with you?"

And just like that, my mind was back in the gutter. The wicked smile on Atticus's face said he was right there with me.

Atticus missed lunch with me on Thursday to attend a resident's birthday party, and I was desperate to see him by the time Friday afternoon rolled around. We didn't explicitly restrict our interactions to our lunchtime chats, but we didn't text often. I wanted to hear Atticus's thoughts through his words and see his expressions shift when he talked. And we both knew our *friendship* was teetering on the edge of something more. The slightest breeze would push us over the edge, and Atticus seemed content to follow my lead. I had to be sure I was truly ready when I made my move, and I grew more certain with every lingering glance, volley of banter, and shared laugh.

"Street tacos and corn salsa from the cafeteria," Atticus called out as he approached.

"Damn, that sounds good." And damn, Atticus looked good. It took all I had not to reach for him. Hell, my hand even shook when I accepted a paper-wrapped taco from him.

"You look really serious right now," Atticus said. "Is everything okay?"

"Yeah. Just had a frustrating morning. I busted a resident smoking in a building."

"Angus McNally?" Atticus asked.

"That's the one. I had to march him into Caitlyn's office. Sometimes I feel like a glorified hall monitor. Angus called me a traitor and said I should get court-martialed. Let's just say I'm ready for the weekend. Do you have any plans?"

Atticus averted his gaze to the pond. "My parents are going out of town to visit my sister's family. It's a spur-of-the-moment thing, which they rarely do. Mom says she misses her grandbabies, but I think Dad just wants to get laid, and he's sick of my interference. I've been hell on their sex life since I moved back home."

It was a good damn thing I hadn't taken a bite of food, or I might've choked to death. The little minx.

"Anyway, Emma invited me out for a drink and live music to make up for last week."

"Are you going?" *Please say no. Please say no.* I had no right to think it, let alone say it out loud, especially when I wasn't prepared to offer him an alternative night out.

Atticus averted his gaze to the pond and licked his lower lip. "I told her it depended on how my day went. I'm slammed with activities this afternoon, so I promised to let her know later." Why wouldn't Atticus look at me? "Wow, it got dark out suddenly. Looks like it might rain." And why had he changed the subject?

I'd just opened my mouth to ask what was going on when the clouds opened and released a torrent of rain. We leaped to our feet, but there was no shelter anywhere nearby except for the big oak tree. I tugged Atticus behind me and abandoned our lunch to the elements. Pressing my back to the rough bark, I folded my arms around Atticus and held him tightly against my chest. A spattering of raindrops cut through the dense treetop, but we were relatively dry compared to the deluge beyond the leafy canopy.

"This will do as long as it doesn't start lightning," I said.

"Mmhmm," Atticus hummed against my chest. "This is a good place to be."

His blissed-out voice jump-started my heart and my libido. I slid my hand up to cup the back of his neck, and Atticus looked up at me. Those gorgeous eyes shimmered with desire I couldn't ignore. Lowering my head, I rubbed my nose against his. "I want to kiss you so damn much. I dream about your lips."

Atticus rose on his tiptoes and pressed his mouth to mine, parting my lips with his tongue and boldly sweeping inside. Groaning, I slid my hand into his hair and angled my head to deepen the kiss. The world around us was soaking wet, but my body went up in flames. That one brief kiss we shared in the closet felt like a lifetime ago instead of two weeks. I needed more of Atticus—his kisses, his body pressed to mine, and the soft mewling sounds he made when he got horny. Everything. I released his hair to skim my hand up and down his back, and Atticus slipped his hand under the hem of my shirt to stroke my stomach.

It was too much and yet not enough. I parted my legs, and Atticus nudged his thigh between mine. His erection pressed against my leg, and his thigh rubbed the underside of my balls. My dick throbbed like it was trying to escape my pants to get to him. Atticus shifted his hips, riding my thigh and rubbing his stomach against my aching erection.

I wanted release; I needed it with him. But not here. Not like this. Not rubbing one out against a tree at work and coming in our pants. A wicked voice in the back of my brain reminded me I could suck him off and swallow the evidence. As soon as the idea occurred, it became the only logical solution to our problem. My fingers gripped his hair again, and Atticus arched his neck. I broke the kiss to nibble the column of his throat. Atticus slid his hands higher up my torso to tease and pinch my nipples. The sharp bite of pleasure brought me back to reality.

I snapped my head up and met his hungry gaze. "We can't do this here."

"No, we can't." I could tell he wanted to ask when and where we could, but he didn't. As if Atticus read my mind, he said, "I won't ask for more than you can give."

This was where I should make my move. Ask him to come home with me or volunteer to go home with him. I didn't. Maybe I would have, if the sound of an approaching golf cart hadn't reached my ears. Shit. Someone had come looking for us in the rain shower. Likely one of my employees, and I didn't want them to find me in this condition, but there was no way my erection would completely deflate by the time they arrived.

"We have company coming," Atticus said.

"A savior we didn't ask for," I growled.

Atticus patted my chest. "Probably for the best since things got a bit out of control."

"A bit?" I teased.

"Well, I dry-humped your magnificent thigh and was a thrust away from coming in my pants."

I closed my eyes and tilted my head back against the tree. "You're not helping the situation I've got in my underwear."

"And I really, really want to help you out of your underwear and get that massive dick in my—"

"Hey, boss," Miller called out as the golf cart came into view.

I narrowed my eyes in the steeliest glare I could manage, daring him to comment on how he'd found us. I also hoped it would prevent him from telling the others.

"Thought you guys might need a rescue," he said less robustly when the cart pulled up under the tree. "Looks like you have it under control."

"I could use a ride back," Atticus said. "I need to get ready for bingo. It'll be a bloodbath if I don't put on a good show. And then I need to prepare for Silver Maple's very first life drawing class."

"You get on the cart, and I'll clean our mess," I told him.

"You're not coming with us?"

"There's only room for two," I pointed out. "You go first so you can set up for bingo, then Miller can double back for me."

"Absolutely," Miller said.

Atticus held my gaze for a few seconds before nodding. He went to step back, but I held him in place, lowering my mouth to his ear.

"Have fun if you go out with Emma, but try not to give your heart to anyone else tonight."

Atticus pulled back and met my gaze. "No chance that will happen." He kissed my cheek and jumped onto the golf cart with Miller. "Let's hit it. Bingo enthusiasts wait for no one and nothing."

Miller hooted with laughter as he pressed down on the accelerator, and I watched them drive off, both chatting and laughing happily. I'd reached the point of no return and could no longer straddle the fence. I could continue to play it safe and guard my heart, as I'd done the past three years, or take a leap of faith and gamble my heart with Atticus.

I had two options but only one choice. Under the oak tree, with rain pouring down all around me, I closed my eyes and took that leap of faith. And there was no way in hell I'd wait until lunchtime on Monday to make my move.

CHAPTER 13

ATTICUS

"I-25," I SAID.

"Louder for the people in the back," Mrs. Hastings yelled from the last row.

"Turn your hearing aids up, Hattie," Mr. Webb suggested.

"Or stop sitting at the farthest table from the bingo caller," Ms. Johansson said.

Mrs. Hastings set down her purple bingo dauber and flipped the room a double bird. "I turned the volume up as high as it will go, and I will plant my ass wherever the hell I want to sit. I'm old, fat, and gassy. Be glad I sat so far away."

"Add self-aware to the mix," Mr. Bauer snarked just loud enough for me to hear him at the caller table.

I needed to put an end to the bickering before it got out of control. WWCD. What would Cammy do? She'd repeat the stupid bingo number and raise her voice to prevent a similar argument from breaking out.

"I-25," I bellowed.

Mr. Bauer in the front row grimaced, so maybe I'd gone too much in the other direction. Mrs. Hastings picked up her dauber and aggressively tagged her bingo card before giving me a thumbs-up.

I reached into the tumbler and pulled out the next ball. "B-12."

"Oh. Reminds me I still need a shot," Mr. Ivans said.

"Bingo!" Mr. Macklin shouted.

The room groaned collectively because Sid Macklin cried wolf a lot. I wasn't sure if it was orneriness or if he wasn't fully cognizant of what we were doing. I was supposed to stop the game and verify just in case because these residents were serious about their prizes. But since I'd only called two numbers so far, achieving bingo was impossible. I was about to stop the game just to appease him, but Mr. Macklin's tablemate waved me off and informed Sid that he didn't have a single match yet.

"Ignore it and call the next number," Ms. Johansson prodded.

These folks were a tough crowd, and the endorphin buzz I got from lunch with Ray was fading quickly. I tightened my grip around the bingo ball, wishing I could hold on to the happiness just as fiercely. Hot damn, that kiss. Every future rain shower would remind me of Ray's hot mouth against mine, the glide of his tongue, and the eagerness in his hands.

God, I loved the feel of Ray's tight abs and muscular chest beneath my fingertips. Heat rushed to my face as I recalled teasing and pinching his nipples. I'd never behaved so boldly in my life. And I'd loved it. Damn, I'd been ready to climb Ray like a tree, and I had no doubt he would've let me. He'd been as hot and horny as—

"Kit!" Mrs. Hastings yelled.

Jolting, I dropped the bingo ball in my hand onto the table, where it bounced and rolled onto the floor. I scrambled after it, snatching the ball before it disappeared under a front-row table. I held it up proudly and said, "B-12!"

"You already called that one," Mr. Ivans snapped. "Pull yourself together, young man."

Mr. Webb rolled his eyes heavenward and declared bingo a disaster. "We need the kid with the tire iron to liven things up."

"It was a crowbar," I reminded him. "And we certainly don't need him to have fun."

"How about we ask your hunky boyfriend to come in here and show us some tackling moves," Mr. Ivans suggested. "We could call it self-defense classes. Surely that counts as an enrichment activity."

I tried not to act like a giddy teenager just because Teddy Ivans had referred to Ray as my boyfriend. "We're not doing that. Ray has serious things to do." But I'd sure as hell offer myself up as the tackling dummy if Ray were giving lessons. I set the B-12 ball in the rack with the other called number and rolled the tumbler a few times. Pulling out the next ball, I cringed at the number. "O-69!"

"That was an exceptional year," Mrs. Hastings yelled. "The cars, the music..."

"The sex position," Ms. Johansson countered.

Mr. Macklin raised a fist in the air. "Bingo!"

The people in the front row pushed their cards away and prepared to get up from the table.

"Please don't," I said. "I'll make this right."

My promise received raised eyebrows and doubtful scowls, but no one abandoned ship. My first task was to pull my head out of my ass. Then I invited Mr. Macklin to be my assistant at the caller's table instead of playing along. He eagerly shuffled up and took a seat behind the tumbler. While he turned the crank, I assessed the prizes. After the many interruptions, the least I could do was hand everyone a little something.

My gaze landed on the stack of prize cards that Bobby had given me. Each one featured Bobby's contact info and offered the bearer a free twenty-minute massage. Bobby had been generous with his time and spirit when he'd given them to Cammy, but he'd likely planned to stretch out the massages over a longer period. I bit my lip to keep from laughing maniacally. Bobby had been a downright shit lately, so I got even the best way I knew how.

"You get a massage. You get a massage. You get a massage," I said, doing my best Oprah impersonation as I passed out the prizes.

"You're not so bad, Kit," Mrs. Hastings said.

"I like you too."

Mrs. Hastings snorted and tucked her free massage card into her bra. "Don't push your luck."

"Yes, ma'am."

Back at the front of the room, Mr. Macklin reached into the tumbler and handed me a numbered ball. "Here you go, Kit."

"Thank you." I looked at the number and said, "N-32!"

Thankfully, the rest of our bingo time passed without a hitch, and I thought my luck was finally making a turn for the good.

My phone rang at two thirty, and my stomach flipped when I saw Cord McDonald's name on the screen. My super-sweet, sexy, and very straight gym friend had agreed to model for the afternoon's life drawing class. It was a new event I'd added to the calendar when Silver Maple hired me, and the enrollment surpassed my wildest dreams. The art room only had space for thirty easels, so I'd had to limit participation. The event had filled up within ten minutes of the posting, and there was even a waiting list for cancelations. Caitlyn promised to green-light more life drawing events if the first one went well. So a phone call from Cord thirty minutes before class was due to start didn't bode well for me.

I accepted the call and said, "Hello," as casually as I could.

"Hey, Kit," Cord rasped.

My self-pity instantly turned to concern. "What's wrong? Are you hurt?"

"I got in a car accident earlier today. The downpour made the road slick, and someone rear-ended me at a traffic light. It seemed like a minor incident at the time, but I'm getting sorer and stiffer the longer the day wears on. I'm afraid I won't make it to the art class. I hate to let you down like this."

"Don't worry about me. I'm just sorry you got hurt. Are you getting checked out?"

"Sierra is taking me now," he said. "I think the seat belt bruised my ribs, and I might have a touch of whiplash."

"Any amount isn't good. I hope you feel better soon."

"I appreciate it," Cody said. "Maybe we can work out a replacement date when I feel better."

"That would be great. Take care of yourself, Cody."

I disconnected the call and checked the time. Determination washed over me because failure wasn't an option. I had something to prove to myself and Silver Maple. I just needed to find a replacement model in thirty minutes. And I knew exactly who I wanted to strip down for life drawing class.

Every encounter I'd had with Ray flitted through my mind, starting with his drenched clothes clinging to him like a second skin and ending with our lunchtime embrace under the oak tree. Mmmm. I'd touched some of those muscles and felt them tremble beneath my fingertips. Cord was a sexy man, but he didn't hold a candle to Ray.

But would he model? There was no way Ray would strip down to his underwear and sit for two hours so the residents could draw charcoal portraits of him. What about just shirtless? No way in hell he'd go for it. He wore long sleeves in ninety-degree weather to avoid displaying his tattoos. I had to pivot.

Think, think, think.

Bobby was hot and had a rocking body, but I'd just passed out his free-massage cards like candy on Halloween night. Those residents had probably already booked their freebies, and Bobby was likely furious with me. Inspiration struck me like a bolt of lightning. Ray might be on the modest side, but I knew at least one member of the security team who would be all too happy to strip down and soak up the attention. I hauled ass to the security office and burst through the door like a shotgun blast. The space was small, so it only took two steps to reach the desk, where I leaned forward and braced my hands on the surface to catch my breath.

Ray leaped to his feet, his body and face going rigid in full-alert mode. "What's wrong?"

"Need help," I said between pants.

Rounding the desk, Ray laid his big, warm hand between my shoulders. "What happened, baby?"

The question hung there in the silence of the room while I panted and Ray panicked. I didn't need to see his face to know how he'd react to that little slip. His hand tensed on my body before it gentled and rubbed circles on my back. Had Ray meant the endearment? Hope was a dangerous thing, but I didn't try to mask the emotion when I turned to face him. Ray's hand fell to my lower back, and he pulled me close.

Please, please, please mean it.

Ray cupped my cheek and said, "Tell me."

Instead of pulling away and acting like a professional, I rubbed my face against his palm like a kitten with his office door hanging open. I should've been terrified about losing a job I desperately needed, and yet I let Ray's warmth soothe me instead of stepping back. "I happened."

Ray narrowed his eyes. "Explain."

"I'm always the problem."

"Bullshit," Ray said with a smirk. "What do you need?"

"Archer's phone number."

"What? Why?" Ray's fingers pressed into my lower back, pulling me tighter against his body. The desperate expression in his blue eyes was the same as when he pleaded with me not to give my heart to someone during a night out with Emma. Silly man. Didn't he know I'd hung a reserved sign on my heart for him?

"Or maybe you can call him for me."

"Again, I ask why?"

"Cowboy Cord can't make it this afternoon. I need someone to stand in for him."

"Cowboy Cord? As in roping and shit? I thought you had bingo and a life drawing class this afternoon."

A man who listened was the sexiest thing on Earth, but I chuckled at the ridiculous turn the conversation had taken. I cycled through a deep breath and tried again. "Cord McDonald is my very-straight friend from the gym who'd volunteered to model for the class this afternoon." I looked at my watch, and panic crept in again. "That starts in fifteen minutes."

"Ah, you need someone to fill in," Ray guessed.

"Yes."

"And Archer was your first pick?" Hurt flashed in his pretty blue eyes.

I rose on my tiptoes and kissed his frowning mouth. "You're my first choice. Always. But I didn't think you'd—"

"I'll do it!" Ray blurted. Then he angled his head and smirked. "But how much stripping are we talking here?"

"Everything goes," I said, waggling my eyebrows.

"Atticus." My name was a growly warning that did wonderful things to my body.

"I meant *anything* goes," I replied with a wink. "Cord was going to strip down to his underwear, but I didn't advertise that as part of the class. You could always just take off your shirt. All your muscle definition and ink would give them a wonderful opportunity to play with shading and dimension."

"So, you're saying you want me to take my shirt off and bare my chest strictly for artistic purposes."

"Uh-huh."

"Mmm. Will you be drawing too?" Ray asked.

There wouldn't be enough easels, but I could grab a notebook and pencil. "Mmhmm."

Ray pressed his lips to my ear and whispered, "You should probably sit where I can't see you. I'd hate for my dick to get hard in front of everyone."

I jerked and would've head-butted Ray if not for his quick reflexes. "That would be awkward."

But I had no intention of listening. I would set up with the perfect view of his chest, consequences be damned. Speaking of chests, mine suddenly felt too small, or maybe my heart had just expanded three times its normal size, beating against its cage and demanding freedom. And if I didn't get a hold of my chemical reaction to this man, another part of me would throb against its confines and demand release too. I took a step back, but Ray came with me instead of letting me break his hold.

"Um, what are you doing?" I asked, sounding as breathless as I felt. Enlarged heart, thickening dick, and all that. Who could breathe properly under these circumstances? "The door is open."

"I know, and I don't care. Let's get something straight."

"There's absolutely nothing straight about the way you make me feel." *Ba-dum tish.* God, I had jokes.

Ray's mouth curved into a sexy smirk as he marched me backward until my ass bumped into his desk. "I want you to come to me."

Of course, my brain heard "come for me." I mean, it wouldn't be the first time he nearly made me jizz myself that afternoon. "When?"

"Whenever you want or need something—anything. I'm your guy. Not Archer or Cowboy Cody or some rando at a bar."

"Cord, not Cody."

"I don't care what his name is." Ray pressed the length of his body against mine, and I nearly combusted on the spot. "Just me," he whispered in my ear.

"Do you talk to all your friends like this?" I pressed. "All bossy and demanding?"

"Nope."

Had Ray just admitted he was ready for more? I cocked my head to the side as I considered what to say next, and that's when he ran his nose along the exposed skin. I couldn't have kept the whimper in my mouth if it saved the world. Cities would burn before I surrendered a single second of this pleasure, and I needed him to know it.

"Is this like a hero complex or something?" I teased. "Do you enjoy saving me from myself?"

Ray growled, and my eyes rolled back in my head. "Nope."

"What's happening, then?" I had to know.

"Ten minutes," Ray rasped.

I pulled back to look into his eyes. "Huh?"

"That's how much longer we have until your class starts."

His words acted like a bucket of cold water. "Fuck. I need to make sure everything's ready to go." I forced myself out of his hold and put as much distance as the small office allowed. "You're really going to do this?"

"Yes. Eight minutes."

"Ugh!" I lunged forward and kissed him hard on the mouth before whirling around and running from the office.

The energy in the art room was the only thing buzzing harder than me. The crowd was a diverse mixture of genders, orientations, races, ages, and religions. They'd broken into a few smaller groups to discuss the upcoming class, and I caught snippets of their conversation. Everyone was curious about the model and eager to get started, so I walked into the center of the circle and stood next to the empty stool I'd provided for the model.

"We're just about ready to get started," I announced.

Mr. Sanchez pinned me with a suspicious glare. "Where's the model?"

"He should be here any minute," I assured everyone. "The original model was involved in a car accident today and couldn't make it, so I had to find a last-minute replacement."

Mrs. Cho, who sat directly across from me, rolled her eyes. "He better not be a dud."

"Oh, I know you're going to love him."

The door swung open as if on cue, and all eyes turned to see who'd joined us. The attendees clapped and cheered as if Ray were a celebrity. I waved him over and gestured to the stool.

"Find a position you can hold for two hours," I said. "We'll stop for stretch breaks, but I don't want you to be uncomfortable."

Ray's brow went up as if to say it was too late for that. Then he leaned into my personal space and said, "Are we still talking about the life drawing class?"

I didn't trust my voice and nodded.

Ray reached for the hem of his shirt and slowly dragged it over his head, baring a mountain of muscle, gorgeous skin, and stunning tattoos I wanted to trace with my tongue. Ray's nipples hardened in the cool air, and I remembered the noise he made when I'd touched them under the tree.

"I feel like I shouldn't be seeing this," Ms. Merriweather said from behind me.

"Hush up, Helen," Mrs. Howard replied. "I want to see more."

Ray raked his teeth over his bottom lip, and I wasn't sure if I wanted to swoon or giggle. "You shouldn't look at me like that when I can't do something about it."

Oh god.

"Stop hogging up your boyfriend, Kit," Mrs. Howard said. "It's our time with him."

Blinking myself back to reality, I hooked a thumb over my shoulder. "I'll just be going now. I'll see you after class." I took a few steps back, never tearing my gaze away from Ray.

"Better watch where you're going," Mrs. Cho called out. "You'll trip and hurt something vital."

The class snickered and pulled me out of my lusty fugue state. I turned and walked over to a side table where I'd set my notebook and pencil. "You guys can begin drawing as soon as Ray gives you a signal that he's ready." God, that sounded naughty.

"Good to go," Ray told the class.

I moseyed over to the front of the room to get the best vantage point, earning a raised brow from Ray. He tipped his head to the other side of the room, but I shook my head. There was no way in hell I was giving up my view.

"Take off your pants," Mr. Brown demanded.

I bit back a laugh and seized control before things got out of hand. "This isn't a strip club, and the model doesn't have to do anything that makes him uncomfortable."

"You just don't want us seeing the goods," Ms. Merriweather challenged. "Keeping him all to yourself."

"That ass would look amazing in underwear," Mrs. Howard added.

"Who says I wear any?" Ray teased.

That's when I lost my balance and bumped into the table, spilling a collection of art supplies onto the floor. "Christ," I muttered. "Nothing to see here. I've got this."

"Good thing," Mr. Brown said. "We're not cutting into *drawing* time with the model to help you clean."

A chorus of "lose your pants" broke out in the room as I bent over to pick up the art supplies rolling around on the floor. The rattle of a belt buckle caught my attention, and I raised my head. Unfortunately for me, I hadn't cleared the stupid table first. *BAM!* Everyone was too busy gaping at Ray as he worked his pants down his long, powerful thighs to notice I'd rung my bell good. Cartoon birds weren't circling my head, but it was damn close.

Ray paused his striptease to stare at me in concern, but I waved him off as I straightened. I wasn't dizzy or nauseated, so I probably hadn't given myself a concussion. Picking up my notebook and pencil, I mouthed, "Lose your pants."

Ray shot me a wink and let them drop. Oh. My. Fucking. God.

CHAPTER 14

RAYDEN

I'D LOST MY MIND. IT WAS THE ONLY PLAUSIBLE EXPLANATION FOR WHY I'd stripped down to my underwear and parked myself on a cold metal stool in the center of a room so that a group of people could draw me. I'd strategically placed my hand between my partially spread thighs and gripped the edge of the stool to hide my junk for a bit of modesty. Atticus, the sexy little minx, alternated between biting and licking his bottom lip while he sketched my almost nude form, and I couldn't stop thinking about where I wanted his tongue and teeth on my body.

"Even your bare feet are hot," Mr. Sanchez said.

The room collectively murmured their agreement as most of them drew my form. Some hadn't stopped staring almost thirty minutes into class, but Atticus didn't seem concerned about their participation, so why should I?

"That's some ass you have," remarked Ms. Merriweather, who hadn't so much as sketched the first line. She turned her head to look over her shoulder at Atticus. "What do you youngsters call a big ass like that these days, Kit?"

"Dump truck," Atticus replied without lifting his head. "You know, so you can back it on up."

I was going to back Atticus up against the nearest surface and do wicked things to him. "Thank you," I said to Ms. Merriweather, even if it was the oddest compliment I'd ever received.

"Your tattoos are amazing works of art," Mrs. Cho said. "Truly remarkable."

Atticus lifted his head and met my gaze long enough to mouth, "Told you," before returning his attention to the drawing.

I kept my head straight so as not to ruin anyone's efforts, but mostly, I couldn't take my eyes off Atticus. That pink tongue, the one I'd just had in my mouth hours ago, poked out of his full lips and spiked my body temperature even higher. I didn't need a powerful imagination to picture his tongue caressing my nipples like his fingers had at lunch. A slight shiver rippled through my body, and I forced my gaze away from Atticus before I made an absolute fool of myself in front of the class. I'd never live this down once the guys found out. Unfortunately, my gaze landed on a smirking older gentleman whose shrewd gaze and impish grin let me know he hadn't missed where my attention had been.

"I bet you served in the military," Mrs. Howard said from my left.

"Yes, ma'am."

"You look like an army man," Mr. Murphy said with a salute. "Special Forces, I bet."

"Yes, sir. I was an Army Ranger."

"A career in security and protection after serving in the military makes a lot of sense," Mr. Murphy said. "Though working here is probably a bit too tame for you."

My gaze returned to Atticus, who watched me with curious eyes. There was nothing tame or safe about my feelings for him. "I don't know about that, sir."

Mr. Murphy laughed. "Did you start your company immediately after the end of active service?"

The question caught me off guard. I didn't like talking about the intervening time between leaving the service and establishing RAVEN Securities. I hated to sound like Dickens, but it was both the best and worst time of my life. I must've waited too long to answer because Atticus spoke up.

"That's enough personal questions," he said. "Ray's done us a huge favor today, and we don't need to pry into his personal life."

"But you might learn something interesting about your sweetie," Ms. Merriweather said.

Atticus held my gaze and said, "I'll let him tell me at his own pace."

His patience meant the world to me and proved Atticus deserved my leap of faith. "I'll answer this one last question," I said. "I spent a few years working private security for embassies and high-risk targets before establishing RAVEN with my best friends."

Mr. Murphy nodded his approval and saluted me again. I risked the wrath of the class to return the gesture.

"Thank you for your service, dear," Mrs. Howard said before humming "God Bless America."

"My pleasure, ma'am."

Atticus slowly raked his teeth over his bottom lip, and I watched with rapt attention as the flesh plumped back up once it was free. His mouth looked darker from the abuse Atticus had put it through, and I wanted to kiss it better. Then I wanted to make his lips redder and puffier from my attention.

"Bet you're really packing some heat, aren't you?" Mrs. Hastings blurted.

"Hattie! Stop being vulgar," Mrs. Cho scolded before Atticus could.

The class laughed together for a few seconds before conversation lulled in favor of…art? I kept my body as still as I could, though it was harder than I imagined. I had several stretch breaks but was relieved when Atticus called an end to the class at exactly the two-hour mark. The group begged for more time, but Atticus wouldn't budge, no matter how persistent they got.

"And take your drawings with you," he reminded them before they left.

Mrs. Hastings looped her arm through Ms. Merriweather's on the way out and asked, "What do you call that kind of ass again?"

I couldn't hear Ms. Merriweather's answer, but I chuckled anyway. "I can't wait to see your sketch," I told Atticus once we were alone in the room.

He closed his notebook and clutched it tightly against his chest. "No chance." Atticus raked his gaze over my body and said, "You can get dressed now." The smoldering expression in his eyes said that was the last thing he wanted.

I stood up and stretched my arms over my head, giving Atticus a real eyeful. "I showed you mine, and now you've gotta show me yours."

Atticus's brow shot up. "Are we still talking about artwork?"

I stalked forward, stepping past my pile of clothes. "Maybe."

Atticus swallowed hard and gripped his notebook tighter, making me even more determined to see it. "I can't draw for shit. My sketch is barely more than a stick figure."

"Uh-huh." I strode forward, took him by the hand, and led him into the art supply closet. I tested the handle, noting it was a little stiff but still functioning. I shut the door and backed Atticus up against the nearest shelf, not stopping until my body pressed against his. I liked the fact that I was all but naked while Atticus was fully dressed. "That was some serious concentration you showed for only drawing a stick figure."

"Some parts of you are enormous and needed extra attention."

My dick knew when it was getting stroked—figuratively and literally. Atticus was doing a bang-up job with the first, and I really wanted to turn him loose on the second. I didn't hold back my reaction to him; I let Atticus feel how hard he made me with a glance and a few casual words. I leaned in and brushed my nose against his temple, his cheek, and pressed my mouth to his ear. "Show me."

"Oh god," Atticus whimpered.

I pinched his chin and tilted his head back so I could kiss his trembling lips. Atticus parted for me and met my tongue with unrivaled eagerness and intention. He melted against me, his limbs turning into noodles, and his notebook would've hit the floor if not for my quick reflexes. I snatched it out of the air and tightly clutched my prize.

Atticus broke the kiss with an affronted gasp. "Did you kiss me just to get your hands on my notebook?"

"No, I just needed to taste those lips again after staring at them for two hours." I stepped back and held the notebook in the air like a trophy. "This is just a bonus." I flipped open the cover and fanned the pages until I found what I was looking for, then stared momentarily stunned at the drawing on the page. "This is…"

"Ugh." Atticus sidestepped me and walked to the center of the closet. "It's terrible."

"No, it's incredible," I told him.

Atticus hadn't gone with the traditional style of sketching; he'd chosen to do… I didn't know for sure. It was like a cartoon, reminding me of the satirical style I'd seen in newspapers. Those subject matters were usually politicians and world leaders, not a massive dick with a ladder leaned against it so a cartoon version of Atticus could climb the rungs to reach its head.

"I'm blushing a little because you've been very generous with my dick size, but damn, this guy on the ladder has your cute nose and pouty, perfect lips. I want to kiss the freckles on his nose." I turned and walked to the real Atticus and kissed his freckles instead. "Do you really want to climb my dick? And what would you do with it once you reached the top?"

Atticus raised his head and stared into my eyes. His pink tongue darted out and swiped over his lower lip before he sank his teeth into it. After a moment, Atticus released the tender flesh and said, "I think you know."

I shook my head. "You'll need to spell it out for me." I cocked my head to the side. "Or you could draw it."

"I want to suck you dry," Atticus said.

I nodded. "Yeah. I want that too." More than I'd ever wanted anything.

Atticus stepped back and gestured to the door. "Not here. Get dressed while I clean up. Then we can leave. My house is close, and my parents are out of town."

I cupped his neck with my free hand and kissed him hard enough to make Atticus sway when I released him. "Take me home with you."

Atticus moved easels and drawing supplies into the storage closet while I got dressed. The art room was otherwise tidy, so I handed his notebook back to him, and we left. The urge to reach for his hand was strong, but we weren't in high school. We'd acted inappropriately in the workplace enough for one day, and I didn't want to push the limits too hard.

"I just need to grab my stuff from my office," I told him.

"Same. I'll meet you in the parking lot. You can follow me."

"My nerves can't take you riding that scooter right now," I said. "The roads will be slick from oil rising to the surface after the downpour this afternoon. I'll stow your scooter in my SUV, and you can ride with me."

Atticus looked like he was going to argue, but he didn't. "Just give me five minutes."

I'd be lucky to last that long after three years of celibacy. A fresh wave of nerves settled in, making me second-guess my sanity. If I didn't get a grip, anxiety would cripple any chance I had of living out the promise Atticus made to suck me dry. A surge of lust spiked my blood, driving away my apprehension. This was right, Atticus and me, and I was done questioning it.

Atticus was already outside and waiting for me by the SUV. I pressed the fob to unlock the doors and open the hatch, then set my gear in the back seat before heading to the rear of the vehicle.

I took the scooter handlebars from Atticus before he tried lifting the machine on his own. "I'll get this."

"I can help."

"Of course you can, but save your strength for the climb." I paused and looked over at him. "Unless you've changed your mind."

Atticus snorted, slapped my shoulder, and then headed to the passenger side of the vehicle. "Heave Blanche into the SUV, and let's go."

The scooter probably weighed close to two hundred pounds, but I easily stowed it away. I had one hell of an incentive, after all. I got behind the wheel and started the engine. "Where to?"

Atticus guided me through the Kirkwood neighborhood with its lovely mixture of architectural styles. The lawns were large, green, and well maintained. It was easy to imagine a younger version of the man beside me, riding his bike down the sidewalks and likely finding a lot of mischief along the way. I didn't let my thoughts linger there since I wanted to get the adult version of Atticus naked and under me as fast as humanly possible.

"It's the second house on the left after you pass the intersection. There," he said, pointing to a lovely Tudor-style home that didn't match the ranch house next to it.

I turned into the driveway, which widened slightly once you drove past the house. A two-car, detached garage with a small carport sat behind the home, and a large expanse of lawn stretched beyond it. "This is a lovely place to grow up."

"Hmm," Atticus said. "It was, but I really hate that I've had to move back." He looked over at me and smiled. "Hmmm. I never got the chance to sneak a boy into my room in high school." Atticus waggled his eyebrows suggestively. "Are you into LARPing?"

"I don't know what that is?"

"Live action role playing," Atticus said with a grin.

I looked at the home's exterior, noting the narrow width of the second-story windows. "I'm not sure I'll fit in such a tight space."

"You're such a dirty talker." Atticus took off his seat belt and leaned over to kiss me hard on the mouth. "We'll use the door like normal people."

I cupped the back of his neck to hold him in place. "My intense need to fuck you feels anything but normal."

Atticus inhaled shakily. "I think I just came in my pants."

"Guess we better get them off so we can start all over again," I teased. "Did you have a car sex fantasy you wanted to test?"

"No. You?"

"Not really." I pressed one last kiss to his lips and released him. "Let's take this inside."

"I have nosy neighbors," Atticus said. "And this isn't the kind of show I want to give them."

I locked the SUV and followed Atticus to the back door, which he unlocked and opened in record time. We stepped inside a gorgeous kitchen that someone had lovingly designed and maintained, yet I couldn't care less. "Bedroom now," I demanded.

Atticus took me by the hand, and we ran through the living room and up the steps with an undeniable eagerness that made us both laugh. We stopped at the top of the staircase and kissed our way down the hall and through a bedroom door I closed and locked. I took a cursory glance around the space, noticing a variety of posters with men on them, a cluttered dresser, and a messy bed. I didn't care about any of that, only the hazel-eyed hottie staring up at me.

I tried to steer Atticus toward the bed, but he dropped to his knees before I could make the next move. He buried his face in my crotch, his hot breath breaching two layers of fabric and revving me up even higher. I tugged my shirt off with shaking hands and tossed it to the floor. Sliding my fingers into his hair, I tilted his head back to stare into his gorgeous eyes.

"You're going to push me over the edge too fast," I warned.

My confession only made his eyes sparkle and his hands braver. Atticus reached for my belt and unbuckled it without breaking eye contact. The button slipped free silently, but the rasp of the zipper sounded loud and sexy in the stillness of the room. Atticus made his intentions clear when he licked his lips. I palmed the back of his head tighter but didn't guide his mouth where I wanted it most. He was in the driver's seat, and I needed him to know it.

With nostrils flaring, Atticus leaned forward and pressed his nose against my boxer briefs, inhaling deeply. My fingers tangled in his hair and pressed against his scalp. I breathed through the urge to rut against his face to get the friction I needed for relief. Atticus kissed my rigid length through the cotton before hooking his fingers in my waistband and tugging my underwear down enough to free my fat cockhead. He tongued me there, and my knees threatened to give out. Atticus's chuckle vibrated my shaft and—

Oh. My. God.

Atticus sucked the tip of my cock into his mouth, and all the air seized in my lungs. I couldn't hold back my groan of pleasure, and why the hell would I? Christ. Atticus jerked my pants and underwear down to my thighs and worked his mouth lower on my dick. The intoxicating wet heat engulfed me as he took my cock deeper, until I bumped up against the back of his throat. Atticus made a soft gagging noise, followed by a sexy groan and a sloppy slurp that was almost my undoing before he eased up.

I carded my fingers through his sexy brown waves, wishing I could fist them in my hands and fuck that glorious mouth, but I wouldn't hurt him. Atticus needed to set the pace, and I needed to respect it. Down he went, licking the underside of my shaft on the descent and swirling his tongue around the head on the ascent. My balls tightened, and my thighs vibrated with restraint. Atticus reached between my legs and palmed me, rolling my balls in his hand.

"Fuck," I moaned. "Won't last if you keep that up."

He chuckled, the little shit, and the vibration, combined with his slurping suction, nearly made me shoot my load right then.

"Atticus," I warned.

Hazel-brown eyes locked on mine as he squeezed my balls a little tighter, and it shredded my self-control. I nudged my hips toward his face, urging him to give me the friction I needed to blow. Atticus brushed his fingers over my taint as he lowered his mouth as far as he could take me. The head of my dick slid into his throat, and he swallowed.

"Atticus, god, please…"

He took that as his sign to do it again. Hollowing his cheeks, Atticus sucked harder and slurped louder, applying the perfect amount of pressure against my taint. His finger slid back further, inching toward my pucker, and I lost it, snapping my hips forward and fucking his mouth.

"Pull back. I'm going to—"

But Atticus stayed with me while I rutted against his tongue and spilled down his throat. Then he wrapped his arms around my thighs to hold me in place as he took his time licking my shaft clean.

I released my grip on his hair and gently caressed his face. "That was. That was…"

Atticus let my dick slide slowly from his mouth and smiled wickedly at me. "Yeah?"

"So fucking good."

His lips, shiny and wet from the combo of saliva and spunk, curved into a blissful smile. There was nothing I wanted more than to taste myself on his tongue.

CHAPTER 15

ATTICUS

NO MAN HAD EVER LOOKED AT ME THE WAY RAY HAD AFTER I MADE him come. His eyes zeroed in on my mouth, so I licked my lips again, capturing his salty essence that remained there. The memory of Ray's surrender as he gripped my head and spilled down my throat elicited a needy whimper.

"Do I taste good?"

No one had ever talked dirty to me like Ray had, and I liked it. No, I fucking loved it. He made me feel powerful, as if all my heart's desires could be mine if I were just brave enough to demand them. Scooting to the center of the bed, I stretched out into a semi-reclined position and braced my elbows against the mattress. "Come down here and find out."

An orgasm had barely softened the intensity in Ray's gaze, and he kept his sexy blue eyes locked on mine as he bent to remove his boots. They hit the floor, one solid thud at a time, sending shivers of excitement pulsing through my body. His socks came off next, and he straightened to his full height. I'd seen Ray's glorious inked chest less than an hour ago, but the beauty of it made me swallow hard. I wished I'd taken the time to rub my face against his happy trail when I gave him head, but maybe I'd get a do-over if I played my cards right. One taste of Ray just wasn't enough.

"Take the rest of your clothes off. I want all of you."

Hooking his thumbs into his waistband, Ray shoved his jeans and underwear down his powerful legs, kicking them to the side to stand proudly in front of me. If I had a body like that, I'd never wear clothes. Even spent, Ray's dick hung large and proud. The beast had just been in my mouth, and yet it still mesmerized me. I wanted to feel him stretching my lips and rubbing against my tongue again.

"You're fantastic for my ego," Ray said.

I snapped my head up and met his hungry gaze. "All I can think about is having you back in my mouth."

Ray wrapped his rugged fingers around my ankle. "Later." Hope soared in my chest with that one word. Ray slipped off my tennis shoe and peeled off my sock. He blinked down at my pastel pink toenails before meeting my gaze. "Cute color."

"Emma wanted to test out some new pedicure products at the salon and volunteered me to be her test dummy." Ray pressed his thumbs into the arch of my foot, and I nearly blew my load right there. My head fell back, and I closed my eyes. "Fuck. Oh fuck. I want to tell you to stop, but I'm scared you'll listen."

Chuckling, Ray moved his thumbs up and pressed again. "How were the products?"

"The what now?" Did he really expect me to carry on a conversation when he was lighting up my insides like a pinball machine?

He shifted his hands lower to just above my heel, and the pleasure was so good I would've done anything Ray wanted. Rob a bank? No question. Scale a mountain? Well, there was only one thing I ached to climb, but I'd have to wait for him to recover.

Ray smirked as if my inability to carry a conversation was cute. "How were the pedicure products you tested?"

"Oh. Good." He hit an erogenous spot, and I moaned like the neediest slut to ever slut. "So fucking good."

He pressed a kiss to my instep before lowering my foot to the bed. I whimpered in protest until Ray's magic hands lifted my other foot.

"Yay!"

Ray met my enthusiasm with a dirty grin as he removed my other shoe and sock. "Do you think I could make you come just from rubbing your feet?"

I wiggled my toes at him since he thought they were cute. "Before today, I would've said no way, but I'm not so sure now."

"Maybe we'll put the question to the test later."

"Mmm. Later. My new favorite word." I flexed my foot in his hand to get his attention.

Strong thumbs pressed right where I needed them, finding the spot that made my cock twitch and my back arch.

"Fuck, I could eat you alive," Ray said. "Starting with your luscious lips."

"You'll get no complaints from me."

Ray massaged my foot for a few more minutes before turning his attention to undressing me. He leaned over the bed and made quick work of my shorts and underwear. My dick slapped against my stomach, smearing precum on my skin. I sat up to take off my shirt, but Ray dropped my pants to the floor and removed it instead. His nostrils flared as he raked his gaze over the length of my body, and he groaned when he spotted my titanium navel piercing.

Meeting my gaze, Ray said, "You decided to wear it."

"I felt inspired after our conversation the other day." I reached down and stroked the cool metal. "I love the way it makes me feel."

"And I love the way it looks."

"You said something about ravaging my mouth," I said, pointing to my lips.

Ray put a knee on the mattress, then crawled his way up my body to straddle my hips. Taking my face in both hands, he lowered his mouth to mine, pressing a few soft kisses to my lips before he licked his way inside, moaning like he'd never tasted anything half as good. One of Ray's hands slid to cup the back of my head, while the other lowered to my neck. My pulse hammered beneath his thumb, revealing how much his kiss affected me.

Ray's hold was commanding but tender, and I never wanted him to let me go. I couldn't get enough, and my slutty little whimpers let Ray know it. When he angled his head and deepened the kiss with a growl, I knew he felt the same way too. My arms shook with the effort it took to keep me upright, and he must've felt my body trembling beneath his.

Ray caressed a path from my neck to the center of my chest, where he pushed with just enough force to get his point across. He followed me down to the mattress, sucking my tongue while pressing his chest against mine, and pinning my throbbing dick between our bodies. Washboard abs would give me the sexiest friction on Earth if I just had enough room to thrust my hips to rut against them. Ray was huge, easily outweighing me by seventy-five pounds of thick muscle, but I wasn't afraid.

The heat of him was everywhere, yet still not enough. I raked my nails over his back and reveled in the thick muscles flexing under his skin. Tangling my fingers in his hair, I held on to Ray as if my very life depended on it. My existence wouldn't physically end if Ray changed his mind, but I'd still die a thousand deaths. The tempo of his kiss slowed, becoming more tender, until he lifted his head to stare down at me.

"Christ, I could kiss you for hours," Ray said.

"Okay."

With a nod toward my dick, Ray said, "I don't think he'd be okay with it…unless…"

My cock twitched as if to say, "Pick me! Pick me!" I brushed my thumb over Ray's swollen lips. "I'll take your mouth anywhere on my body."

Ray raised an eyebrow and pitched his voice low. "Anywhere?"

It seemed like he'd taken my words as a challenge and upped the ante. God, this man made me feel sexy and wild. I got high on the desire smoldering in his gorgeous eyes. Notching my chin higher, I said, "And everywhere." Because nothing would be off-limits to him.

A low growl rumbled in his chest, and Ray lowered his mouth to my neck. "How I resisted you this long is a mystery." The words vibrated against my skin, seeped into my soul, and curled my toes. "We could've been doing this for months if I'd been braver."

A verbal seduction was something I would've scoffed at before I met Ray, but he made me a believer. "You'd be sick of me already if that were the case."

Ray's mouth moved lower, and he nipped the tender skin where my neck curved into my shoulder. My full-body shiver made him chuckle. Those skillful lips kissed a trail across my collarbone before rocking my universe with the words that tumbled through them. "You wouldn't say that if you knew all the ways I've imagined having you." Ray paused at my sternum to breathe me in before kissing me there too. "Fucking my fist and wishing it was your sweet ass." His warm breath ghosted over my nipple, and I whimpered for him to continue. But I also wanted to look into his eyes when he confessed such filthy things.

"Ray—"

He cut off my protest with a single swipe of his tongue over my nipple.

I fisted my hand in his hair and arched my back, wanting his mouth right back where it had been. But Ray lifted his head and pinned me with his hot blue gaze. "That's exactly how you sounded all the times I made you come."

"Oh god," I whimpered.

"Yeah, you said that a lot too."

Ray inhaled deeply, his nostrils flaring with unnecessary restraint. He could ravage me now and savor me later. I was about to tell him so when he lowered his head and sucked my nipple between his lips. The tug sent bolts of electricity straight to my balls, and I wriggled beneath him. Ray swirled his tongue around the hardened bud, nipped it lightly, then blew on it. I bucked my hips, seeking the friction I needed to get off.

"And fuck if the reality of you isn't so much better than fiction." Ray kissed a trail lower, stopping to nip and lick along the way until my entire body trembled. My dick was so close to his mouth, the wet heat that could put me out of my misery. Ray kissed my navel, then lightly tugged on my piercing with his teeth before licking my precum off my belly. "Which is why I can't decide how I want to make you come this first time." Ray kissed my hip, trailed his nose over my pelvis, and nuzzled his face in the trimmed curls at the base of my cock.

"W-what are m-my options?" I stammered.

Ray inhaled deeply again, as if he couldn't get enough of my scent. "There was the time I got you off just by pegging your prostate while sucking your balls." He rubbed his goatee against my nutsack, and I nearly shot off like a rocket.

"N-not a terrible start."

Chuckling, Ray kissed my taint. "Then there was the time I tongue-fucked you while jerking you off."

"O-oh."

"Ever been rimmed?" Ray asked as he brushed his thumb over my puckered entrance.

"No."

"Noted." Ray brushed his beard over my inner thigh. "I've sucked you off in several fantasies."

"Did I like it?"

Ray flattened his tongue at the base of my cock and licked a path upward, circling the head to capture the proof of my excitement. "Tastes like you do."

"Show me. Make me come."

"Soon," he promised before sucking my dick down to the base. I wasn't nearly as long or thick, but Ray moaned around my length as if it was the best he'd ever had in his mouth. That was more than enough for me. He worked me up and down a few times before he pulled off me. "Lube and condoms?"

"Huh?"

"I want to fuck you." Ray stood from the bed, and his dick was hard again and ready to go. "Lube and condoms?"

Incapable of speech, I pointed at the nightstand on the right side of the bed. There was only one drawer, so he wouldn't need additional instruction. Ray opened it and smiled down at the contents before lifting a vibrating butt plug. "Maybe the fucking can wait."

I shook my head vehemently. "I need you to fuck me."

Ray's grin turned wicked. "Pretty sure you said that in more than one of my fantasies." The way he calmly spoke about jerking off while thinking about me was such a turn-on, and I wanted to return the favor.

"I used that at least once a day while thinking of you."

His brow went up. "Just once a day? Amateur."

"I have a lockbox full of toys that have gotten a workout in your honor," I replied.

"Show me."

I would've been mortified if not for the heat in his eyes. I sat up and scooted off the bed to stand beside him. Then I dropped to my knees, putting me too close to that glorious cock to ignore, so I sucked it into my mouth. The vibrating butt plug landed back in the drawer with a *thud*, and Ray's fist was in my hair once again. This time, he gently eased my mouth off him.

"The next time I come, it will be in your ass," he said. "Show me your fuck toys."

I dragged the box from under the bed and turned the lock tumblers with trembling fingers until I got the right combination. I hesitated before opening it and looked up at him. "Don't judge me."

He cupped my face and stroked my cheek. "I would never."

Opening the lid, I gestured at my assortment of toys like a game show host.

Ray didn't look right away; he held my gaze and continued lazily stroking my cheek with his thumb. He finally broke eye contact to check out my assortment of dildos, vibrators, and butt plugs. There was a pair of vibrating nipple clips that were still in the package and a variety of lubricants. I knew the minute he spotted Fat Bastard because he inhaled a deep breath, making his chest rise. "Feeling intimidated now."

I closed the box and slid it back under the bed. "Don't be," I said as I stood up. "It's got nothing on you." I grabbed his hand and tugged him toward the bed. "Consider it prep for the fucking you're about to give me."

Nostrils flaring, Ray grabbed the lube and a strip of condoms before following me down to the mattress.

"Looks like you plan to live out several fantasies," I said when Ray stretched out beside me. "And you're too far away."

Closing the distance, Ray cupped the back of my head and kissed me passionately. Never had I ever felt so damn desired and cherished. I moaned into his mouth and hooked a leg over his hip, bringing our erections into contact. The slick glide of two leaking heads was so much better than one, and I couldn't resist rutting against him. Ray rolled me onto my back and positioned himself between my thighs, pinning our erections between our stomachs.

I broke our kiss to breathe. "Dare you to move."

"No fucking way. I told you I want to be inside you when I come." Ray pressed one last kiss to my lips before he sat back on his haunches and reached for the lube. After opening the cap, he drizzled a generous amount onto two fingers and rubbed them against his thumb.

I lifted my legs to my chest, thighs spread widely, to give him access to what we both wanted more than our next breaths. "I don't need a lot of prep."

Ray leaned forward, pressed a kiss to my calf, and said, "Yes, you do. We both do. You need to stretch, and I need to get myself under control so I don't come too fast and embarrass myself."

"I—" A blunt, slick finger pressing against my puckered rim made me forget what I was about to say.

"You'll just lie there and enjoy it." Ray spread the cool liquid around and around, stirring every nerve ending to life. "Feel good?"

My toes curled hard enough to snap off. "It's okay."

Laughter rumbled in that broad, sexy chest. "I'll try harder." Ray pressed a finger against my opening and inserted just the tip, slowly working it in and out and circling the quivering ring of muscles.

I wrapped a hand around my dick and said, "Speaking of hard..."

Ray stilled his finger and pinned me with a dark glare. "Hands off your dick. This is my fantasy I'm living out, so I'm going to make you come without you touching yourself." I obeyed him, letting my hand fall back to the bed.

"Is that right?" I asked.

Ray reached for my right foot and propped my ankle on his shoulder, then did the same with the left. I'd never felt so exposed, so vulnerable, or so alive. "Yes." Ray slid his thick digit deeper inside me and pressed against my prostate. I gasped and rocked into him, seeking more, but he eased back, leaving just his fingertip inside me. I whimpered in protest, and he pushed back in, deeper and a little harder. "Look at the way your cock jerks and leaks for me."

I couldn't see it with my eyes rolled back in my head, but I eventually recovered from sensory overload and saw the trail of precum dripping onto my belly. "Self-lubing in case you need me to tag in," I teased.

"You won't." Ray pulled all the way out but returned with two digits before I could complain. "Too much?"

"God no. Give me more."

Ray kept his gaze locked on mine, working those two fingers in and out of me and teasing my prostate. I undulated my hips and fucked his fingers until he settled a hand on my pelvis to hold me still. His fingers landed in my precum, and he licked it clean. "Next time you come, it will be in my mouth," Ray said.

"Oh god." The visual alone was enough to take me to the brink of orgasm.

"Almost there," Ray said. "You need me to work you open with another finger, or are you—"

"Give me your monster cock."

"You're so good for my ego," Ray said as he eased his fingers from my ass. He tore open a condom packet and rolled it on with quick efficiency. Then he reached for the lube and slicked his dick with short, jerky strokes. "Fuck, that's almost enough to make me blow."

Tucking my hands under my head, I spread my thighs wide. "Better get to it, then."

Ray growled sexily as he lined up his dick to my entrance. "Tell me if this gets to be too much."

"I'll let ya know. Now, fuck—"

Ray pushed the fat head of his cock inside me, stealing my breath, my words, and my sanity.

"Oh my god," I moaned when I could speak again.

"Too fast?" Ray asked, his whole body tensing.

I shook my head. "More. Please."

Leaning forward, Ray braced his hands on either side of my head and captured my mouth in a deep kiss. Then he pushed his dick inside me until it bottomed out, and fuck me, nothing had ever felt so good. "Okay?"

I nodded, incapable of speech again. Cupping the back of Ray's neck, I pulled him down, wanting as much of his body touching mine as possible, but he stopped before his chest was flush against mine. I pouted in protest, and he kissed me.

"No friction," he reminded me, then adjusted his angle to nudge my prostate, turning my nervous system into a Vegas slot machine.

"Fuck me!" I yelled, more in surprise than demand, but it got me the result I wanted most.

"Happily." Ray pulled back and nailed my gland again and again, reducing me to incoherent moaning as my pleasure built and my channel tightened around him. "You're so close."

"Kiss me," I begged.

Ray dominated my mouth just as hungrily as he fucked my ass, and it's what tipped me over the edge. My entire body tightened with tension, like a rubber band stretched too thin. His body was both the source of the tempest whirling inside me and the only thing that could silence the madness.

"I've got you," he growled. "Come for me."

"Oh god! Oh—" The tension snapped, and pleasure flooded my body. My cock jerked and painted my stomach with milky stripes of cum. "Oh fuck. Don't stop."

"Never." Ray hitched my legs up and pounded into me, driving me into a higher frenzy as my pleasure hit another peak, then another. Once I stopped spurting, Ray finally gave me his full weight. "So tight. I don't want to stop, but I don't want to hurt you."

"Use me." I wrapped both arms around Ray's back, holding him tightly against me as he fucked me mercilessly. Ray buried his head in my shoulder, and I kissed his temple. "Fill me up." And he would, if not for the condom.

With a low snarl, Ray thrust hard one last time and cried out.

"That's it. Give me everything."

He pumped in and out of me a few more times, breathing hard against my skin while I held on to him as hard as I could. Ray went boneless and smashed me into the mattress. The heft surprised me at first, but I took shallow breaths to prove I wasn't suffocating.

"Should get off you. Heavy." Ray's words were sluggish and not very convincing.

I hooked both legs around him just in case. "Stay."

He lifted his head to look at me, and it seemed like the effort had cost him a lot. "On top of you or stick around for a while?"

"Yes."

Ray smiled at me and cupped my face. "Told you I'd make you come without touching your dick."

"I didn't put up much of a fight," I told him. "Maybe next time."

Ray stiffened, and I wondered if I'd pushed for too much. He'd been the one who'd used words like "later," and "next time," but it had been during the heat of passion. I wanted to take the words back, but—

"Okay, but I need to get cleaned up, and we should probably think about food."

"I can't cook worth a damn, but I excel at ordering food through an app that magically appears on the doorstep."

"Sounds perfect."

"My bathroom is downstairs, but so are all the takeout menus. Why don't we go down and get cleaned up. You can shower while I order food."

"Why can't we shower together?" Ray asked.

I told my heart to settle down and not read too much into it. "Tight fit."

Ray rocked his hips, and his softening dick rasped over my sensitive nerve endings. "I'm a big fan of tight spaces." He pressed a kiss to my lips, then eased out of my ass. Ray rolled onto his back beside me and looked up at the ceiling. His fingers found mine, and we laced them together. "After we eat—"

"We live out one of my fantasies," I said.

Ray shook his head. "I called dibs already. I want to suck you off."

I rolled onto my side, pressed a kiss to his chest, and then sat up. "You're in luck. That was the same fantasy I wanted to live out next."

"I won't be long," Ray said as we parted ways outside the kitchen. The man had the most beautiful bare ass I had ever seen.

"Towels are in the hallway closet," I called after him. "I'll fish out the menus from the junk drawer. Is there anything you're not in the mood for?"

"I only want to avoid food that will prevent me from tapping your tight little ass again."

"Good to know," I said, my words calm even though my heart was doing a happy dance.

Don't read too much into it. Take what he can give and nothing more. But damn it. Rayden Freaking James wanted me. Again. Now I was the one bopping in the kitchen as I sorted the menus into two different categories: "yes before anal sex" and "hell no before anal sex."

The bathroom was just on the other side of the eat-in kitchen nook, so I knew the moment Ray turned on the shower. I probably lost about five minutes picturing what he looked like under the running water. Rivulets would stream down every dip and valley of his sculpted muscles. Oh god. I should've gone with him, even if it was to sit on the toilet and watch. I shook myself out of my daydream and focused on the task: feed Ray so he could tap my ass again later, possibly after sucking me off. *Focus, dumbass.*

"Mexican, Thai, and Indian could be too spicy," I said. Those started my "hell no before anal sex" pile. "Italian could be iffy, but—"

A car door shut nearby, cutting through my debate. It could've come from the neighbor's house, but it sounded way too close. It wouldn't be my parents. They'd headed out of town and would've let me know if their plans had changed. Then again, when was the last time I'd checked my text messages or missed calls? Another door shut, this one louder. It had definitely come from just outside the house.

My mom's raised voice carried from the driveway. "I can't believe our luck."

My dad mumbled something in response I couldn't hear.

What the fuck? I stood in my boxers and nothing else. I'd only given my stomach a cursory wipe with a dirty T-shirt to remove my cum. The streaks probably could've passed for dried Elmer's glue, but no one with two brain cells to rub together would mistake my cum for glue smears. My parents continued to talk as they approached the house, and then a new sound came from down the hallway. I cocked my head to the side as I tried to make out what it was, then smiled when I realized Ray was whistling in the shower. I'd made him happy enough to whistle while he washed. *Aww.*

The utility room door flew open, and I had just enough time to angle my body so my parents wouldn't see the dried cum smears on my stomach. My mom entered the kitchen, looking bedraggled. Damp, wrinkled clothes plastered against her body. Mascara smeared under her eyes and streaked down her cheeks, and her frizzy hair stuck up all over as if she'd been electrocuted.

"Mom! What the hell happened?" I asked.

Dad stepped into the room behind Mom, looking just as bad, minus the mascara smears. He raised an eyebrow at my state of undress but didn't say anything. He looked like he barely had enough energy to stand.

"What happened?" I asked again. "I thought you were going to Tess's?"

"We were," Dad said. "I thought it would be a great idea to take a new route. Change of scenery is supposed to be good for the soul, they say." Dad slumped even more, like that little outburst had been all the energy he'd had left. Then he rallied to add, "They're full of bullshit."

Mom patted his shoulder and sighed. "We broke down in a rural part of the state, couldn't get cell service, and had to walk a million miles to the nearest little town. It's hotter than hell out there, and I'm afraid to look in the mirror."

"Must've been Mayberry or a ghost town because everything had already closed," Dad said.

"On a Friday night," Mom added. "Can you believe it?"

"Wow, that's wild. How'd you get home?"

"A delightful couple about our age passed through and offered help," Dad said. "They drove us to the next city so we could hire a tow truck and rent a car to come home. What a night."

The water turned off down the hall with a slight squeak, grabbing my parents' attention. They both flicked their gazes to the kitchen nook wall, as if they could see through to the bathroom. Dad's gaze slid back to me, and a slight smile tugged at his lips.

Mom looked at me and blinked. "Is someone here? I saw that SUV outside and thought you'd come to your senses and bought reliable transportation."

"Uh…"

Mom narrowed her eyes, making her look like a psychotic killer. "That had better not be Chad in our home."

Dad's smile turned into a scowl. "You deserve so much better, Kit."

"Not Chad," I assured them and nearly laughed when they sighed in relief. "Never again with that guy. I promise."

Mom turned to look at Dad over her shoulder. "You should've let me take a baseball bat to his car like I wanted to."

"Well, you told me I couldn't set his car on fire, so we're even," Dad told her.

Their support both warmed my heart and worried me, but I would need to have that conversation later. It was possible for them to walk through the living room and get upstairs before Ray exited the bathroom. I could whisk him up to my room, where we could get dressed and escape without my parents bombarding him with a thousand questions.

Mom crossed her arms over her chest. "Who is it, then?"

I looked to the doorway and sighed when there was no sign of Ray, but my relief was short-lived because he hadn't brought clothes down with him. Oh god, oh god, oh god. My parents were about to get a real eyeful. "Can we please talk about this later? Can you go upstairs so I can—"

Footsteps approached, and we all turned in time to watch Ray reach the kitchen archway and jerk to a stop. Thank god he'd wrapped a towel around his waist, but the closure looked precariously loose.

Mom sucked in a breath, and I turned to see if she was okay. Dad had covered her eyes with his hands while his own bugged out of his head. "Get off me, Steven. I want to introduce myself to Kit's friend."

"I bet you do," Dad said. "I think there might be a better time or situation to get to know him better." He nudged Mom forward, still covering her eyes. "We'll just go on upstairs so the two of you can…"

Ray sidestepped to clear a path for my parents.

"I'm Valerie, and this brute is Steven," Mom said as they passed.

"Rayden James. Nice to meet you both."

"The pleasure is, um, yeah," Dad replied awkwardly. "It's good to meet you too."

"That's a very sexy name," Mom purred.

Ray rubbed the back of his neck. "Thank you."

"Keep it moving, Val," Dad urged.

And once they cleared the doorway, Mom held up two thumbs for me to see. Ray had his back to them and didn't notice it or the wink Dad shot me over his shoulder. Probably for the best since the situation was weird enough. I expected Ray to make a mad dash for his clothes as soon as the coast was clear so he could bail. But he just grinned at me and said, "So, my place, yeah?"

CHAPTER 16

Rayden

Atticus blinked a few times in surprise, and I understood because I was right there with him. But I'd imagined Atticus in nearly every inch of my personal space, and I wanted to live that reality with him. I didn't just want it; I needed it. Holding my breath while waiting for him to answer, I watched a myriad of emotions flash in his expressive eyes. Surprise made way for hope, which quickly faded into a heartbreaking uncertainty that triggered every protective instinct I possessed.

Crossing the distance between us, I pulled Atticus into my arms and kissed him. His lips trembled beneath mine, then parted with an invitation I happily accepted. Yes, his parents were in the house, and the towel barely clung to my waist, but I didn't care. Atticus clearly needed assurances from me, and that was more important than my modesty. I kissed him until there was no room for any doubt about what I'd asked or what I wanted. But just in case, I pulled back and held his gaze. "Please come home with me."

When Atticus finally spoke, his voice was soft with tenuous hope. "My parents' unexpected arrival didn't kill the mood?"

"Not even close."

Atticus rose on his tiptoes to get at my mouth again, and the motion loosened the knot on the towel. My quick reflexes kicked in, and our sanity returned. I retightened the towel and regretfully stepped back from him.

"We should get dressed and go." Atticus sidestepped around me, grabbed my hand, and tugged me out of the kitchen. "My dad won't be able to hold my mother back for long."

"Judging by their appearances, they've lived through something tonight."

"My bad luck is rubbing off on them." Atticus paused at the base of the steps and looked over his shoulder at me. "Sure you don't want to get out while you still can?"

Wrapping my arm around his waist, I pulled Atticus back against my chest. "This has been the luckiest day I've had in a very long time."

"How long?"

"Three years." Sadness washed over me, but it was more of a trickle than the tsunami that had flooded my soul for so long. Javier had been a wonderful person who'd died tragically and much too young. I'd loved and mourned him with everything I had, but spending time with Atticus helped me admit to myself that I needed more from life. I rubbed my nose through his hair and kissed his head. "There's a lot of living I want to do with you, so you better pack a bag."

It took longer to get dressed than I'd expected, but that's what happened when you couldn't keep your hands and mouth off someone long enough to do the most menial tasks. Atticus threw random items in a bag in between stealing my kisses, and we headed back out to my SUV. But we had to unload his scooter beneath the carport and move vehicles around before we could leave.

"So embarrassing," Atticus groaned when his dad all but skipped out to the driveway to move his car.

"Seems like your parents are supportive and cool."

"Yeah," Atticus sighed. "Until you realize at least one of them might know more about gay sex than you do."

"What?"

Atticus proceeded to tell me about the audiobook incident on his way to our hookup.

"So, I was extra horny by the time I parked Mom's car," he said.

I reached over and squeezed his thigh. "I'm truly sorry I disappointed you."

Atticus laced his fingers through mine. "Don't be. I like how things turned out."

Neither of us said much for the rest of the drive, until I pulled into the warehouse parking lot.

"Did you need to pick something up from the office?" Atticus asked.

I'd never explained my living situation to him, and there was no way to avoid it now. I could probably get by with simply telling him we all lived above our offices with little fuss, but getting by wasn't good enough. That had been my existence for too long. If I admitted to wanting more out of life, then I needed to put more into it, especially when it came to exploring my growing feelings for Atticus. Starting with the truth was the easiest option, so that's what I chose.

Parking my SUV in its usual spot, I left the engine running to keep the interior cool. I unbuckled my seat belt and angled my body toward Atticus to see every expression that crossed his face. "The guys and I live above our security office. Vaughn's family has owned several warehouses in Columbus for hundreds of years, and they sold this one to us at a bargain. We each have our own loft apartments on the third floor," I rushed to say.

Atticus tilted his head to the side and raised an eyebrow. "Okay," he drew out slowly, sounding uncertain of where the conversation was heading.

"We have a communal space on the second floor where we get together to hang out, eat, and watch television."

Atticus said nothing at first, just continued to watch me with curious eyes. When the silence stretched on a beat too long, he removed his seat belt and angled toward me too. "You don't have to tell me anything that makes you uncomfortable. Who the hell am I to judge? I live with my parents again after blowing up my life. At least you have a place to call your own." Atticus leaned forward and kissed me softly. "And I'm glad you share it with people who are so important to you. I think your friendships are beautiful."

"Our bond runs much deeper than a typical friendship." Realizing how that sounded, I rushed to add, "It's not romantic or sexual. We've never—"

Atticus raised his hand. "Again, not my business." He placed his palm over my heart and added, "But I want you to be my business though. I really, really care about what you do from now on."

I chuckled to relieve the pressure in my chest. "It's important that I explain some things, and I probably should've already done this...before we...you know." Why had I suddenly found it hard to talk about sex?

"Shared amazing orgasms?" Atticus suggested.

"'Life-altering' is a better adjective," I said. "I want you to understand why I fought my attraction to you so hard and why some things are going to be challenging if you're willing to take a chance on me."

"Nothing you can say is a deal-breaker," Atticus told me. "But I'm just curious what kinds of things you mean."

"I just want to keep you safe." My throat dried as if suddenly pitched into the desert without water. I cleared my throat a few times and generated enough saliva to speak without sounding like a chain-smoker. "I *need* to keep you safe. I worry that my motivation will come across as overbearing or controlling. I never want to do those things. I just need you to be careful."

Atticus searched my eyes for a long time, then nodded. "Okay. I'll double down on my efforts to replace Blanche."

The sigh I sighed was so ridiculous and dramatic that it made us both laugh. My relief didn't last long because Atticus's expression turned sad again.

"I saw the title of the book you read about overcoming survivor's guilt," he said. "Considering your military career, I'm sure you've witnessed some truly heinous things. Your need to keep me safe is understandable." Atticus smiled softly and added, "And a little sexy."

My traumatic heartbreak hadn't started with my military service, but we could peel the bandages off that twenty-three-year-old wound another time. The most pressing issues needed to come first. Atticus was cool with my tight connection with the guys, but I needed him to understand the depth of the bond before I got in too deep with him.

"I met Vaughn, Archer, Ethan, and Nico at the Army Ranger School at Fort Benning. We became immediate friends. Some call us platonic soulmates, but I don't know about all that. I'm sure you overheard me talking about our transition to the private security company after we left the army."

"I did."

"Well, that was my idea," I said. "The pay and benefits were much higher, and we were supposed to be stateside more frequently. The guys came with me without hesitation, and we met some incredible people who became very significant in our lives. There was a group of ten to twelve of us who worked together on foreign details for dignitaries and ambassadors overseas. Some jobs were like taking walks in the park, and others..."

Atticus squeezed my hand, and I looked down at our tangled fingers, remembering the charred, twisted-metal fate Javi had suffered. Alarm bells clanged, and my heart pounded, reminding me of what was at risk if I ever fell in love again. I raised my gaze, and soulful hazel eyes promised me that the fear was worth it. "Did you lose many people on your team?"

I nodded. "During an ambush in Budapest, when insurgents attacked the ambassador's envoy while en route to the airport. We were heading home for a long break before our next stint. We all had exciting plans we were looking forward to one minute…and bam."

Atticus flinched and swallowed hard. "How many of you didn't make it home?"

"Too many," I replied. "The five of us were the only survivors on the security detail. We saved the ambassador's life, but all her support staff died." I shook my head. "I don't know how any of us survived. The attack was extremely organized, merciless, and came with no warning from the State Department. Everything happened so fast…" My mind tried to replay the horrible images, but I visualized a bright red stop sign instead.

"Did this attack happen three years ago?" Atticus asked.

My mouth became as dry as the Sahara Desert. Other than a few mental health specialists, I'd never discussed the attacks with anyone outside the group of men who'd survived it. "Yes. We lived through something most people wouldn't understand, not that they didn't try. It's just the kind of fire you must walk through to comprehend it. The same friendship bond that originally united us is what saved our lives overseas, so we relied on the connection to rebuild our lives and heal. And we are stronger for our bond, even if we're deeply scarred." I took a deep breath. "And scared, in my case."

Atticus cupped my face so I couldn't look away from him. "You lost someone very important in the attack, didn't you? Someone you loved romantically?"

My broken inhale was the only answer he needed. The next thing I knew, Atticus climbed over the console to straddle my lap. His ass hit the horn, so I scooted my seat back as far as it would go to prevent everyone from rushing out of the building to see what was going on.

"Tell me about him."

"His name was Javier, but we called him Javi. We'd been dating for a little over a year, and I had planned to propose when we got back home. I had the ring and his mama's blessing. It's terrifying how quickly your life can get turned upside down. One minute, you're on top of the world, and the next, you're burying the person you wanted to spend your life with."

"I'm so sorry," Atticus whispered as unshed tears shimmered in his eyes.

He hadn't known Javi, but he would grieve for him alongside me if that's what I wanted. But I needed so much more than existing in the shadows of sadness and despair, and I craved the light Atticus offered me. I held him in my arms as tightly as I could, soaking up his affection like a greedy sponge. Then I cupped his face and kissed him. Atticus was hesitant at first, his lips stiff for a few seconds before he yielded. He swirled his tongue around mine, sucking it into his mouth and reminding me of all the wicked things I wanted to do with him. *Honk!* But we needed to get the hell out of the SUV first.

Atticus jolted back and covered his mouth in mortification. "We don't have to do anything you feel is too much or too soon." We both knew we were heading into deeper waters, and he was throwing me a life raft I didn't want or need.

"I want to see you in my space. It's all I've thought about since that first day at Silver Maple."

"Seriously?"

"You've left your mark here," I said, tapping my temple with two fingers. Then I lowered my hand to cover my heart. "And I want you imprinted here too."

Atticus swallowed hard and inhaled shakily. "Oh, wow."

"You breathed new life into me." I nodded toward the building and added, "And the guys know it too, so they're going to be eager to know more about you."

"Me?"

"Yes, you. And there are security cameras all over the warehouse, so they'll know we're here."

"Cameras?"

"Not in the living spaces," I replied. "Just the business offices, the corridors, entrances, the elevator, and the stairwell."

"Oh my."

"Yeah. It's a lot, but safety and security are our business." I scanned the row of cars parked near the building and sighed. "And damn, everyone is home already. The guys are going to invade our sanctuary at some point." I ran my thumb over his cheek. "There's still so much I want to do to you tonight."

Atticus pressed his lips to mine in a quick kiss. "Then why the hell are we wasting time in the parking lot?"

I glared at every camera we encountered as I escorted Atticus through the building. I didn't know if the guys were watching our progression, but if so, my look promised hell's fire if they dared interrupt us. My antics might've bought us an hour because that's how long it would take for Archer and Nico to wear Vaughn down. Ethan would stay neutral until Vaughn caved, and then he'd be just as eager to make trouble as the other two. We made it to my apartment without interruption, and an internal clock started ticking in my head as soon as I shut the door and locked it. We deposited our gear on the kitchen island, and Atticus wandered deeper into my loft while I debated how to ravish Atticus first.

I owed him a blowjob and had a sudden image of sucking him off in my shower.

"Wow!" Atticus said.

For a second, I thought I'd mentioned the shower blowjob out loud, but it seemed Atticus only had eyes for my apartment. He stood in the center of the living room, slowly turning in a circle to take it all in. I tried to see the loft through his eyes and let my gaze wander around the space. The floor plan was wide open, with furniture groups dividing up the living areas instead of walls. High ceilings and exposed ductwork gave the space an industrial vibe that I'd softened with warm hardwood flooring and light-colored furniture. The few walls that existed were the original rough brick that we'd sandblasted clean. I accented the kitchen wall with blue-gray cabinetry and butcher-block countertops that matched the island. The accent wall in the living room had floating black shelves to hold my books, a few collectibles, and framed pictures.

Atticus slowly looked up, his gaze climbing the iron staircase to the open mezzanine where my bedroom and bathroom were located, the latter being the only room closed off from view from the rest of the loft. But once inside the bathroom, the exterior wall was all dark-tinted glass that let light in while maintaining my privacy. I pictured dropping to my knees in the shower to eat Atticus's ass while he pressed his palms to the glass wall for support. I'd wait until his legs threatened to give out, and then I'd turn Atticus around and suck him off.

"This view is something special."

Atticus stood at the floor-to-ceiling wall of windows overlooking the Chattahoochee River. The glass was tinted for ultimate privacy, just like the bathroom, but it gave the illusion of being exposed to anyone who drifted down the river. God, he looked so damn good in my space.

"I'll say." I crossed the room and wrapped my arms around him from behind. Atticus smelled like sex and me.

"This place is stunning." Atticus turned to look at me. "Did you design it?"

I shrugged. "I got input from Vaughn and his sister. They took my vision and gave it a glow-up."

Atticus gripped my shirt and tugged me down. "I think you're being modest."

"I think I owe you a blowjob."

Whimpering softly, Atticus leaned his forehead against my chest. "How private are we?"

"Very private unless we go out onto the balcony." I dropped my hand and cupped his growing erection through his athletic shorts. "I could suck you off right here, and no one would know. But by the time I'm through with you, you won't care who's watching."

A hard shudder rocked his body. "Okay. But maybe I should get cleaned up first."

"Too many steps." I shoved his shorts and underwear to his thighs and took his cock in hand. "I want you now. Here."

I lifted his T-shirt off and tossed it aside, then dropped to my knees in front of him. Seeing the evidence of the orgasm I gave Atticus earlier drove me mad. I rubbed my nose against his stomach and pressed kisses to the sensitive skin while Atticus carded his fingers through my hair. I wanted to take my time and tease him until he was painfully aroused, but I was still mindful of that ticking clock in my head. Gripping firm ass cheeks in both hands, I licked and sucked the head of Atticus's dick, savoring the burst of his excitement.

Atticus moaned and said, "I shouldn't be this hard after the orgasm you gave me, or on the verge of coming so fast."

My skills were rusty after years of celibacy, but giving head was something I'd always loved. I took my time learning his taste and adjusting to his size, taking him deeper with every pass. When his cock nudged against my throat, I relaxed and breathed through my nose, then took him deeper.

Atticus tightened his fingers in my hair and tensed his entire body. I stayed right there, his cock buried in my throat, and pressed my nose into his trimmed hair. "Oh my god," Atticus moaned. The muscles in his ass flexed with his restraint, and I didn't want him to hold back. I wanted him to fuck my face and needed his balls to slap against my chin as he chased his orgasm. I swallowed around his cock, and Atticus released an animalistic growl. He eased back and thrust forward. "You want this?"

I swallowed again in response, begging him with my eyes.

Atticus fisted both hands in my hair and gave me what I wanted, pulling out and snapping his hips forward, using my mouth to get off. His cadence was short and choppy at first, but then he settled into long strokes. Atticus watched his dick glide in and out of my mouth, lust twisting his handsome face into a savage mask of need.

I swallowed around his cockhead every time it reached my throat and hummed when his eyes rolled back. Atticus was lost in passion, not caring about the boats going up and down the river. I wanted to fuck him right up against the window until his spunk painted the glass. Atticus went up on his toes, changing the angle and fucking deeper and faster until his balls slapped against my chin.

"Gonna come. Do you want me to pull out?"

I gripped his ass harder, holding him in place. Atticus pumped twice more and shot his load down my throat, riding out his orgasm on my greedy tongue. His legs turned to jelly, and he collapsed back against the window once he eased from my mouth. Getting him off helped me reach an aroused state I would have to ignore until after dinner. I wanted a sex marathon, not a sprint. Pressing a kiss to his pelvis, I rose to my feet and pulled his shorts back up to his waist.

"Appetizer," I said before kissing him deeply.

Atticus looped both arms around my neck and melted against my chest. God, he was so warm and sexy. If I had my way, we wouldn't see another soul until at least Monday morning. Then, as if I'd conjured them out of thin air, a loud knock landed on my door. Atticus lifted his head from my chest and stared at me with wide eyes. Another knock followed, this one even louder than the first. I needed to think fast because Atticus smelled like sex and wore an orgasm face.

"Go away," I yelled.

The third knock sounded more like a battering ram. "We know the code," Archer said.

"Um, this is intense," Atticus said, blinking owlishly.

I chuckled and stroked his jawline. "You're not in any danger...from them." I aimed for a smoldering look, and it must've worked because Atticus relaxed his head against my chest.

Bang! Bang! Bang!

"We won't hesitate to let ourselves in," Nico added.

Bang! Bang! Bang!

"You can't hog him all to yourself," Ethan said.

"Come on, Hawk," Vaughn cajoled. "I want to meet your man."

Atticus snapped his head up at that. "Your man?"

I couldn't tell if the idea thrilled or terrified him, so I kissed him deeply, passionately, and without concern for the nuisances loitering outside my apartment.

"My man," I agreed.

Bang! Bang! Bang!

Atticus pulled back with a huge smile. "They're not going away, so we might as well get this over with. I'll go upstairs and get cleaned up while you get the door. Hopefully, they won't stay long."

I nearly whimpered at the intrusion into our night, but Atticus was right. It was best to get the meet and greet over with so we could get on with our night. I swatted his ass and kissed him fiercely. "The bathroom is attached to my bedroom. Far-right door. Enjoy the view."

"More windows?" Atticus asked.

I waggled my eyebrows in response. "So many dirty things I'm going to do to you in there."

"Yeah? Like what?"

Bang! Bang! Bang!

"That's it!" Archer yelled. "We're coming in!"

Atticus pecked a kiss against my cheek and ran for the stairs. I waited until he was inside the bathroom before I crossed to the door and opened it.

"I hate each and every one of you right now."

CHAPTER 17

ATTICUS

I didn't realize my mistake until I stood naked in the shower, the hot water pounding against my skin with the same intensity as my heart thrashing against its cage. I really wanted to focus on the incredible view outside the window and the amazing water pressure, but that's when I remembered I'd left my backpack downstairs. I'd dropped the clothes I'd been wearing on Ray's bedroom floor, so there was no way for me to exit the bathroom without showing my ass, literally, to the people I desperately wanted to impress. I could do the towel-around-the-waist thing that Ray had done in front of my parents, but he hadn't done it intentionally. I lacked both the confidence and the grace to pull off such a bold move on purpose. Fuck!

And why was I so nervous about spending time with Ray's best friends? I'd already met three out of the four. Not formally, and we'd only exchanged casual greetings when our paths crossed, but I'd seen nothing on those occasions to warrant such panic. Maybe it was the idea of meeting Vaughn. There was something in his voice that stood out more than the others, a warm persuasion that reached Ray when the others hadn't. I had this irrationally strong pressure to make a good impression on him. That meant I'd need to step up my game, and I'd have to do it on wobbly, just-sexed-within-an-inch-of-my-life legs.

Get it together, man.

Instead, I sat in the center of the shower floor. *Real mature.* But what else was there to do when the world spun around me? Everything had shifted between Ray and me so dizzyingly fast, taking us from strangers to friends to…boyfriends? *Whoa! Reel it in, pal.* I was getting ahead of myself while everyone waited for me.

Hell, those super soldiers could probably smell my fear from downstairs. No, fear wasn't the right word. I wasn't afraid of them or even my growing feelings for Ray, though I should've been terrified of how badly I wanted *this*—whatever it was—to work out between us. I needed to be chill and let them get to know me. No biggie. Except I'd never been chill a day in my life.

The door opened, and Ray stepped into the bathroom with my backpack in his hand. He wore a bemused smile until he saw me sitting on the shower floor. Ray's brow furrowed, and the light left his eyes. "Did I hurt you?"

I scrambled to my feet, eager to ease his worry. "God no." Taking a deep breath, I said, "I'm just freaking out a little. I want your friends to like me." I cringed as soon as the words left my mouth. "God, that sounded so whiny and desperate."

Ray dropped my backpack on the closed toilet lid and came to the shower door. His intense expression made me think he was coming in fully dressed, but he stopped. "You don't sound whiny, and you don't have anything to worry about with the guys. They already like you."

"They don't really know me," I told him.

"But they know me, and I really like you." Ray's voice was low and velvety, and I nearly slid to the shower floor for a different reason.

Bracing my hand on the glass wall, I stared into his gorgeous blue eyes. "I really like you too."

"The sooner you come downstairs, the faster we order pizza and get rid of them."

"Pizza?" I asked.

Ray groaned and rolled his eyes. "I couldn't reason with them to leave, though I tried like hell. They agreed to limit their visit if we ordered pizzas." He raked his gaze over me, slowly and thoroughly. Every cell in my body felt caressed during his perusal. "Because there are things I want to do to you."

That got me moving like nothing else could. I reached for his bodywash and squirted a generous amount into my palms, rubbing them together to get a good lather. Ray's nostrils flared, and a menacing little devil stirred inside me. Keeping my eyes locked on his, I made a sensual production of washing my arms and chest, slowing my motions as I reached my stomach and soaped my cock and balls.

Ray growled and reached for the door handle but stopped himself before opening it. "Turn around and show me your ass."

Arousal stirred in my belly as I obeyed him, though nothing else was ready to rise to the occasion. Spreading my legs, I slid soapy hands over my ass and fingered the crease between my cheeks. My fingertip brushed over my sensitive pucker, and I couldn't hold back a moan. The door opened behind me, and cool air washed over my skin as feverish hands gripped my hips and yanked me back against a hard body. Ray's hands roamed over my chest, then down over my belly and into my pubic hair to circle around the base of my cock. He stroked me once before sliding his hands up to tease my nipples. Then Ray gripped my chin and turned my head so that his mouth was against my ear.

"I like that you're using my soap, but soon, every part of you will smell like me for a different reason."

"Yes," I whimpered.

"I'm giving them an hour max before I throw them out the door or shove them through a window." Ray nipped my earlobe. "I need you."

I didn't know what to do with the things this man made me feel. How was it possible someone like Ray could want me so badly? I couldn't wrap my overheated mind around it, so I didn't try. Giving in to my instincts, I met his dirty talk with some of my own. I turned in Ray's embrace and looped my arms around his neck. If he didn't care that his shirt was getting soaked, then neither did I.

"Maybe you can just push them off the balcony since you promised to fuck me up against the windows."

"The balcony seems too tame. Besides, there are tons of windows to choose from." Ray slid both hands down to grip my cheeks, pulling them apart and pushing them together in an erotic massage that drove me wild. And then he said, "Kinda wish I grabbed the butt plug I saw in your toy box. Imagine you squirming with arousal every time the tip nudged against your prostate over the next hour. Mmmmm."

Ray captured my mouth in a hot, wet kiss before I could respond beyond a needy moan. He swallowed the sound and continued massaging my ass until a burst of laughter from downstairs caught his attention. Reluctantly breaking the kiss, he dropped his hands from my body with a heavy sigh. "Better get down there."

"I guess." The pout in my voice made him grin.

"What do you like on your pizza?" Ray asked.

"I'm not picky."

Ray's brow shot up. "You'd eat anchovies?"

"It's not my favorite thing," I admitted. "And I don't have food allergies." Thank goodness, or I'd surely eat the one thing I shouldn't and ruin our night with a major medical event.

"Good to know." Ray kissed me hard and swatted my ass once more before stepping back and shutting the shower door.

"Might want to change your shirt and pants," I said. Could we be more obvious?

Ray winked as he backed out of the bathroom. "They already know what's taking me so damn long." He shut the door, leaving me alone to finish my shower.

Suddenly, the idea of eating pizza and getting to know Ray's friends didn't seem so scary.

All eyes swung in my direction as I approached the steps, and the confidence I'd found in the shower fizzled a bit. I inhaled a good, deep breath and tried to recall a scene from a movie where a glamorous woman or a debonair man descended a staircase. An image of Kate Winslet sprang to mind, and I channeled her gracefulness as I took the first step, and then the next. I was halfway down when I realized the scene had come from *Titanic*, and my stomach sank faster than that ship had.

My next step was a little shaky, and I nearly missed the one after that. Ray's eyes widened in alarm, and he moved toward the bottom of the staircase as if prepared to break my fall. That sweet gesture calmed my nerves and steadied my legs so that I reached him unscathed. Strong hands landed on my hips, and Ray greeted me with a devastating smile.

"Hi," I said breathlessly.

"Hi." Ray kissed me once, twice, and likely would've taken more if not for the giddy laughter coming from the oversized sofa. Releasing my lips with a soft growl, Ray whispered, "I might kill them."

"With kindness?" I teased.

Ray tilted his head to the wall of glass. "If I launch one of them through the window, the other three should scatter on their own."

"But which one would you choose?" I whispered.

"Won't be me," Archer called out. "I'm bottom-heavy."

"That's one way to describe that juicy ass," Nico told him. "And I'm afraid of heights, so I'm not going out the window."

Ethan smiled and shook his head. "Won't be me. I'm Ray's favorite."

"It's true," Ray said.

Vaughn shook his head and stood up. "No one is going out the window. Too much of a mess when there's a perfectly good balcony to hurl Archer over."

"Hey!" Archer protested.

Vaughn crossed the room, extending his hand to me when he reached us. His big palm engulfed mine when we shook, but he kept the pressure friendly. "I'm Vaughn."

"Kit," I replied. Only Ray called me Atticus, and I liked it that way. "Nice to meet you."

"Likewise."

"He's the daddy," Archer said. "Sugar and otherwise."

Vaughn shook his head firmly. "Nope."

"He's our fearless leader," Ethan amended with an easy smile.

"Reckon that means y'all better close your mouths and behave, then," Vaughn told them. "This is an important night."

The guys grumbled for a few seconds before promising to be on their best behavior.

Moving toward the kitchen, Vaughn said, "What's everyone want to drink?"

Ethan wanted a root beer, Archer wanted an IPA I'd never heard of, and Nico just asked for water.

"Sprite Zero," Ray said.

Vaughn looked at me over the top of the refrigerator door. "How about you, Kit?"

"What are my options?" I asked.

"A little bit of everything."

A refrigerator's contents said a lot about a person, and it sounded as if Ray kept his stocked like a convenience store to take good care of his friends. It made me even more curious about the man I was falling for, so I kissed Ray's cheek before crossing the room to peer inside the appliance. I grabbed a Cheer Wine and a few of the other requested drinks and stepped back so Vaughn could get the rest. But he wrapped a brawny arm around my shoulders and kissed my temple.

"We've been waiting a long time for you, Kit," Vaughn said. "Thank you for giving Ray back to us."

I was too stunned to speak, so I just stared up at him.

"Vaughn is trying to steal your man, Hawk," Archer teased.

I pulled free of the innocent embrace and spun around to face the rest of the guys.

Ray snorted and followed it with a playful smack on Archer's leg. "Behave." He patted the empty cushion next to him, and I made a beeline for it, stopping to pass out the root beer to Ethan and Sprite Zero to Ray.

"Me?" Archer asked. "I'm not the one putting hands and lips on Kit. Is that allowed? Do we all get turns?"

Ray held up a hand, his thumb and forefinger an inch apart. "You're this close to going out the window."

"Over the balcony," Vaughn corrected as he passed out the remaining drinks.

I curled up next to Ray and rested my head against his chest. His heavy arm wrapped around my shoulder, holding me close.

"You'll change your mind when you try the new ice cream recipe I made today." Archer leaned into Ray's personal space and whispered, "Nutella with fudge swirl."

"Wow," I said. "Do you all cook?"

Ethan snorted, and Nico shook his head.

"Vaughn and I do most of the heavy lifting when it comes to cooking, but Archer is getting damn good at making ice cream." Ray turned to his friend. "Okay, maybe you can hang out here a little longer."

They ended up staying for a few hours, entertaining me with shared stories that required both verbal and physical reenactments as we killed three pizzas and at least a gallon of that insane Nutella ice cream. I couldn't remember a time when I'd laughed so hard or eaten so much, and I didn't know which made my stomach hurt more. When the sun went down, Ray escorted them to the door, saying out loud what everyone already knew.

"I want to be alone with Atticus now."

My face heated from anticipation instead of embarrassment. Ray had held me close, stroking my arm or rubbing my leg all night, to keep me aware of his presence beside me. I waited until the last man was through the door before I pulled my shirt off and tossed it onto the floor. By the time Ray turned the dead bolt, I'd already shucked my pants and underwear and stood completely nude in the dimly lit space. I turned to face the wall of windows, watching the lit boats drift by on the river.

Ray's footfalls grew louder as he approached from the kitchen, and I caught his reflection in the window. His body and face were tense with desire as he raked his gaze over me. Ray stopped directly behind me, his body so close I could feel the heat rising from it. He snaked an arm around my waist and settled a hand low on my belly. Ray dipped his free hand between our bodies and cupped my ass with the other.

"I don't store supplies down here, and I don't want to pause to go get them," Ray rasped into my ear. "I am going to drop to my knees and open you with my tongue. Then I'm going to take you upstairs so you can ride my dick. Does that sound good to you?"

"Yes," I whimpered and pushed my ass against his palm.

Ray took my earlobe between his teeth and tugged, sending a spark of pleasure straight to my balls. "How do you feel about reverse cowboy?"

I reached behind me and cupped Ray's thick erection. "Big fan."

"Makes two of us."

Ray pressed a kiss to my ear and patted my ass. Then he released me long enough to circle his fingers around my wrists and place my hands on the window. "For support."

"Good thinking."

Ray dropped to his knees, still fully dressed, and the reflection of me standing naked before him was so damn sexy. Gripping my cheeks in both hands, Ray pulled them apart and moaned as if there was nothing he wanted more than to eat my ass. I thought I'd be prepared for the sensation of a hot, wet tongue against my pucker, but I'd been so damn wrong.

"Oh! Oh my god!"

Ray's laugh vibrated against my sensitive flesh as he circled the rim again and again, slowly and sensually, his hot breath stimulating me to new heights.

When he sucked on my pucker, I nearly lost my legs. Leaning forward, I braced my forearms on the cool glass, and Ray came with me, burying his face deeper between my cheeks and wiggling the tip of his tongue into the tight ring of muscles. Ray growled and worked deeper inside me, licking, sucking, and tongue-fucking me until I became a whimpering mass of bone, muscle, and flesh. I arched into the pleasure, pushing my ass in his face for more.

"Please," I said when I couldn't take the shallow penetration another minute.

My begging made him chuckle, but Ray withdrew his tongue and slapped my ass as he stood up behind me. The erection straining against his jeans looked painful, and I really, really wanted to make him feel better. I reached for his belt, but he stopped me with a gentle hand on my wrist. "I've thought of nothing else but getting you alone for the past few hours, and hearing your needy little moans while I tongue-fucked you has me primed and ready to go off."

"Just one little kiss?" I asked.

Ray answered by hoisting me over his shoulder like a fireman. "No."

I couldn't resist fondling his magnificent ass as he took the steps two at a time. Ray carefully set me on the ground and immediately tackled his clothes.

"Top drawer," he growled when he was down to his boxers. "Condoms and lube."

I felt his eyes on me, so I bent over farther than necessary to remove the protection and lube from the drawer.

"You're so wet from my tongue. I want to make you even wetter with my cum."

Spinning toward him, I said, "I get tested regularly and take PrEP. You can come inside me."

Ray was on me, cupping my face and kissing me deeply. "Same. I get tested and take the meds, even though it's been three years since..." He kissed me again, slower and so tender it made my heart ache. When Ray pulled back, he just stared into my eyes. "I want that intimacy with you, no more barriers, but only if you're sure."

I understood he hadn't only meant the thin layer of latex; Ray had meant the walls he'd built to keep his heart safe. I was ready to tear his defenses down, one brick at a time if needed, but it meant so much more to me that Ray had voluntarily let me in. I didn't trust myself to speak without crying, so I tossed the condoms back in the drawer and slammed it shut.

Ray hooked his thumb in his boxer briefs and shoved them down his legs. His erection slapped against his abdomen, thick and ready to fuck me. He stretched out on the bed and crooked a finger for me to follow. I straddled his thighs, facing away from him, and braced my hands above his knees while he stretched and prepped my ass with lube. Once his thick fingers disappeared from my channel, I looked over my shoulder and watched Ray slick himself, his mouth slack and eyes half-closed.

"Better save some of that for me."

Meeting my gaze, Ray gripped my hip with one hand and lined his dick up to my entrance with the other. "Nice and slow," he cautioned, guiding me onto his thick head.

My breath snagged in my throat as Ray groaned. The burn and pressure were a lot at this angle, but I loved the way I stretched around his dick. Judging by the sexy little snarls, Ray enjoyed the view as much as I loved the penetration. His fingers tightened on my hip, and he lowered me further.

"So sexy taking me in. Damn, your ass is so hot and greedy."

"Give me more," I demanded. "Please."

Ray snapped his hips up, burying his cock to the hilt inside me. I cried out, digging my fingers into his legs as my ass settled onto his pelvis. "You okay?" he asked.

"So good." I undulated my hips, rocking myself on his shaft. "Ready for more."

Ray's hands disappeared from my body, and I whimpered from the loss. "You wanted to climb this cock, now show me what you wanted to do with it."

I set an easy pace at first because I'd never felt so stretched and full. The pressure could've turned to pain in an instant, and I didn't want anything to spoil the delirious pleasure building inside me. Up and down, long and slow, I rode that magnificent cock.

"I won't last," Ray warned. "Get yourself off."

"Going to pump me full?" I sat fully on his cock, arched my back, and rode him with shallow thrusts, knowing it wouldn't give him all the friction he craved.

"Oh Christ. Fuck yes," Ray growled as he gripped my hips and lifted me up and down his shaft. "Jerk yourself off."

I spat in my palm and stroked my dick as Ray controlled the pace of our fucking. My head fell back, and my balls tightened as pleasure peaked to the point of pain. Ray pulled me down as he bucked up once more, driving himself to the hilt and holding me still as he jetted his release inside me. Feeling him flood my channel was enough to trigger my release. I put my hand on the mattress between his thighs and chased my orgasm, giving him a view as I rode his wet, dripping cock. I eased off him, squeezed my pucker, and felt some of his spunk drip down my balls.

"Fuck," Ray growled. He snatched my waist and pulled me down on top of him, then rolled us onto our sides to spoon behind me. "I know we need to clean up, but I want to hold you for a minute."

"Mmmm," I said dreamily. "I could stay like this forever."

Ray pressed a kiss to the back of my neck. "Careful what you offer me because I might just take you up on it."

Nestling deeper into his embrace, I smiled. "Not afraid."

CHAPTER 18

RAYDEN

Rolling onto my stomach, I tucked my arms under the pillow and burrowed my face into the cool cotton. I'd just had the best night of sleep in probably my entire adult life, and I wasn't ready to surrender to daylight's invasion. And maybe I was afraid that everything I'd shared with Atticus the previous night had been nothing more than a delicious dream.

Intrusive thoughts were an enemy I refused to battle before coffee, so I squeezed my eyes tighter and inhaled deeply. Atticus's scent was everywhere, stirring a growl in my chest and a different rumbling below the belly button. I snaked an arm out from under the pillow and reached for him but only found cool, empty sheets where a warm body should be. My brain registered alarm a half second before it detected freshly brewed coffee.

Lifting my head off the pillow, I scanned the loft as apprehension hummed under my skin. The noise quieted as soon as I found Atticus curled up in a club chair with a throw blanket around his shoulders. He lifted a mug to his lips, blew softly, then sipped his coffee while looking out the windows. It was early, maybe around six in the morning, so the sun hadn't risen yet, but there was already plenty of activity on the river. The lights on the smaller vessels looked like fireflies hovering over the black water.

The sky was just beginning to lighten at the horizon, a mere hint of promise or pain, the outcome yet to be determined. I'd fallen into the latter camp for so long, viewing each new day as nothing more than a tragic reminder of all I'd lost. Now, the silvery ribbon of light represented persistence and pushing against the darkness to let the light in. It would grow bigger and brighter, unwilling to be denied or ignored, like the feelings I'd developed for the beautiful man in my loft.

I rolled onto my side so I could observe Atticus as he watched the world come alive. He pulled the throw blanket tighter around his shoulders as if he were chilly and lifted the coffee cup to his mouth again. Then Atticus set the mug on the end table and swiped a hand under his eye. It was too dark to tell if he was crying, but the slight sniffle gave him away. Panic momentarily paralyzed me as I wondered what had happened.

Did I have a nightmare and scare him? They were rare these days, but maybe my intense emotions for Atticus triggered one. But I didn't feel the lingering disorientation I typically experienced after a nightmare. Atticus wiped his face again, breaking me from my frozen state. I whipped back the covers and leaped from bed, moving before thinking and taking the stairs buck-ass naked.

Atticus looked in my direction when I was about halfway to the first floor. His eyes widened in surprise, but then his mouth curved into the most beautiful smile I'd ever seen. "Hey," he whispered. "Did I wake you?"

I dropped to my knees on the rug before Atticus, cupping his face. "What's wrong?" I husked.

"Nothing is wrong." Atticus turned his head to kiss my palm before opening the throw blanket in invitation.

I slid both hands under his ass and lifted him in the air so I could sit down with him on my lap. The leather chair was cold, and I shivered before Atticus's blanket-wrapped body could warm me. "Something is wrong if you're crying. Did I have a nightmare or upset you?" I brushed back the hair from his face and worried that he'd gotten scared or felt trapped without transportation. Any of the guys would've taken him home with no questions asked, but Atticus wouldn't have known that. Then a different concern hit me. "Was I too rough last night?"

Atticus wriggled so he could see my face. "God no. These are tears of joy." He laughed as more tears sprang to his eyes. "I can't seem to turn them off." Swallowing hard, he said, "I woke up feeling happy and hopeful for the first time in so damn long. Maybe the happiest and most hopeful I've ever been in my life. And it hurts." Atticus rubbed his sternum as if that would ease his discomfort. "And that's not all I felt." Atticus waggled his eyebrows and said, "I also woke up horny. You were sleeping so soundly, and I didn't want to wake you up, so I came downstairs and woke you anyway. Was it the coffee? I tried to be quiet when I made it."

I ran a thumb over the lips I was dying to kiss again. "I woke up when I realized you weren't in bed."

"Sorry. Guess I can never leave it again."

"Works for me," I said. "But rewind a minute. Tell me about these happy tears." I lifted my hand and brushed a fresh cascade off his cheeks. "Something about happy and hopeful."

Atticus wriggled on my lap, pressing his sweet ass against my hardening length. "Don't forget horny."

I recognized a diversion tactic when I saw one and couldn't let it slide. "I haven't forgotten that, and we will circle back to it." Kissing Atticus's temple, I said, "Tell me what hurts."

"This hope," Atticus replied with a chuckle. "You've given me something so beautiful and miraculous, and I'm afraid of messing up. I'm scared to believe in myself." He twisted on my lap to face me better. "I love the way you look at me. You make me feel important and valued, and I want to look at myself with the same level of affection." Atticus took a deep breath and swallowed hard. "I need to get my shit together and prove something to myself. That's what I've been thinking about as I watched the boats go by." Atticus pressed a quick kiss on my lips. "You've set a new standard for me and raised the bar." He dropped his gaze lower and wriggled his eyebrows again. "You upped it high, and it's scary. And then I feel foolish because you're so brave."

I tightened my arms around Atticus, and he rested his head against my shoulder. The blanket fell away from his neck on one side, and I caressed the delicate skin there, smiling when he shivered and nestled closer. I wrapped him up again and rubbed his back through the blanket. Atticus had made himself completely vulnerable to me, emotionally and physically, and I wanted to do the same. "I've spent a lifetime being afraid of something. I just learned to mask the fear at an early age."

Atticus raised his head and looked at me. "How young?"

"Thirteen," I replied. "That's when my mom died, and I went into the foster care system."

"Oh no." Atticus somehow maneuvered his body to straddle my thighs without getting tangled in the blanket. Cupping my face in both hands, he said, "I'm so sorry. What happened?"

"Single mothers take the jobs that pay the bills and put food on the table," I told him. "My mom worked at a factory in Florida where improper ventilation systems exposed the employees to deadly chemicals. She, uh, developed what she thought was a terrible cold, but it kept getting worse. We both knew her condition was severe when she started coughing up blood, but neither of us expected her to die within a few months from an aggressive form of lung cancer."

Atticus gasped so softly that I barely heard it. He nestled as close to me as he could get. "I'm so sorry," he whispered. "God, that's so unfair."

"Yeah," I said. "It's the kind of devastation that changes you forever. I went into foster care, which isn't easy for a thirteen-year-old kid who was already wrestling with surging hormones and confusion about his sexual identity. Throw in devastating grief and depression, and it could've been so much worse than it was. But I ended up in a group home run by an ex-marine who ran the place like it was boot camp."

Atticus stiffened in my embrace, so I ran a hand over his back and kissed the top of his head to soothe him.

"It was what I needed," I told him. "And Sarge was a strict man, but he wasn't without kindness. He gave me outlets to burn off my steam by teaching me how to lift weights and box."

"Sounds like a recipe for disaster," Atticus said. "He could've turned your grief and confusion into aggression."

I considered his point for a few seconds. "It would've been a big risk without proper guidance," I replied. "Sarge—"

Atticus sat up and looked at me. "He made you call him that?"

I chuckled and shook my head. "His name is Henry, but the kids called him Sarge. It was the most passive-aggressive thing he permitted from us." Brushing my fingertips over his cheeks, I said, "He also taught us about service to others, especially our community through volunteering."

"You mean he volunteered you?" Atticus asked with a wry smile.

"Of course. No teenager offers to get out of bed early on weekends to mow grass at local parks or shovel dog shit from kennels at animal shelters."

"Yeah, you've got a point there." Atticus curled up against my chest again and tucked his head under my chin. "Did you enjoy it?"

"Enjoyment is a stretch," I said. "But I felt a sense of pride from a job well done. I liked it when Sarge praised us for our work. I wanted to make him happy with me."

Atticus jerked back up and looked at me with an ornery expression. "Was he hot, this Sarge?"

I laughed, picturing the grizzled older man with a gray buzz cut, steely blue eyes, and leathery skin from too much time in the sun without SPF. "Not at all. Sarge was just a reliable, positive presence in my life when I needed it most. Making him happy or proud felt like the best way to thank him."

Hazel eyes softened and grew suspiciously damp again. "You've known a lot of loss."

"I have," I agreed. "But each time, someone has helped stitch the pieces of my tattered heart together. There was Sarge after my mom died, and then there were my guys when I lost Javi." But if something happened to this beautiful, sweet man in my lap—

Atticus kissed me before I could complete the thought. Had he known where my mind had gone, or did he just want to comfort me? I wrapped my arms around him and sank into the moment instead of worrying. The blanket fell away from his shoulders, and he shivered. I tried wrapping him back up, but Atticus whipped off the blanket and pressed his bare chest against mine. He moaned, wriggled on my lap, and deepened the kiss. My dick went from soft to semi-aroused in a flash.

I pulled back from the kiss and cupped his face. "Careful, you'll get something started."

Atticus arched a brow. "And?"

"You've got to be sore after last night, and I only want to give you pleasure."

Shaking his head slowly as if I were the densest person on Earth, Atticus said, "We can stick to handsy and mouthy things today." He gripped my biceps in both hands. "Then I'm going to put these to use."

That got my attention. "You need me to do some heavy lifting?"

"Yes, actually."

"Can I have a hint?" I asked.

Atticus slid from my lap to land on his knees at my feet. "And scare you off before we do handsy and mouthy things to each other?"

I wanted to push for more information, but Atticus wrapped those lush lips around my dick, and I was a goner.

CHAPTER 19

ATTICUS

THE ECHO OF OUR FOOTSTEPS ON CONCRETE FLOORS WAS LOUD INSIDE the storage complex. My footfalls were lighter and more of a slap than Ray's heavy thuds, my shorter legs taking two steps to his one.

Slap. Slap. Thud. Slap. Slap. Thud.

Our footwear, my flip-flops versus Ray's combat boots, was just one example of how different we were. But damn, we fit. My pucker flexed with the reminder of how snugly Ray had fit inside me, and I faltered on the next step.

Slap. Thud. Thud. Slap.

Ray's arm snaked around my waist, and his hand landed low on my stomach, tugging me against the rocking body I couldn't stop craving. I pushed my ass against his groin and moaned because he felt so damn good. I'd just had Ray's monster dick in my mouth less than an hour ago, milking him to the last drop, and here I was, ready to go again. My eyes clocked the security cameras in the nick of time.

"You good?" Ray asked.

Twisting in his embrace, I looked up at him with a smug smile that heated his cheeks. "You know I am."

Ray licked his bottom lip, his pink tongue reminding me of the favor he repaid by bending me over the coffee table and eating my ass while he stroked me off. He had the mouthy and handsy things down to an art form. Lucky me.

"And so are you," I said.

My compliment made him blush a deeper shade of pink, and I wanted to drag him back to his SUV to do naughty things to him. Did Ray enjoy anal play on himself? His demeanor screamed top, but maybe he was verse or at least liked a good prostate pegging now and then. I imagined Ray on his knees for me, ass up and cheeks spread, my finger buried inside his quivering hole as his big body trembled with pleasure from my touch and my filthy praise. I swallowed hard as my head tilted back to rest on his broad chest. Squeezing my eyes shut, I willed the poorly timed fantasy to go away, but it was no good. The sexy imagery gripped my brain as tightly as Ray's pucker would clench my finger when I found his sweet spot.

"Yes," Ray whispered huskily in my ear at the same time the fantasy version of him cried out with his release. "I want whatever it is you're thinking."

My eyes snapped open and locked onto the cameras again. Pulling myself together, I eased out of Ray's embrace before we got tossed out of the place. I turned and smiled up at him. "Not sure you'd be into it," I teased, walking backward, even though it was a disaster waiting to happen in flip-flops. But Ray's affection made me bold. "I'd sure like to try though."

"I will do anything you want after..." He paused and gestured at storage units around us. "We accomplish your mission."

Ray's steadfast personality was a major turn-on for me. I'd said I needed his help, and here we were. His lobelia eyes sparkled with curiosity, good humor, and more than a little lust.

His allure was too great to resist. "Anything?" I asked.

He opened his arms wide in surrender. "I'm all yours."

I could've taken his hand and led him out of the building, but I turned and headed down the corridor to my unit instead. "Let's do this." My courage waned, and my steps slowed as I neared my unit. Why in the hell had I asked for Ray's help when I could've just as easily swung by after work to photograph the inventory I wanted to sell? I stopped suddenly two doors down from my spot and whirled to face him. Ray was closer than I realized, probably because of my slowed pace, and he plowed into me before he could fully stop his big body.

Wrapping me in a protective embrace, Ray said, "Whoa. I'm built like a freight train and need time to stop."

"Sorry." I burrowed my face against his chest and mumbled, "I've changed my mind. Let's go back to your place."

"Hey," he said gently. "Look at me." When I hesitated, Ray slid his fingers into the wavy mess my hair had become and tilted my head back. I met his gaze head-on because it's what he deserved. "What's in the storage unit you don't want me to see?" His mouth curved up playfully on one side. "Please tell me you're not stashing bodies in there."

"No," I said with a snort.

"Body parts?"

I laughed and shook my head. "There's nothing morbid in there, but that might be less embarrassing." When Ray only blinked, I realized how weird that sounded. "I'm screwing this up like I do everything. There's nothing sinister in my storage unit, but I'm worried you're going to think I'm a dork."

Ray kissed me tenderly. "Enough of that talk." He cocked his head to the side. "I'm curious as hell, but we can leave if you're uncomfortable. I won't pressure you to do something you're not ready for."

And that's when I knew I was ready. "I want to do this. Selling off my inventory is part of my big plan to get my life together."

Ray furrowed his brow. "But these things must mean something to you if you're paying for a climate-controlled unit."

"They did once. I think I'm hanging on to things because they remind me of a simpler time, when I really need to focus on my future. The money I got from Chad is a good start toward buying a reliable car, and listing these items on eBay could generate the rest of the money I need. I might even have enough left over to pay down some college debt and possibly lease my own apartment." I tilted my head to the side and said, "The last two things might have to wait until I find a permanent job after Cammy comes back from maternity leave."

"You really do have a lot on your mind. No wonder you felt so overwhelmed this morning."

"I do, but the overriding emotions this morning were happiness and hopefulness." Gesturing down the corridor, I said, "Come on, while I still feel brave."

Ray dropped his arm and swatted my ass. "Fine, but no sudden stops."

"Don't power up to full speed because my unit is close," I cautioned.

"Got it."

We walked the short distance and stopped next to the door so I could enter the code. I waited for the keypad numbers to change from white to green before turning the knob. Flipping on the light, I stepped into the unit and waited for Ray to join me. He said nothing when he walked in, just quietly looked around. What did it look like through his eyes? A graveyard of old gaming systems, games, DVDs, and records? I'd carefully organized these things when I rented the unit, so it wouldn't take me long to snap some photos of the things that would sell fastest and bring the most money.

"Wow," Ray said. "This is impressive. It's like stepping back in time. Did you buy this stuff when you went yard-saling with Emma and Ramona?"

I adored a man who freaking listened. "Most of it, yes. We also hit up flea markets, swap meets, and estate sales too. I had my own neighborhood lawn-mowing business when I was a kid. I used the money to buy gaming systems with minor issues. The goal was to repair them cheaply and resell them." Shrugging, I said, "But as you can see, I collected more than I sold. Newer systems with cooler graphics replaced these, and no one wanted to buy them. I saw their value and hung on to them. And guess what people are looking to buy now?" Looking around the unit, I said. "Nostalgia, I guess. The graphics are still outdated as hell; maybe that's part of their charm."

Ray moved further into the room, stopping at the shelving unit with one of the Nintendo GameCube systems. "Damn, I haven't seen one of these in ages." He reached out and reverently touched the box. "My mom worked her ass off to buy me one of these for my eleventh birthday." Ray tipped his head back and laughed heartily. "She ended up playing the GameCube as much or more than I did. Damn, she loved the Scooby-Doo games. She used to laugh and curse that cartoon dog like it was his fault the missions failed when she was the one holding the controller." Ray smiled, lost in a memory I couldn't see but somehow felt. Just as quickly, his joy was gone. "After she died, the social worker told me to shove my clothes in a trash bag and take nothing else. I was too devastated to even consider taking my gaming system anyway. I never even wondered what happened to it. It probably ended up at someone's yard sale."

I had never felt a connection like this with another person, and it was terrifying. I joined him at the shelving unit and stood on my tiptoes to kiss his cheek. "Which game was her favorite? *Night of 100 Frights*?"

Ray jolted and looked at me as if remembering he wasn't alone. His smile was big and immediate. "Yeah. That's the one."

"It was my favorite too." I moved deeper among the shelves to find the rotating racks of games I had for the GameCube. Half a spin later, I lifted the treasure over my head victoriously. "Got it! Pick out a gaming system, and we'll take it and the Scooby-Doo game back to your place."

"Seriously?" Ray asked. "Modern televisions aren't compatible with these old systems, are they?"

"No, but they make adapters." I stepped over to a plastic storage caddy with a variety of cords, adapters, and accessories. "Aha!" I returned to his side and showed him the adapter kit. "This is all we need to play. Grab the console color you want, and we'll set these things aside."

"Are you sure?"

"I'm positive. I really want to relive this memory with you." But then I reconsidered. What if he didn't want to share it with me? "Or not. I can, um…"

"Leave me alone to game with my mother's ghost?" Ray shook his head. "No way. This will be a fun way to honor her memory." He leaned forward and kissed me hard. "And I want to do it with you."

"I would love that."

I had multiple console color options, but Ray chose the silver one because it was just like his. Ray took the game and adapter kit from me and set everything by the door. Then he turned to face the unit with hands on his hips. "What next?"

I looked around the room, trying to decide where to start, when Ray released a short exhale. I turned in his direction and saw that he'd discovered the DVD racks.

"Find something you like?"

Ray pointed to *Say Anything,* a classic John Cusack movie.

"You know that one?" I asked.

"Do *you*?"

I laughed at his expression. "You're only ten years older than I am."

"Yeah, but at least I was born a few years after the movie came out. Your parents might not have even met yet in the late eighties."

I snorted. "My mom has loved my dad since kindergarten. It took him until second grade to catch up and marry her at recess. They were well acquainted when this movie released."

And very little had changed since then, if my untimely interruptions since moving back home were anything to go by. I cringed because I didn't want to wade too deep into those weeds. But the conversation made me wonder about Ray's dad and extended family. Had there been no one who could've taken him in instead of letting him get placed in foster care? I didn't want to wander too far down that path either. If someone could've taken him in, they would have. Right?

Ray's bright smile slashed through the shadows cast by my dark thoughts. "That's really sweet," he said. "It sounds like you and your sister had an idyllic childhood."

"It would seem so, but I've always marched to a different beat, and it caused a lot of problems. I'm too much of one thing and not enough of another. But computers and electronics didn't care about any of that stuff. They operated the same way for everyone. Figuring out how things ticked fascinated me, but my parents were not nearly as enthusiastic about my curiosity. I took apart so many things and ruined them before I learned how circuit boards and wiring worked."

I smiled up at Ray, knowing the gesture hadn't reached my eyes. "It took me a long time, like maybe right this minute, to understand why I was so hell-bent on fixing the stuff that people no longer wanted when something newer and shinier came along. Where they saw junk, I saw possibilities. And if I could fix those electronics, then maybe I could figure out why my brain's circuit boards misfired, and my wires always seemed crossed." I shrugged as if the barbs of old hurts weren't permanently anchored in my soul. "I was a lonely-ass kid who collected things instead of forming friendships," I said, gesturing around the room. "Until Emma moved to town in third grade and declared I was her person."

"Did you follow in your parents' footsteps and try to marry Emma at recess?"

Laughing, I shook my head. "I realized I loved boys instead of girls at a young age." I blew out a breath because the next part still hurt. "I thought I hit the lottery when I met Chad in high school."

Scrunching his face, Ray said, "The guy I tackled after he bashed your car in with a crowbar? The one who barely acknowledged he'd fucked you over six ways to Sunday and definitely didn't apologize for it? That Chad?"

His outrage made me laugh. "Yes. He wasn't always a complete douchebag. Chad used to be loving and kind. I thought we wanted the same things out of life. We did once," I amended. "We had the same interests and hobbies. He understood and loved my interest in electronics and computers. I don't even know when we started planning a future together. Eleventh grade, maybe. We went to the same college and shared an apartment instead of living in dorms. We got hired by the same software engineering company after graduation. It was supposed to be our dream careers, but the pay sucked, and I hated the work. It sucked the soul right out of me. I'd much rather hang out with the residents at Silver Maple."

I shook my head because I'd gone off on an unexpected tangent. "Anyway, Chad and I just rushed into a relationship we weren't prepared for, and I hadn't recognized the signs that critical parts had broken until I saw the evidence that he'd found someone newer and shinier." I took a shuddering breath. "Chad knew about my deep-rooted insecurities and still threw me away instead of trying to fix what had broken. That felt more like a betrayal to me than the cheating. It's what I can't forgive."

"And you don't have to." Ray pulled me into a tight embrace, resting his chin on top of my head. "Do you think I'm a guy who keeps his word?"

"Absolutely." It was silly to be so resolute about a man I hardly knew, but I felt his goodness down to my bone marrow.

Ray let go just enough to look into my eyes. He cupped my jaw with one hand and brushed his thumb over my cheekbone. Forehead kisses and cheek caresses were quickly becoming my favorite form of touching. "I will never betray you like that. If something isn't working for me, I will do the honorable thing and talk to you about it."

Tears filled my eyes and stung the back of my nose. Trying to blink them back, I failed, and they cascaded down my cheeks. I lowered my head to hide my reaction, but Ray gently tucked his finger under my chin and lifted it. I bravely opened my eyes and met his beautiful blue gaze.

"I'm not done having my say." Ray paused to kiss me softly, once, twice, and then lingered long enough that hiding was the last thing I wanted to do. He pulled back and swiped his thumb over my lips. "You're not broken, your circuit boards aren't...whatever you called them, and there's nothing wrong with your wires. You're neither too much of this nor not enough of that. Fucking perfect is what you are. Chad is an idiot, but his loss is my gain. That fucker isn't getting you back."

"I don't think—"

Ray briefly covered my mouth with his finger. "Yes, someday, that dumbass will figure out that he royally fucked up and will want you back. But you won't fall for his crap because you know you deserve better." He tapped my temple, my heart, and then a few inches below my sternum. "Wherever your soul is supposed to be located. It knows the truth too."

"I wouldn't take Chad back. Not after the way he hurt me, gaslit me about our breakup, and beat sweet Sadie to a pulp." Sighing, I said, "I really miss that damn car."

"You can borrow my vehicle," Ray said.

"Your work SUV?"

He shook his head. "I have a pickup truck I drive for personal use. You're welcome to borrow it whenever you want."

"That's so sweet of you to offer." It was on the tip of my tongue to refuse, but I said, "Is it fully insured?"

Ray tipped his head back and laughed. "Yes, but I'm not worried." He looked around the room, then said, "Where do we start?"

"With the highest-priority items first," I told him. "I have at least two thousand dollars' worth of GameCube systems and a tiny fortune in games. And the Wii systems and games are hot commodities right now too."

"Then you should sell the stuff you set aside for me."

"No way," I replied. "We're going to have so much fun playing the Scooby-Doo game this weekend. And we're taking *Say Anything* with us to watch in your mother's honor." I snagged the DVD box off the rack and carried the movie over to our pile. "Besides, I'm not looking to buy a luxury vehicle. I want to offload the highest-value items to people who can appreciate them while putting myself in a better financial position." And once the words left my mouth, I knew they were true. The things I'd held on to for so long weren't what mattered to me anymore. "I'll buy a reasonable car like Sadie and tuck the rest away. Then I'll sell another batch of treasures and so on until nothing remains."

Ray inhaled deeply and nodded. "Put me to work."

So I did. "Tell me more about your mom," I said as I snapped the latest round of photos for my online eBay store.

Ray returned the Wii system to the shelf and grabbed the next one. His shirt had a thin layer of dust covering the front, and beads of moisture dotted his upper lip. How did he look even hotter when all mussed and sweaty? I fully planned to reward his efforts beyond his wildest dreams as soon as we got home—er, back to his place. "What do you want to know?"

"Anything you want to tell me," I said. "What was her name?"

"Delia James." Ray's voice was soft and reverent, as if saying a prayer. His eyes lost focus for a few seconds, and then he blinked himself back to me. "My mom was vibrant and so much fun. She would do the silliest impulsive things like mixing sugary cereals in odd combinations."

"I think I saw that in a movie once."

"That might be where she got the idea," Ray said with a shrug. "Some combinations made sense. Peanut Butter Captain Crunch with Cocoa Puffs were pretty good. Apple Jacks and Cinnamon Cheerios were decent too. But then she'd mix some granola crap with something equally healthy and gross." His smile dimmed as if a shadow had crossed his face. "I used to think she did the weird combos to entertain me, but now I realize she did it because we were low on money. Mom saved the good stuff for me and ate whatever was left. I wish I had at least five minutes with her again to thank her for how hard she worked to put a roof over our heads and food on the table. I want to hear her laugh again."

The question of where the hell his father or extended family was sprang to mind again, but I didn't let my outrage on his behalf insert itself into the situation. "She sounds like a wonderful mom."

"She was," Ray said, looking away as his voice broke. He sniffed and cleared his throat and met my gaze again before continuing. "She loved love. Man, she adored the big, romantic gestures in movies like the one from *Say Anything*. And she was always positive, no matter what. And life had dealt my mom some really shitty cards." Ray puffed out his cheeks and exhaled. "I don't know the full details about my parents' relationship. Hell, I don't even know my dad's name because Mom refused to list it on my birth certificate. She once told me it wasn't because he was a bad person. They'd had a fling, and he moved on before she found out she was pregnant. She claimed she didn't have a way to contact him and didn't want to share me with him anyway." Ray tilted his head to the side and smiled wryly. "My best guess is that she hooked up with a professional baseball player during spring training in Florida. It's something I would've asked her as an adult if I'd gotten the chance."

"What about her family?" I asked, unable to hold back my question any longer. "Where the hell were they when you guys needed them?"

"Religious fanatics," Ray replied. "I don't stomp on people's beliefs, but I have a real problem when folks use religion as an excuse to hurt others. Mom's parents kicked her out of the house when they found out she was pregnant, and they told her not to come back until she married her baby's daddy. I reckon that wasn't an option because Mom lived in a women's shelter. After I was born, she got the factory job that would eventually kill her. Damn, she was proud of working there too. We didn't have much, but what we had was ours, and no one was going to take anything from her again."

"And your grandparents or someone in your extended family wouldn't take you in after she passed? You were an innocent kid, for fuck's sake."

"I'm sure the state attempted to place me with family, but they wouldn't have taken me in. It's like that old saying about throwing the baby out with the bathwater. But I didn't want them either." Crossing to me, Ray took the phone from my hand and set it on the table. "You've taken about a hundred photos of that Wii system already."

I looked down at my hand in surprise. "I did?"

Nodding, Ray said, "You were too outraged on my behalf to notice."

"I am furious, damn it."

Ray bit his bottom lip, probably to keep from laughing. I narrowed my eyes, and he lost his shit, cracking up at my fury. "Sorry," he said, holding up his hands in surrender. "You just look so cute when you're angry. All puffed up like a little kit—"

His eyes widened as I narrowed mine.

"Don't," I warned. "I already have a million nicknames."

"Kitten," Ray said anyway.

"Ugh, no."

"But it fits. You got all hissy on my behalf, and I really liked it."

"Hissy, huh?" I asked. "Well, I have claws, and I'm not afraid to use them."

Ray planted a hard kiss on my mouth. "I can't wait for you to really dig in and hold on, kitten."

"Archer once called me that," I announced, hoping it would put an end to the nickname for good. He actually called me a kitty cat or something, but why split hairs?

"I'll beat his ass if he uses that nickname ever again."

Ray pressed kisses along my neck, and I arched to give him better access. And yes, I released a happy hum that sounded too much like a kitten's purr. Ray made a different noise in response, a predatory growl that let me know he was about to lay me down across the nearest surface and—

The shrill sound of Ray's cell phone cut through the lust fog, and he released me with a snarl. "Speak of the devil," Ray said. "I'll tell the asshole right now that I don't want him calling you anything cutesy ever again."

"That's not—"

"Listen here, Archibald," Ray said instead of a normal greeting.

Archer's voice cut him off, but I couldn't hear what he said. The one-sided conversation lasted less than fifteen seconds before Ray tapped the screen and returned his phone to his pocket. "Brunch will be ready in twenty minutes. I guess Vaughn pulled out all the stops. There are pancakes, waffles, three different breakfast meats, and enough eggs for an army. Arch said there's fresh-squeezed orange juice and yogurt parfaits too." Ray smiled and kissed me. "We don't have to go if you don't want to. No pressure."

I took him by the hand and led him to the door. "I have plenty of pictures to get me started. Feed me. We'll need fuel for our afternoon and evening activities."

The guys were waiting in the communal room on the second story of the warehouse. I was immediately blown away by the beauty and comfort of the space these guys gathered in to show love to one another, even if it came as snarky banter and a little roughhousing. They were kind of like overgrown kids when they wound each other up, and I was immensely happy to witness it firsthand.

Vaughn met my gaze with a smirk and shook his head. "All right. That's enough, you hooligans." He set a massive platter of breakfast meats on the large farmhouse-style dining room table that had long benches tucked under it instead of chairs. "Or you can at least carry food to the table while you provide Atticus with cheap entertainment."

"Who are you calling cheap?" Archer asked as he got Nico in a headlock after he suggested they invite Bobby over for brunch too. "I have impeccable taste…most of the time."

Ray wrestled Nico away to freedom and pulled Archer into some kind of chokehold. The bulge of Ray's biceps sent lightning bolts of lust straight to my groin. "No more using cutesy nicknames for my guy."

Archer sighed heavily, proving the grip around his neck wasn't that tight. "Aw, man."

"You heard him," Vaughn said to Archer, then looked at me with apology. "Forgive us. We know how to behave like adults. It's just been a hot minute since any of us has brought someone special around."

The remark both warmed my heart and made me sad. These wonderful men deserved exceptional love. "It's no problem," I said. "This is the happiest I've ever been in my life."

Ray immediately released his friend to gloat, raising his arms in the air and grinning smugly.

Archer clapped Ray on his shoulder. "Attaboy, Ray Ray."

"Let's eat," Vaughn called.

Once the food was on the table, all the chaos settled into hums of happiness.

"This is amazing," I said after sampling the waffles.

Vaughn beamed his appreciation. "Thank you."

"I helped," Ethan said.

Nico and Archer snorted.

Ethan narrowed his eyes and bounced his gaze between them. "I did," he insisted.

"Barking out tips on how to fold egg whites into the batter isn't helping," Nico said.

Notching his chin higher, Ethan said, "It is too."

Archer and Ray watched the argument with barely suppressed laughter.

It didn't take long for the six of us to devour Vaughn's hard work, and then the guys bickered over who had cleanup duties. That's when Ray took my hand and quietly led me out the door. We grabbed the gaming stuff and the DVD we'd stashed in the hallway when we arrived.

"Game or movie first?" Ray asked once we were alone in his apartment.

"I vote movie while we digest that massive brunch."

"Works for me," Ray said, then stripped down to his boxers.

What else could I do but follow his lead? We cuddled together in the center of the sofa, wrapped in the fluffy throw blanket, and watched as a very young John Cusack stumbled his way through love.

"Pretty sure he's the reason I knew I was gay," Ray said.

"Really?" I tried to twist around to look at him, but he'd wrapped me up tighter than a burrito.

"Yeah. My mom loved this movie so much and watched it all the time."

When it got to the boom box serenade, Ray's chest vibrated with a chuckle.

"Was this her favorite part?" I asked.

"Oh yeah. She was a real sucker for grand gestures. Mom never gave up hope that she'd find a big love like that."

It broke my heart that Delia never got to experience her epic love story, but it wasn't too late for Ray. I was more than willing to give him the happily ever after they both deserved.

CHAPTER 20

Rayden

Someone knocked on my open door just as I reached for my lunch bag. I jerked my head up, expecting to see Kit, but found Caitlyn there instead. Her once-crisp linen suit looked like she'd wrestled a tiger, and her normally tan skin had a sickly pallor that her makeup couldn't hide.

"Cait, what's wrong?"

"This is the worst day of my professional career," she said before slumping into a chair. "The Monday-est Monday to ever Monday."

Caitlyn had approached me when I arrived at work this morning and asked me to attend a meeting with a resident's family after lunch. Their mother had assaulted one of our security guards over the weekend, and he'd required several stitches in his face. Since it was the resident's third and most violent incident, Caitlyn had no choice but to present two tough options to the resident's family. They could take their loved one's worsening dementia more seriously and place them in the memory care unit or find a different facility. But going off Caitlyn's present condition, her day had only gotten worse since we talked.

"What's happened?"

Caitlyn's eyes widened. "You mean you haven't heard?"

"Obviously not."

My phone vibrated with an incoming text. I checked it quickly and saw it was from Atticus. "Excuse me for one second," I told Caitlyn. Atticus just wanted me to know he was heading to the cafeteria early to grab our fried chicken while it was fresh out of the fryer. My mouth watered as I replied that I'd meet him at the pond with the side dishes we prepared together before bed. We'd been dating and basically living together for two weeks, and I'd never been happier in my life. But Caitlyn obviously needed my help or at least my attention while she vented, so I set my phone down. "Give me the tea or whatever it is people say now."

"I wish this was just idle office gossip," Caitlyn said, "but this could be a major scandal."

"Involving RAVEN?"

"Well, maybe one of you," she teased.

There was only one of us who could bring shame upon our good name, and I had to fight the urge to call Archer and demand answers before I even knew what he might've gotten caught up in this time. "I'm afraid to ask."

"So, I'll just tell you." Caitlyn held up her index finger and pulled her phone from her pocket. "Better yet, I'll show you." She tapped and swiped for a few seconds before turning the phone around for me to see the breaking news headline from an hour ago.

"Columbus, Georgia, massage therapist charged with prostitution and solicitation during undercover sting," I read aloud. Beneath the heading was a picture of Bobby, looking pouty and rebellious. "Holy fuck!"

"That's what I said." Caitlyn nodded and rocked the phone back and forth. "Want to read more?"

Shaking my head, I instructed her to give me the recap.

"It seems Bobby did freelance work as a private massage therapist and offered extra services for the right amount of money. It's only a matter of time before the media connects him to Silver Maple." She covered her face with both hands. "We can't afford a scandal like this."

I wanted to say something that would ease her strain, but encouraging words failed me. "I guess the best thing to do is inform the board so they can get ahead of it."

Caitlyn worried her bottom lip between her teeth, then nodded. "Yeah. I don't have any other choice. I just hope none of the board members are his…customers. Can you imagine if he kept a scandalous client list like a Hollywood madam?"

I remembered the time he'd freed Atticus and me from the art supply closet. Bobby had been cagey about why he was still on campus, claiming he had to give extra attention to certain clients. Caitlyn's fears might not be that far-fetched, but I wouldn't throw gasoline on the fire. "I'm sure the board has an excellent attorney or someone with public relations experience to guide them."

Caitlyn looked slightly less gray as she got to her feet. "True. Thanks for letting me vent."

"No problem." I stood up and picked up my lunch bag.

"Meeting Kit?"

"Unless you need anything else," I replied.

"No, no. Go ahead." She paused on her way to the door and smiled at me. "You guys are so cute together. Couple goals for the rest of us less fortunate souls."

Heat bloomed in my chest and spread up my neck. "Thanks."

"And I'm making things weird. Bye!"

Caitlyn ducked out before I could respond, and I just shook my head. *Couple goals.* I liked that she called us that and couldn't wait to tell Atticus.

I found Atticus at the pond, phone in hand and a shocked expression on his face. Pretty sure I knew what he was reading.

I bent to kiss his cheek before sitting next to him on the bench. "I'm never letting Archer live this down."

Atticus turned his stunned expression on me and narrowed his hazel eyes in accusation. "You knew?"

Raising my hands in surrender, I said, "Just found out from Caitlyn. She also referred to us as couple goals."

"Aww, how sweet. I love that for us." Atticus looked back down at his phone with disbelief still etched on his gorgeous features. "I can't believe it."

But when he set his phone down, Atticus remembered it was fried chicken day, and Bobby's plight was all but forgotten. He reached into the bag and pulled out a drumstick, sinking his teeth into it with a soft whimper of delight. The smug grin said he knew the effect those noises had on me, and he loved every minute of it. I reached into the cafeteria bag and pulled out a piece for myself, biting through the crispy skin and into the juicy meat. Christ, it was a near-orgasmic experience. Hazel eyes widened as they watched me chew, and I realized I'd probably made slutty noises too.

"I never thought of eating as foreplay until I met you," Atticus said. "Now everything is a form of stimulation."

Leaning forward, I kissed him hard before he could take another bite of chicken. "It's because you've turned me into a horny bastard."

Atticus snorted and shook his head. "You're not sick of me? We live, commute, and work together."

"We also shower, eat, and share lots and lots of orgasms together," I added. "I love every minute of it, but it sounds like maybe you're sick of me."

"No way." Atticus sounded firm, worried even. "I just don't want to overstay my welcome."

"Impossible."

"You say that now," Atticus said, "but I think we're still living in a honeymoon bubble. You're bound to want your space, and I need you to know that's okay. Like I should probably want independence too. I went from living at home to moving in with Chad, then I moved back home before practically moving in with you. Shouldn't I want to try living on my own?"

I cocked an eyebrow at him. "You're talking to a man who couldn't sleep unless he shared a home with his four best friends. I'm the last person to judge anyone for not wanting to live alone."

Atticus scowled at my glib remark. "Hey now. Our situations aren't the same. Look at the hell you guys survived."

"Living with Chad doesn't sound like a cakewalk."

Sighing, Atticus said, "It wasn't, but it's not nearly the same trauma you experienced. I moved home because I was jobless with a fuck ton of college debt and had nowhere else to go. And you know what? I'm grateful for my parents, but shouldn't I want to make it on my own?"

"But don't let pride make your comeback unnecessarily harder," I said.

"What do you mean?"

"The money you would pay on rent could go toward your college debt. It makes more sense to save money by living with your parents or spending most of your nights with a guy who thinks you're the most amazing person." I pointed to my chest. "It's me. I'm the guy who thinks that."

Atticus smiled and shook his head. "I don't know why you feel that way, but I'm so glad you do."

"You will understand someday. I promise you."

And I saw in his gaze that he believed me, which was a temporary victory I'd happily claim. I kissed Atticus deeply, not caring we were on campus. He melted into me and lost himself in our embrace, whacking my chest with his drumstick. That yanked me back to reality with a laugh. We both took a bite of chicken and worked to unpack the sides while we chewed. We kept our conversation light, chatting about our mornings and upcoming afternoon plans. Atticus had organized a weekly series where local artists would visit Silver Maple and teach their various art mediums to the residents. The first class kicked off later that afternoon and featured watercolor painting.

"Need me to model?" I offered. "That worked out pretty well for us last time."

"Yeah, but now I don't need to take such drastic measures to get you to take off your clothes."

"Hard to believe that was two weeks ago," I said. "I can't remember what my apartment was like before sharing it with you."

"Bet it had a lot less clutter and chaos."

"You're neither messy nor chaotic," I told him. "I wish I could snatch those negative thoughts right out of your head."

"Maybe you could try to fuck them out."

I huffed a laugh. "I'll give it my best shot." But we both knew it wouldn't be that easy. "Have you ever worked with a therapist?"

Atticus shook his head. "What about you?"

"Yeah," I admitted. "I've worked with a few different therapists on cognitive-behavioral therapies. I benefitted from the sessions, but the therapists didn't approve of my trauma bonding with the guys."

"Why?"

"They thought we were too codependent, existing in a hive that prevented us from forming healthy relationships with anyone else." I tilted my head to the side. "And maybe there's some truth to their concerns. Until now, none of us has brought new people into the fold or even expressed a desire to do so."

"It's because none of you have been ready," Atticus said. "But you're showing them what's possible when you take chances."

I wasn't so sure about that, so I said, "Maybe." Then I forked a bite of macaroni salad and held it up for Atticus to eat. "Good?"

Atticus nodded enthusiastically as he chewed. "Mmmm."

I took a bite and had to agree it was excellent. "It seems you're slated to have a much better afternoon than I am."

"Really? Why?"

Atticus knew about the incident that occurred over the weekend since we were all together when Vaughn got the call about our security guard's injury. What Atticus likely didn't know was that it wasn't the resident's first occurrence, so I brought him up to speed and told him about the upcoming conversation Caitlyn and I both dreaded.

"Woof. That is hard. I'm sorry." He reached down and lifted the brown butter chocolate chip cookies we bought from the bakery yesterday afternoon. "Maybe this will make it a little better."

"Dragging you off to a secluded spot is the only thing that will make me happy."

I stole a quick kiss from Atticus before I accepted the oversized cookie. I broke it in two and gave half to Atticus. "Sexy time with you can be my incentive to get me through the day."

"Good idea."

Matilda and Marty showed up as we finished our lunch, providing us with cheap entertainment while we snuggled together under the shade. It was too hot outside to be pressed so tightly together, but wild horses couldn't have dragged me away from Atticus. Besides, we were both headed into air-conditioned buildings and could cool off then. I reached for his hand and laced my fingers through his on our way back to the main buildings. I nodded at the few employees we passed on their way to lunch and clocked the cute smiles they sent our way. Maybe handholding and canoodling at the pond wasn't very professional, but fuck if I gave a damn what anyone thought.

I retreated to the sanctuary of my office after the meeting with the irate family ended. The resident's son, daughter, and their spouses had been apologetic at first, offering to cover the medical bills for our security guard. I'd accepted their apologies and declined their offer before turning the conversation over to Caitlyn. And that's when it got ugly. The "oh my goodness" and "we're so sorry" turned into "you must be mistaken" and "our mother would never do that."

Caitlyn stayed firm, fair, and friendly, never losing her cool, even when the family raised their voices and made accusations. I'd been ready to jump in if necessary, but Caitlyn hadn't needed my help. The family agreed to discuss the situation among themselves once they'd allowed time to digest the information. They were in deep denial about their mother's rapid decline, and I felt terrible for them. By the end of the conversation, cooler heads had prevailed, and they reverted to using civil tongues and Southern manners. They promised to get back to Caitlyn with a decision in forty-eight hours.

My ass had barely landed in my chair when an internal alarm rang in to the monitoring system. Bolting upright, I saw the flashing message on the screen and nearly lost my lunch. **Smoke detected in the Arts and Literature building. Fire suppression system engaged. Fire Department Notified.**

I pulled up the security cameras in the building's lobby and saw smoke coming from the art classroom. Jesus Christ. Atticus was hosting his watercolor class in there. I saw no indication that the fire suppression system had kicked in, and if that was faulty, the direct call to the fire department might not have worked either. One of the first things we did when taking over the account was to review all the safety inspections and protocols performed by our predecessors. The smoke alarms and fire suppression systems were marked as inspected with no issues. I never should've taken their word for it.

"Fuck!"

I jumped from my chair and ran from my office, dialing 911 on the way. A female dispatcher came on the line and collected my information.

"Are there people in the building?" Her voice was calm and authoritative, which was exactly what my panicked brain needed.

"I'm on my way to find out," I said as I burst through the front door, hitting the sidewalk at a dead sprint. Up ahead, I saw a cluster of residents gathered a safe distance from the building where smoke billowed from the open door. "Did everyone make it out?" I asked when I reached the group.

"I think so," Mrs. Cho replied. "Class has been over for a while."

I searched the crowd for messy brown hair and hazel eyes but came up short. "Damn it. Where's Atticus?"

"Who?" Mrs. Hastings asked.

"Kit!" I yelled. "Where is Kit?"

"Haven't seen him," Mr. Sanchez said.

"He was teaching the class, Rico," Ms. Johansson said, turning to me with worry in her eyes. "The building wasn't on fire when we left, and the rest of us are all accounted for, including the guest instructor, Sarah Jo." She pointed to a lady with lavender braids as if I had time for introductions. "She's just been telling us about her latest art pilgrimage."

"Have you seen Kit?" I asked Sarah Jo.

The artist pressed both hands to her chest. "He was putting the art supplies away in the closet when we left."

Not that motherfucking supply closet again. "There might be someone inside the building," I told the dispatcher.

"Help is on the way and will be there within minutes. Don't go—"

Fuck that! I disconnected and dialed Atticus. The phone rang in my ear and somewhere nearby. I whipped around, expecting to see the man I'd fallen for, but only saw Angus McNally, holding Atticus's phone. "Hey!" I yelled, charging toward him. "Where'd you get that?"

Angus clutched the still-ringing phone to his chest. "Finders keepers." Besides smoking in the worst places, had the guy turned into a kleptomaniac?

I needed to keep calm because Atticus needed me. I disconnected the call and tucked my phone away. "Did you see Kit inside the art room?"

"No. There was no one there. I ducked in for a quick smoke and found this cool phone. I m-must've dropped my cigarette in my excitement." Tears filled the older man's eyes, but I didn't have time to console him. I eased Kit's phone from his trembling hands and tucked it in my pocket.

"Do you know where the supply closet is in the art room?" I asked.

"Uh-huh. The door was open when I went into the room, but I closed it on my way out."

I didn't need to hear anything more. I turned and ran into the burning building.

CHAPTER 21

ATTICUS

AN EAR-SPLITTING SHRIEK RENT THE AIR AND SCARED THE HELL out of me. I dropped the supplies and tripped over a rolling bottle of paint. Staggering sideways, I slammed into a metal shelving unit hard enough to topple the supplies onto the concrete with a jarring clatter. I wasn't sure what hurt worse: the instant headache from the shrill alarm or my throbbing ribs from the impact with the shelving unit. What the hell was going on? Was that an air-raid siren? Were we under imminent attack? It took me a moment to collect my equilibrium, and I rounded the corner of the L-shaped closet, only to discover the door was closed.

What the hell? I hadn't shut it. Rushing forward, I grabbed the handle and pulled down hard, but the damn thing wouldn't budge. I reached for my phone, but it wasn't in my pocket. I'd left it on a table in the art room. *Fuck me.* I yanked and pulled on the handle in vain, then switched tactics. I banged on the door, shouting for help until my mouth went dry, but no one responded to my pleas.

"Okay, don't panic."

But my wrecked voice and racing pulse said I was beyond that. I took a deep breath to calm myself but coughed instead. There had to be a reasonable explanation for this. Had one of the wily seniors thought it would be funny to trap me inside the closet and pull the fire alarm? While there were a few hell-raisers living on Silver Maple's campus, none of them had attended my art class, and a sick prank such as this felt too cruel for one of them. It had to be a short in the system. Faulty wiring. Yeah, that was it. After all, the fire suppression system hadn't engaged, or I'd be covered in water, foam, or whatever the hell was supposed to spray out of the overhead nozzles.

I coughed again and registered the first hint of smoke. Glancing down, I saw tendrils creeping under the door and rising toward me. They looked sinister, like something paranormal trying to penetrate my body and possess me. But this was so much worse. There was a fire in the building, and the fire suppression system wasn't working. It was time to panic! More banging, more shouting, more smoke. All I got for my effort was a dry throat, a worsening headache, and burning lungs.

No, I was not going out like this. I reached for the handle again, but the metal was already warm and would be hot soon. *Oh fuck. That's not good.* I covered my mouth with my arm and tried to remember a single safety tip I'd learned in school. Stop, drop, and roll? Or was that for when a person was already on fire? I held my breath and watched as more smoke snaked its way under the door, looking thicker and darker on its way toward the ceiling. That was it! I needed to get lower to the ground, so I dropped to my knees and backed away from the door a little. The air was fresher, and I sucked a lungful in while trying to figure out other ways to... delay the inevitable? I would be a goner if someone didn't rescue me soon. The smoke would kill me before the flames did.

With fresh lungs, I shouted for help again. But who the hell was I yelling to? The residents had already left. None of them were going to charge into a burning building to save me, nor would I want them to. Wouldn't Ray get an alert in his office? But wait. If the fire suppression system hadn't worked, then maybe the other safety measures failed too.

Holy shit. I was going to die.

The fire alarm seemed to shriek louder, my headache thumped harder, and breathing became more difficult. Was I running out of clean air, or had a panic attack reduced my airflow? I lay down flat on the ground, the concrete cool against my cheek. I fixed my gaze on a dropped bottle of blue paint that nearly matched Ray's eye color. If this were to be the end for me,

I wanted that blue to be the last thing I saw. A scene from a movie popped into my head, and I remembered the lead actor covering his nose with a cloth while trying to escape a burning building.

I pulled my T-shirt up over my nose and mouth and worked on getting air into my lungs, one slow cycle of breath at a time. The discomfort in my chest lessened with each new inhale, and I just kept my gaze trained on the blue paint, recalling the range of emotions I'd seen in Ray's eyes since meeting him. I tried to choose a favorite but decided I couldn't. All of them were equally precious to me, from the initial recognition by the pool to the shimmering adoration just hours ago. I would miss the way his blue eyes burned with lust whenever he got me naked. Did dead people miss things?

Dead? Oh no. I couldn't die.

Ray had already lost too much. I would not be just another person who crushed his soul. Pushing to my knees, I looked for something, anything I could use to pry that damn door open. My gaze landed on something metallic under the shelf across from me. It was maybe four or five inches long and slender. One end had a ringlike circle, and the other hooked slightly. It was a paint key! I scrambled over and pulled it out from under the shelf. It wouldn't be strong enough to pry the door open, but maybe I could insert it into the release hole in the handle. Tess used bobby pins to break into my bedroom whenever I locked her out when we were kids.

Crawling to the door, I reached up and shoved the paint key into the small hole and wiggled it around. I couldn't hear a fucking thing over that screaming alarm, but I felt the moment the lock disengaged. *Holy shit! I did it.* Tucking the paint key into my pocket, I pulled my shirt off over my head and wrapped it around my hand. I pulled the handle and eased the door open to assess the room beyond, but all I saw was billowing black smoke. The fire was a heavy beast growling nearby.

Fuck. It was now or never, so I tied it around my nose and mouth like a bandana and army-crawled out of the closet. The fire raged in the opposite direction of the exit, and I thanked my lucky stars. I knew I wasn't out of the woods yet because burning debris and ashes cascaded all around me. The fire made a heaving sound, and embers rained down on top of me, scorching my flesh. Scooting on my stomach as fast as I could, I made my way toward safety. More embers singed my skin, but I didn't slow down to acknowledge the pain.

"Atticus!" Ray yelled.

My name had never sounded so beautiful, and tears of relief filled my eyes. I was going to make it. I would stare into the blue eyes and discover even more expressions.

"Here!" I yelled as I neared the front of the room. The door was right there. Just a few more feet and—

A burning piece of ceiling tile landed six inches from my head, setting the low-pile carpet ablaze. Crawling was no longer an option, so I jumped to my feet, prepared to hurdle the low flames and dart for the door when Ray appeared out of nowhere, brandishing a massive fire extinguisher. He blasted the floor in front of me and yelled for me to run. He continued to battle the encroaching flames while I made a mad dash for freedom. When I reached him, Ray dropped the fire extinguisher and scooped me into his massive arms and bolted toward safety. He didn't stop running until we were safely away from the burning building.

Ray dropped to his knees and carefully laid me in the grass. "Atticus," he panted. "Baby, are you okay?"

Baby. I thought I'd hate that cutesy name, but it sounded so sexy when Ray said it. "Yeah," I wheezed before the coughing started.

Sirens wailed in the distance, and my vision dimmed. Or had it gotten cloudy? I looked up and noticed that a large crowd had gathered overhead. One cough led to another, and I couldn't seem to stop.

"Everyone, back up and give him room to breathe." Ray's voice was urgent but calm.

"So sexy when you're bossy," I croaked before coughing again.

Ray gently brushed the hair off my forehead. His misery and pain were expressions I never wanted to see again. I wrapped my hand around Ray's wrist, needing to touch some part of him. I tried to say something, but he shook his head. "Try not to talk right now." Then he raised his head and asked if anyone had water. Several arms thrust bottles toward him, and Ray took the fullest one. He uncapped the water, raised my head, and held the bottle to my lips. "Easy sips. I need to ask some questions and assess your injuries. Just nod or shake your head. Okay?"

I nodded as the cool water soothed my parched throat. He let me have a few sips before he eased it away.

"Did you inhale a lot of smoke?"

I wasn't sure what he defined as a lot, so I held up my hand and rocked it from side to side. That's when Ray saw the tiny burns from falling debris. They were superficial and sore, nothing that worried me too much, but Ray made a pitiful groan as he inspected each one.

"It's not too bad," Ray said, cupping my face. I wasn't sure if he was trying to comfort himself or me, but I leaned into his touch and stared into his turbulent eyes. "Do you hurt anywhere else?"

Pointing to my head, I tried to sit up, then gasped when I felt a twinge in my ribs. That triggered another round of coughing, which Ray eased with more sips of water before he helped me into a sitting position. The thunderous expression in his eyes gave away the storm raging in his mind. Ray was going to blame himself for this entire incident and use my injuries as an excuse to build walls between us again. It was happening before my very eyes. The loving touches Ray had given me had grown clinical as he searched for signs of injury.

Clink, clink, clink went the bricks. "Point to where it hurts," Ray said, his voice terse from strain.

I carefully tapped my rib cage and tried to whisper what happened, but Ray held the water to my lips instead. I took two more sips, then pulled back.

"No talking," he said. "Did you fall?"

I nodded and reached for the bottle, wanting to down the rest of it so I could explain what happened.

Ray eased it away. "Slowly," he reminded me as he kept a firm grip on the bottle.

I nodded, and he helped me drink some more. With each passing second, Ray's defenses crept higher until I barely recognized the man in front of me as the same one who'd made tender love to me just that morning.

Ray shuttered his expression and said, "I knew the door handle should've been replaced. Accepting a repair instead almost killed you." Ray's voice broke on the last two words, and he closed his eyes.

I gripped his arm tightly, hoping he'd meet my gaze, but Ray only lowered his head. Damn it. I couldn't lose him now. Not after crawling through a burning building to get to him. I wanted to say that, but my voice was a mere croak by that point. The noise was enough to grab Ray's attention, and his shattered expression shredded my heart into a million little pieces. It was too late. I'd lost him.

The emergency vehicles roared up to the building, and we got caught up in a flurry of activity. One minute, Ray was within arm's reach, and the next, he was talking to a first responder while the firemen battled the flames coming out of the building's roof. Holy fuck. The reality of how close I'd come to dying hit me like a ton of bricks. My pulse must've spiked because the EMT assessing my vitals looked at me with concern. I couldn't remember her name, but she had kind brown eyes.

"Drink some more water," she said. "Try to take slow, even breaths between sips."

She handed me a bottle of coconut water, explaining that it would help restore the electrolytes I'd lost while inhaling smoke. She'd cautioned me to go slow, and I sipped the water while I watched Ray. He was only a dozen feet from my gurney, but he might as well have been a hundred miles away. His body language was tense, and he'd completely shut down his emotions, running purely on his training.

It hurt too much to look at him, so I glanced at the large group of people barricaded off to the side for their safety. Caitlyn stood in front with several of the staff members to ensure the residents stayed safely out of the way. A wave of dizziness washed over me, so I closed my eyes and willed myself to calm down. I was roughed up but not injured. I'd probably sound like a chain-smoker for a few days, but everything would heal, and I'd be back to myself in no time. And where would that get me? Back in my bedroom at my parents' house? Returned to a time before Ray showed me how good life could be? Tears filled my eyes and pushed against my eyelids. I was seconds away from bawling like a baby and making a massive fool of myself.

The EMT lifted the stethoscope from my chest, but I kept my eyes shut. "I don't like the way your lungs sound. I think it's best you head to the hospital for further evaluation."

Unable to speak without giving my devastation away, I just shook my head. Footsteps approached from Ray's direction, and I hoped it was the other first responder coming over to assess the situation. But I recognized the no-nonsense stride, which only made my eyes well up more. I'd fallen in love with Ray, and I'd never get the chance to tell him. The surrounding air stirred as Ray reached the gurney, and the remaining hair on my arms stood at attention to salute him.

"Atticus." Ray's voice was gentle, but I knew the look I'd see if I gave in and opened my eyes. "Please go to the hospital and get checked out." Then he said the one thing that would guarantee my cooperation. "Do it for me, okay?"

I squeezed my eyelids tighter but gave him a slight nod.

"Do you want me to call your parents for you?" Ray asked.

The sudden panic nearly made me capitulate and meet his gaze, but I held steady and simply shook my head. "I only want you," I whispered hoarsely.

Warm lips landed on my forehead, and the tears I'd held in check cascaded down my cheeks. Gentle fingers brushed them away, but they just kept coming. Ray withdrew his hand and said, "I have to stick around here for a little while longer, but I'll be at the hospital as soon as I can."

I forced my eyes open and met his gaze. Maybe Ray believed his words, but his somber eyes told the truth. Someone from RAVEN would show up at the hospital, but it wouldn't be him. I was too devastated to say or do anything but give him a slight nod. Ray kept his eyes locked on mine for a few seconds before one of the firemen called him away. The EMT strapped me to the gurney for transport, and they loaded me into the back of the ambulance. Ray kept his back to me the entire time, and I wanted to howl at the unfairness of it all.

The rig rolled forward, and a siren split the air once more, taking my last nerve and running it through a paper shredder. To distract myself, I tried to guess which guy would show up in Ray's place. Archer would seduce someone, Ethan would bring his golden retriever energy, Nico would offer comedic relief, and Vaughn would bring a calm assurance that everything would be all right. I knew in my heart who Ray would choose and was proven right when the medical team finally allowed my visitor back after what seemed like hours. They hadn't told me who had been pacing the waiting room floors, but they hadn't needed to.

The curtain whisked to the side, and Vaughn entered my triage area with the ease of someone who'd known me for years, not weeks. I'd run through a gauntlet of emotions while waiting for this moment, trying to figure out how I wanted to handle the situation. By sending Vaughn, Ray signaled we were through, and I didn't fucking accept that.

"No," I simply said. My voice was a little raspy, but much stronger than it had been before my breathing treatment.

Vaughn's brow rose as he dropped into the chair next to my bed.

"Hell no. Ray's not getting away with this."

"What do you have in mind?" Vaughn asked.

"This situation calls for a grand gesture, and I know just the thing."

Vaughn's mouth curved into a huge smile. "I knew you were worthy of him."

CHAPTER 22

RAYDEN

I CHECKED MY PHONE AGAIN FOR THE UMPTEENTH TIME, HOPING FOR an update from Vaughn or a text from Atticus, but I knew neither would happen. Vaughn had been very disappointed by my cowardice when I asked him to go to the hospital to be with Atticus, though he hadn't said it. The words had been unnecessary because the sadness in Vaughn's expression had told me everything I needed to know.

As for Atticus, I still had his phone, so there was no way for him to text me, even if he wanted to. And why should he? I'd proven myself to be unworthy of him in so many ways. I'd failed to keep Atticus safe, and worse, I hadn't kept the promises I'd made to him just a few weeks ago. So much for my commitment to communication and honesty.

I'd used the fire as an excuse to resurrect old walls because it had been safer and less scary. Telling Atticus I needed to remain at Silver Maple to answer questions and supervise the situation wasn't a lie, but it was only half the truth. Stand and deliver had been my motto for as long as I could remember, but I'd misplaced my priorities, choosing duty over his well-being. And that was almost as unforgivable as telling Atticus I'd meet him at the hospital.

Atticus had known the truth; it shimmered in his sad eyes as he wept.

I'd tried to comfort him but had only smeared the soot and offered a half-baked promise. I would see his heartbroken hazel eyes every night in my sleep, but damn it, Atticus lived to love again, even though it wouldn't be me. And with that depressing thought, I took myself to the kitchen to get a beer.

When I turned back to the living room, I saw Atticus's influence everywhere. His favorite flip-flops were next to the balcony door, waiting for him to slide into them and enjoy a glass of wine at sunset. His current book was open and upside down on the coffee table, ready for him to pick up where he'd left off. The throw blanket was still draped over the captain's chair, where Atticus had flung it to sit on my lap, and later my—

I wouldn't let myself go there. Tears and boners didn't go well together.

Not that I'd actually cried…yet. That would come after I said the words we both knew were coming. I wouldn't suggest we stay friends because I couldn't do friendship with Atticus. He would move on and meet the love of his life, and I didn't want a front- or even a second-row seat. I didn't even want to be in the same stadium or even the same city when it happened. Hell, being on the same planet when Atticus fell in love and started a life with someone else was too much for me to take.

Then why the fuck aren't you fighting for him, dumbass?

The question came out of nowhere, the voice once as familiar as my own. *Javi.* He sounded so close that I spun around, expecting to find him standing in the apartment, but the room was empty. For years, I'd tried to recall the sound of Javi's voice, but I never could without replaying old videos on my phone. I'd once read that it was my brain's way of protecting me from trauma. Dissociative amnesia or something.

But my brain chose this exact moment to recall the playful derision Javi could inject into his voice when I was on the verge of doing something stupid. I could even picture how he'd look if he were with me just then, arms crossed over his chest and shaking his head slowly. Closing my eyes, I imagined what he'd say to me if he could. Would he say he was proud of me for not giving up after he died? Or maybe Javi would promise me that happier days lay ahead if I were brave enough to try. He'd probably say he liked Atticus and would compliment my good taste. Or he'd say—

It's about damn time.

My bark of laughter echoed through the silent room because that sounded more like the Javi I loved. And damn it, I had loved him. I would've given my life for Javi's, but fate hadn't given me the opportunity to trade places. Tears of misery burned my eyes and spilled down my face. I'd lived three years in a hellish purgatory of my own choosing until Atticus came along and made me want to take chances. I let my guard down and invited Atticus in. And I got careless. I never should have taken anyone's word that the fire detection, alert, and suppression systems had been properly maintained and inspected.

And what about that fucking door handle on the art supply closet? Damn it. I should've insisted it get replaced after Atticus and I got trapped in there the first time. That stupid temporary fix had nearly cost Atticus his life. My chest hurt so badly that I had to set my beer down before I dropped it. Was this a heart attack? Was that why I heard Javi's voice so damn clearly in my head after all this time?

You're an idiot, Ray. You're having a fucking panic attack because you're going to lose the best damn thing that's happened to you since…forever.

Gritting my teeth against the pain, I pressed a hand to my chest. "Thanks, Jav," I wheezed.

Box breathing, super stud. You know what to do.

I breathed in, held, breathed out, and held again for four seconds each. I felt a little better, but not good enough. I repeated the cycle until the trembling subsided. I opened my eyes, feeling centered and present.

"Thanks, Jav."

Did I really want to return to the way things were before Atticus crashed into my life? Could I really give up the laughter and kisses we shared? Did I want to wake up to an empty bed in the morning? Would sacrificing our happiness guarantee his safety? The answer to all my questions was no, so why the hell was I moping around my apartment and allowing Atticus to believe we were over? That's exactly the signal I sent to him when I asked Vaughn to go to the hospital in my place. He'd survived a fire only to have me stomp on his heart. Maybe Atticus was truly better off without me.

Fuck that! It was my voice ringing through my head this time, and I sounded damn sure of my decision.

I reached for my keys just as music filtered into my apartment from somewhere. The song was familiar, but my sluggish brain struggled to name it. The music grew louder, and recognition kicked in like a jolt of electricity. "In Your Eyes" by Peter Gabriel. The song got louder as if the music was getting closer to the building. Was it coming from a moving vehicle? Who was jamming out to eighties love ballads outside my apartment? And why did it have to be that song? An irrational hope bloomed in my heart as I moved to the wall of windows overlooking the property.

My breath caught in my throat when I saw Atticus standing on the lawn, holding a boom box over his head. And he wasn't alone. My faithful, ride-or-die guys stood nearby, wearing ridiculous grins on their faces as they stared up at my windows. They couldn't see me, I was certain, yet they knew I was there because the four of them waved for me to come out.

I ignored them and turned my attention to Atticus, who wore an oversized trench coat over a scrub top and the khaki cargo shorts he'd worn to work. Where the hell had he gotten the coat and boom box? The latter might've been in his storage unit, but it looked like a new version. I knew I was right when Archer aimed something small in his hand toward the radio and turned the music down. Fuck. Who'd given him the remote control?

"Get your ass out here!" Archer yelled. "Kitten has something he wants to say."

I growled as I made my way to the sliding door and stepped onto the balcony. "I told you not to call him cutesy names."

Archer shrugged and said, "And I told you not to fuck this up."

He had. At least once a day since I brought Atticus home the first time.

"But I—"

Archer aimed the remote at the boom box, and the music went up a few notches. Vaughn, Nico, and Ethan all swayed to the music and laughed as if this was the best thing they'd ever seen. Ignoring them, I turned my full attention to Atticus. They'd cleaned his face, but he looked pale and drawn, and that damn boom box looked heavy. I noted a slight tremor in his arms and gestured for him to put it down, but he shook his head. Archer aimed the remote at the boom box and turned the music down.

"There's only one play here, Ray Ray. Don't let us down." Then he cranked the volume back up before I could respond.

I locked my gaze with Atticus and saw his determination. He'd stand out there all night if he had to, but I wouldn't do that to him. Instead of ducking inside the apartment and exiting like a sane person would, I swung my legs over the side of the balcony, released the emergency stairs, and rode them down to the ground. One grand gesture deserved another. Vaughn, Ethan, and Nico cheered loudly while Archer swooned with his hand over his heart. I could've done without the audience when I ate crow, but fuck it.

Hazel eyes and a wide smile greeted me as I approached Atticus. His mouth moved, but I couldn't hear a damn thing he said over the music.

Turning my head, I hollered, "Turn the music down!"

Instead of aiming the remote at the radio, Archer cupped his ear and mouthed, "What?"

"*Turn the music down!*"

Archer squinted at me, then looked at the other guys, shaking his head as if he didn't have a clue what I'd said. Vaughn, Ethan, and Nico were laughing too hard at our antics to be of any help. With a growl, I took the boom box from Atticus and marched toward the river. That got Archer's attention because he turned off the music completely. I returned to Atticus and set the radio on the ground by his feet. Cupping his face, I pressed our lips together for a quick kiss before meeting his eyes. I poured every ounce of emotion I felt into this one glance. I needed him to see not only the regret I felt for the way I behaved, but the hope Atticus instilled in my heart and the adoration I felt for him.

"Please forgive me," I whispered as I wrapped my arms around him and pressed my forehead to his. "I was scared and stupid and…" Words failed me. "So damn wrong. You are everything I want, everything I need. And damn, it's terrifying. But the idea of not having you in my life is far scarier. I'd reached the realization and was about to come find you just before you John Cusack-ed me."

"Well," Atticus sighed. "It's a good thing you came around to my way of thinking because I wasn't giving up on us without a fight." He kissed me hard, lingering for a long time before pulling back. "We have some things to work out."

"We do," I agreed. "It won't be easy. I'm a lot of work."

"Easy is lame, and I'm not afraid to get dirty." Atticus looked over at our audience and chuckled. "Maybe we can continue this conversation someplace more private?"

"If not for your injured ribs, I'd throw you over my shoulder and carry you up the fire escape," I said.

"Not in this lifetime."

"We'll do this the normal way, then." I laced my fingers with his and led Atticus toward the building, leaving the guys to deal with the boom box. I figured it would end up in the communal room for get-togethers and barbecues. Once inside the building, I backed into the elevator, tugging Atticus in with me. I captured his mouth in a hot, greedy kiss, noting that he still smelled of acrid smoke. My pulse raced, and my brain tried to conjure up all the horrible things that could've happened to him, but I held Atticus tighter instead of pushing him away.

The elevator stopped on the third floor, and the door opened with a chime. I didn't stop kissing Atticus as we navigated the corridor or when I punched in the code to my apartment. I barely separated our mouths when I stripped off his clothes before working on mine. By the time we reached the mezzanine, we were both completely naked. Atticus stepped toward the bed, but I guided him to the shower instead.

He pulled back then and wrinkled his nose. "Yeah, I smell like smoke and hospital antiseptic."

"I only smell the smoke," I said. "I want you to smell like me again."

Atticus practically purred and wrapped his arms around my waist. "I really want to smell like you too."

On our way to the bathroom, I glanced down at the loft and noticed the trench coat lying on the floor. "The boom box is easy to figure out, but where the hell did you get that coat?"

"We swung by a thrift store."

I swatted him on the ass. "Promise me you'll never change."

"Okay."

I took my time washing Atticus from head to toe, shampooing his hair twice because he loved the way it felt, and because I loved making him purr like a kitten. Atticus tried to take the towel from my hand and dry himself, but I wrestled it away from him and rubbed the terry cloth over his skin.

"Are you going to get oversolicitous every time you get scared where I'm concerned?" Atticus asked.

I looked up from my task to see if he was upset, but his half-lidded eyes sparkled with adoration. "Is that going to be a problem?"

He looked down at his crotch, and I followed his gaze to his erection. "Doesn't seem that way."

Tossing the towel to the floor, I said, "I don't want to be an overbearing ass."

"You won't be."

"How do you know?" I asked.

"Because it's one thing we're going to work on." Atticus took my hand and wrapped it around the base of his dick. "But later. The best remedy after a traumatic event is to remind ourselves that we're safe and alive." He rose on his toes and kissed me.

I placed my free hand on his hip and guided him toward the bed. "Healthy and horny?"

"Exactly. So fuck me already."

"Huh-uh," I said. A fast, hard tumble wasn't what the moment called for.

"No?" Atticus arched a brow while his mouth formed a cute little pout.

He was so damn adorable and precious, and that is what I wanted him to feel when I put my hands, mouth, and body on his. I could tell Atticus my intentions, or I could show him what was in my heart. I lowered my head and kissed him as I guided him onto the bed. The tension melted from Atticus's body when I covered his, and he hooked his legs around the back of my thighs to keep me near. As if I were going anywhere. He'd need time to believe I was in this for the long haul because I'd screwed up. And I'd likely fuck up again, but I silently vowed that Atticus would never question my commitment.

Kissing a trail down his neck, I felt his pulse hammering beneath my lips. Atticus tangled his fingers in my hair to guide me lower, but I ignored his urgency to relearn every inch of his beautiful body. I eventually licked a path to his belly button, nuzzled my nose in his happy trail, and kissed across his pelvis until his erection brushed against my cheek.

"Please suck me," Atticus begged.

I kissed the tip of his dick but didn't take him into my mouth. "Not yet."

"You're so mean."

Chuckling at his outrage, I eased lower to kiss the juncture of his thigh and sink my teeth into his tender skin. My nose bumped up against his taut balls as I sucked on his taint.

"Oh god. Suck me."

I lifted my head and said, "Almost."

Atticus pressed the head of his cock against my mouth and smeared his precum across my lips. "Now."

I sucked him down to the root, finally giving Atticus what he wanted, but I drew back slowly, taking the blowjob at the pace I needed. Gentle fingers tensed and tugged at my hair, but I took my time, loving Atticus slowly and thoroughly until his body quivered with need. Only then did I let his dick slide free from my mouth.

Atticus whimpered his protest, and I kissed his stomach as I retrieved the lube.

"I've got you, baby," I promised.

He sighed in relief when I slicked my fingers, and I bit back a grin because I knew his frustrations would return. Several minutes of prep later, Atticus slapped his hand against my shoulder.

"How many dicks do you plan to shove in there? I'm open and ready for business." And in case I didn't know what he meant, he wrapped a fist around my dick and stroked.

I closed my eyes and moaned as stars exploded behind my eyelids. I thrust into the tight sleeve of his fist, and Atticus released me to thrust the bottle of lube at me.

"Huh-uh," he said. "Slick up that monster dick and give us what we both want."

Who was I to refuse or refute him? I made quick work of slicking up my dick because anything longer would've ended the party much too quickly. Poising at his entrance, I locked my gaze on his and pushed past the tight ring of muscles, easing into his snug heat. I rested my forehead against his while he adjusted to the penetration, and I reined in the urge to rut like an animal.

"Please," Atticus whimpered.

And I would not make him beg again. Capturing his mouth, I kissed Atticus deeply, my tongue rubbing against his as I worked my dick in and out of him. Arousal built as my pace quickened. Atticus vibrated under me, and his entrance tightened around my shaft. He broke our kiss to cry out, pushing his head against the pillow and arching his neck so beautifully.

"Don't stop."

"Never." I powered into Atticus, thrusting deeply as I watched his expression morph from desperation to exquisite pleasure.

Atticus opened his mouth in a silent cry as his hot release splattered between us. His channel clenched tightly around my dick and triggered my orgasm. My balls tightened and emptied as I gave in to the urge to rut and fuck and claim him. Sinking my teeth into his neck, I marked Atticus. *Mine, mine, mine.* The word echoed around in my brain, its rhythm matching the wild pounding of my heart, and I loved the way it sounded. Spent, I collapsed on top of Atticus, though careful not to give him my full weight, and buried my nose against his neck.

Atticus stroked his hands up and down my back, then slid his fingers into my hair. "Yours, yours, yours."

I hadn't realized I'd said the word out loud, but I didn't want to take it back. Lifting my head, I stared into his beautiful eyes. "I am yours if you'll have me."

Atticus snorted and dug his feet into my ass, nudging my softening dick a little deeper inside him. "Every fucking chance I get." His expression sharpened around the edges, though his eyes remained soft. "I'm going to prove that your heart is safe with me."

"You have nothing to prove," I replied before kissing him softly. Easing my dick free, I lay on the bed beside Atticus and pulled him into my arms. "It's the universe that has some explaining to do." Pressing my lips to his temple, I added, "And I have a lot of healing to do." I couldn't do it on my own. Previous therapists might not have worked, but that didn't mean none of them would. I just needed to find the right fit. But living without fear and being the best version of myself was something I wanted, not just for Atticus, but for myself. "Can you be patient with me?"

"Yes," Atticus said and kissed me. "But can you promise the same? My desire for independence is going to conflict with your need to keep me safe."

"Yes, I will." I stroked my hand up and down his back. "We deserve this happiness." To admit as much felt like the biggest leap forward I'd taken in a very long time.

"We deserve each other," Atticus said. "And something delicious to eat for dinner. Maybe some ice cream."

"How does delivery sound?" The idea of leaving my apartment didn't appeal to me. Hell, I didn't want to leave my bed, but bedside delivery wasn't an option unless I wanted to involve the guys. And fuck no.

Those assholes probably wouldn't leave. I could put on a pair of pants long enough to meet the delivery driver downstairs.

"Perfect."

A song started playing somewhere in the apartment. It took me a second to recognize the tune, and then I burst into laughter as Atticus tensed in my embrace. "'Parents Just Don't Understand'?" I asked when the music stopped as suddenly as it had started.

Groaning, Atticus plastered himself tighter against my body as if he were trying to burrow beneath my skin. "It's the ringtone for my parents."

"I figured that one out for myself."

Atticus jerked and raised his head. "That's my phone. I thought I'd lost it in the fire."

I cupped his cheek and pulled him down for a kiss. "Angus had stolen it from the art room when he'd snuck in to smoke." Christ, Atticus had almost died. The panic swelled in my chest, pushing against my rib cage. I would not give in to fear. I would not.

"Breathe," Atticus whispered. "I'm right here. And I'm not going anywhere."

His phone rang again, and he huffed out a frustrated sigh. "Okay. Maybe I'm going downstairs to answer my phone, but I promise not to go any farther. And I'll be right back." By the time he stood up, the call had switched over to his voicemail.

I forced myself to sit up. "I'll go with you to find my phone and order dinner. What sounds good?"

"Anything. And I have a feeling I'm going to need chocolate."

The perfect restaurant came to mind. I could order a delicious steak dinner for two and a massive piece of chocolate cake to share. Or would he want his own? The Fresh Prince started serenading us again before Atticus was halfway down the stairs. Irritation lengthened his stride and straightened his spine, and Atticus caught the third call before it rolled over.

"Hi, Mom. Sorry, I—"

A discernible sob came from the other end of the connection.

I bolted out of bed and took the stairs as quickly as I could, coming to a stop next to Atticus, who scrunched up his face in concern as he tried to make out what she was saying. I couldn't distinguish individual words, just complete devastation. She took a breath, and I heard the words "on the news" and "fire."

"Oh no," Atticus said. "Mom, I'm okay. I didn't realize my name would get released, or I would've called you." More sounds came through the phone, but it sounded more like the wah-wah-wah sounds the teacher made on *Charlie Brown*. "I'm fine. I promise. Did Aunt Ronni tell you about the fire?" His hazel eyes went wide, and Atticus said, "Picture? What picture?"

I retrieved my phone from the counter to do a quick internet search, but it wasn't necessary. I had more than a dozen messages in the RAVEN group chat and knew the picture would be in there somewhere. Sure enough, Archer shared a photo of me running out of the burning building with Atticus cradled in my arms. There was a link to an article touting my heroics, but I didn't click on that nonsense. Atticus had saved himself. I'd just come in at the end to give him an assist. I rolled my eyes and turned the phone around so he could see it. Atticus waggled his eyebrows and licked his lips.

"Yes, Ray is very strong," he told his mom. "And the bravest man I know."

I rolled my eyes, and Atticus tweaked my nipple hard in retaliation.

"Dinner?" Atticus asked. "Um, well, we were about to order in and—"

The tone of voice changed on the other end of the connection, from worry to formidable.

"Yes, ma'am. Ray and I will be there in thirty minutes." Atticus disconnected the call and stared down at his phone. "I'm in so much trouble. I might never hear the end of this."

I bit back my laugh as I turned to go upstairs.

"Where are you going?" Atticus called out.

"Upstairs to shower. I didn't make a good impression on your parents when we met. I want to change that."

Atticus snorted. "You made a great impression on them. My mom couldn't quit ogling you, and even my dad had given his approval."

I stopped on the stairs and faced him. "Really?"

"Uh-huh." Atticus started up the steps, stopping when he reached me. "And they'll probably build a shrine in your honor now that you pulled me out of a burning building—"

I silenced him with a firm kiss. "I didn't save you."

"Oh yes, you did."

"No. You got yourself out of the closet."

"But you would've kicked down the door," Atticus countered.

"I didn't have to because you got it open." Cocking my head to the side, I said, "How did you get it open?"

"I found a paint key under a shelving unit when I dropped to the ground to get fresher air. It's still in my pants pocket, I think."

Pulling Atticus in for a hug, I said, "I'm going to build a shrine around that damn paint key."

A hand landed swiftly on my backside. "Better get moving. The quicker we assure my parents I'm alive, the faster we get back here and celebrate privately."

"After we stop for chocolate cake," I added as I hoisted Atticus into my arms.

Looping his arms around my neck, Atticus pressed his forehead to my cheek. "See, you are my hero."

EPILOGUE

ATTICUS

September

WHAT WAS BETTER THAN THE FRIDAY AFTERNOON BEFORE A THREE-day weekend? A Friday afternoon before a three-day weekend that included a birthday party with punch and cupcakes.

I raised my plastic cup to toast Gabby, our birthday girl. "May this be your best year yet."

She clinked her cup against mine. "Hear, hear!" Gabby looked at the variety of cupcake flavors in wide-eyed wonder. "They all look so delicious. How will I pick one?"

"It's your birthday," I reminded her. "Why choose?"

"You are a genius. I'll start with the chocolate."

"Can't go wrong there," I said. "I think I'll go with key lime."

We finished our punch and ate our cupcakes while chatting about our Labor Day weekend plans. Gabby came from an enormous family who would host endless barbecues and pool parties over the next three days. My plans with Ray were much tamer in comparison, with only two barbecues planned—one with my family and one with the guys. My sister and her husband were coming home for the holidays, bringing my nephew and niece, and I couldn't wait for everyone to meet Ray. He was an exceptional man, and I was the luckiest person in the world to call him mine.

He'd be heading out for a therapy session soon, and I wanted him to enjoy a cupcake before he left. I wished Gabby a wonderful weekend and picked a fluffy pink strawberry cupcake for him. I debated grabbing one for Vaughn too, but he'd vowed to cut back on refined sugar. When I turned toward the door, I spotted Cammy and baby Amelia entering the room. She visited frequently since both the staff and residents loved to see her and the baby. Cammy's face lit up when her gaze connected with mine, and I made a beeline for her and Amelia.

"Hey," I said, giving them a one-armed hug so I didn't drop Ray's cupcake. "How are you?"

"The best I've ever been," Cammy replied, and her megawatt smile proved it.

I stroked a finger over Amelia's chubby arm. "And how's this sweet angel?"

"She's amazing."

"Are you the Amazing Amelia?"

She smiled at me, and my heart swelled. "Oh my god. I just can't with your cuteness. How do you ever put her down?"

"I don't." Cammy kissed the top of her daughter's head and patted her bottom.

"Because she's the prettiest little cutie ever," I declared.

The baby giggled softly, and I nearly swooned on the spot.

"Looks like Millie is a big fan of yours." Cammy smiled at me and said, "And I am too. Knowing you're here with the residents has made it so much easier to enjoy time at home with my daughter."

"Thank you. That's one of the loveliest compliments I've ever received."

"Well, you've earned it. The Silver Maple residents and staff absolutely adore you."

Swallowing hard, I said. "I love them too." I would miss them so much when my interim position ended in November.

Cammy smiled and smoothed her hand over Amelia's red gingham romper. "I know you do, and that's why I resigned from my position without guilt."

"What?"

My pulse spiked with excitement, and I didn't bother tempering it.

Cammy's resignation didn't automatically mean I'd get the position, but it allowed me to put myself out there and go for it.

Cammy smiled and nodded. "I want to focus my attention on Amelia, and I'm fortunate enough to have the opportunity."

"I'm so happy for you."

Caitlyn entered the room and smiled when she saw the two of us chatting. "Just the person I was looking for," she said to me. "Do you have a few minutes to chat in my office?"

"Sure."

"Great." Eyeing Ray's strawberry cupcake, Caitlyn held up a finger. "Let me just grab one of those first."

She chose a lemon meringue and gestured toward the exit.

Cammy squeezed my arm and whispered, "Congratulations. You deserve this, Kit."

"Thank you."

"I assume Cammy told you her news," Caitlyn said when I caught up to her.

"She did. I'm thrilled for her."

"I am too. And I'm just as happy about the conversation we're about to have," Caitlyn said.

"That sounds promising."

My impending unemployment had been weighing heavily on me, even though I'd padded my savings account with the proceeds from my eBay store. I'd researched freelance jobs in computer engineering fields, but none of it appealed to me after working at Silver Maple.

"Let's cut to the chase." Caitlyn gestured for me to have a seat as she settled in behind her desk. "I want to offer you the permanent position as Silver Maple's activities coordinator."

"I accept," I replied before my ass touched the chair.

Laughing, Caitlyn pushed a folder toward me. "You didn't even look at the contract to know what you're agreeing to."

"Doesn't matter. I love working with the residents and staff here. I'm all in."

Caitlyn shook her head. "Love your enthusiasm, but let me go over some highlights. You can take the contract home and read it over the weekend."

"Okay."

"You'll go from an hourly to a salary position with a substantial raise," Caitlyn said.

I couldn't imagine it would get better than that, but then she started detailing the benefit package that came with the position. "I'm ready to sign," I said in disbelief.

Caitlyn nudged the folder closer and smiled. "Take this home and let me know if you have questions. If not, we'll sign the contract on Tuesday. Your new salary and benefits would go into effect immediately."

"Wow. This is incredible. Thank you for taking a chance on me, even if my Aunt Ronni nudged you to hire me originally."

Frowning, Caitlyn said, "No, she didn't. Ronni handed me your resume and said that you're a good egg. Frankly, I think she undersold your talents." Caitlyn placed her elbows on her desk and leaned toward me. "You're the one who bowled me over during your interview. I knew the moment you sat down that you were the perfect fit for Silver Maple. In fact, I'd already talked to the board about expanding the budget to include a second position for you once Cammy returned. I still think you could use help, even part-time, but that's something we can talk about later." She pointed at me. "It's one thing for someone else to understate your talents, but you need to stop underselling yourself."

Smiling wryly, I said, "I'm working on it."

"Good, now get out of here before I snatch that cupcake and eat it."

"Thank you, Caitlyn."

"No, thank you."

I tucked the folder under my arm and headed toward her door. When I pulled it open, a guy about my age stood on the other side with his hand raised as if prepared to knock. He was a few inches taller than me and had blond hair, pretty brown eyes, and the most flawless skin I'd ever seen. I lived with the sexiest man on Earth, and even this guy's appearance flustered me.

"Oh, hello," the stranger said.

"Hi. Are you looking for Caitlyn?" *Duh, dumbass. He's standing outside her door.*

"Dorian!" Caitlyn exclaimed. "I'm so glad you're here. I want to introduce you to Kit, who is our activities coordinator at Silver Maple."

What were the odds Dorian's parents had named him after a fictional character too? Maybe I'd get to know him well enough to ask. I extended my hand, and Dorian shook it. "Nice to meet you."

"Same," he replied.

"We've hired Dorian to help us with our public relations issues," Caitlyn said with a light grimace. Ray's heroic rescue replaced Bobby's coverage in the media for a while, but salaciousness would always prevail. "Dorian's primary focus is managing Silver Maple's social media presence, so I imagine the two of you will work together frequently."

"And I already have ideas for our first campaign," Dorian told Caitlyn.

I gestured to the hallway with the cupcake. "I'll let you get to it."

Dorian stepped aside so I could exit Caitlyn's office, and I called out, "Have a good weekend."

Ray grinned broadly when he spotted me.

"Are you happy to see me or the cupcake?" I asked.

"Always you."

Vaughn looked up from the monitors and zeroed in on the pink confection in my hand. "Did I say I wanted to cut back on refined sugar?"

"Yes," Ray and I said together.

"I hate you both," Vaughn snarled and reached for the flavored sparkling water he took everywhere.

"You love us," Ray teased.

Vaughn rolled his eyes. "Yeah, but get out of here, and take that gross cupcake with you."

Out in the corridor, Ray peeled off the cupcake liner and devoured it in three bites.

I wiped the icing smear off his mouth and licked my fingers. "Mmm. That might be better than the key lime."

"Oh man. Key lime? Too bad there's not enough time for me to help set up for the life drawing class *and* mow through the rest of the cupcakes."

"You don't have to help me," I told him.

Ray draped his arm around my lower back and pulled me closer as we walked. "You're much sweeter than any cupcake."

"Charmer."

"Nah, that's Archer," Ray said.

"And speak of the devil," I said, pointing to Archer walking ahead of us.

Ray stuck two fingers in his mouth and whistled shrilly to get his attention.

Archer stopped and waited for us to catch up. Then he grinned like the

Cheshire cat, showing off a mouthful of brilliant teeth. "I'm ready for my modeling debut."

"Dude," Ray said. "Did you whiten your teeth for this gig?"

Shrugging, Archer said, "I want to give the people their money's worth."

I looked between Archer and Ray and wondered if some wires got crossed. "The attendees didn't pay for the class."

"Not directly," Archer said. "But they pay a fuck ton to live here, so it's fair to say they funded the class."

Ray leaned closer and narrowed his eyes. "Why does your face look shiny? Did you run here?"

"I used a face mask to give me glass skin," Archer replied.

"What?" Ray poked Archer's cheek with his finger. "Feels real to me."

Smacking his hand away, Archer said, "Don't be obtuse."

"I'm not," Ray said. "I don't have a clue what you're talking about."

"You're going to wake up one day and regret the way you've neglected your skin," Archer said.

Ray just grinned. "Today's not that day."

Archer waved him off and walked ahead of us.

"I'm glad he's taking your life drawing class seriously," Ray said.

"Maybe too seriously."

"He's told everyone that you had to move the class to the auditorium because of his popularity," Ray said. "Not because the new arts and literature building is still under construction or because your first class was so successful. It's all because of him."

"Archer's participation sure doesn't hurt attendance," I said.

"Can't you let me be annoyed with him?" Ray asked.

"Sure, but can it wait until after I tell you about my amazing news?"

"Of course."

I showed him the folder and relayed the conversation I had with Caitlyn. He stopped in his tracks and wrapped me in an enormous bear hug.

"I'm so happy for you, baby," Ray said. "You deserve this."

"Thank you."

"Let's go out and celebrate tonight. Just the two of us."

"Sounds perfect," I said. Movement to my right caught my attention, and I turned to find Dorian approaching us. "Oh, hey."

Dorian smiled and volleyed his doe eyes between us before introducing himself to Ray. "I was just heading to the auditorium to talk to the model posing for your life drawing class," he told me. "This would make the perfect story for Silver Maple's social media accounts, but I need them to sign a release before I can use their images."

Ray snorted. "You won't have any issues getting that prancing peacock to sign the release. I'll introduce you."

The three of us continued to the auditorium, making small talk to avoid an awkward silence. Once we got there, I pointed out Archer to Dorian, who groaned wearily.

Uh-oh. "Do you know Archer?" I asked.

Dorian's cheeks turned pink, and he said, "In a roundabout way." Then he straightened his shoulders, notched his chin up higher, and marched forward.

Archer turned as Dorian approached and blasted the sexy blond with a brilliant smile. Where most men would melt into a puddle, Dorian remained unaffected, at least externally.

"What do you think their deal is?" I asked.

Ray tugged me around to face him. "Don't know, but you can bet we'll find out." He brushed wayward strands of hair off my forehead and smiled. "I should get going to my session, but I'll meet you at home afterward to make plans." He kissed me once more, lingering a little longer this time. "I love you."

God, I'd never get sick of hearing that. "I love you too."

Walking backward so I could watch him go, I thought of all the beautiful ways my life had changed since meeting Ray. Then I bumped into a row of seats and nearly flipped backward over them. I stood up quickly and dusted myself off. Well, fuck a duck. Some things sure as hell hadn't changed.

The End!

Staying in touch is easier than ever and prettier too! Would you like to follow me on all the socials, signup for my newsletter, or join my Facebook reader's group? You can do all those things by checking out this handy hub on my website @ www.aimeenicolewalker.com/links

OTHER BOOKS BY
AIMEE NICOLE WALKER

Curl Up and Dye Mysteries

Dyeing to be Loved

Something to Dye For

Dyed and Gone to Heaven

I Do, or Dye Trying

A Dye Hard Holiday

Ride or Dye

Curl Up and Dye Box Set

Road to Blissville Series

Unscripted Love

Someone to Call My Own

Nobody's Prince Charming

This Time Around

Smoke in the Mirror

Inside Out

Prescription for Love

Welcome to Blissville Collection (Both M/M Blissville series)

Volume One

Volume Two

The Lady is Mine Series

The Lady is a Thief

The Lady Stole My Heart

Queen City Rogue Series

Broken Halos

Wicked Games

Beautiful Trauma

Zero Hour Series

Ground Zero

Devil's Hour

Zero Divergence

Zero Hour Box Set

Sawyer and Royce: Matrimony and Mayhem

The Magnolia Murders

Marriage is Murder

Killer Honeymoon

Matrimony and Mayhem Box Set

Sawyer and Royce: Felonies and Fatherhood

The Paternity Puzzle

The Sinner's Son

Brokered Beytrayals

Sinister in Savannah Series

Ride the Lightning

Mr. Perfect

Pretty Poison

Sinister in Savannah Box Set

Savannah Universe Standalone Books

Invisible Strings

Bad at Love

About Last Night

Just Say When

Single in Savannah Box Set

Standalone Novels

Second Wind

Fated Hearts Series

Chasing Mr. Wright

Rhythm of Us

Surrender Your Heart

Perfect Fit

Redemption Ridge Series

Guys Like Him

The Fortunate Son

Saints Like Him

Friends Like Them

The Keeper

The Beautiful Mess

Starts With a Bang

Redemption Ridge Volume I

Coauthored with Nicholas Bella

Undisputed

Circle of Darkness (Genesis Circle, Book 1)

Circle of Trust (Genesis Circle, Book 2)

ACKNOWLEDGMENTS

Many, many thanks to Charity, Sandra, and Lori for your editing services and for keeping me in line. These ladies are consummate professionals and are pure joy to work with. And much love to Natasha Snow and Wander Aguiar for this gorgeous cover and to Stacey Ryan Blake for her stunning interior designs. All of you make my books sparkle and shine so beautifully—inside and out. I thank my lucky stars that I get to work with such wonderfully talented people.

Sending much love to Melinda James Rueter and Racheal Yunk for bravely reading my rough drafts and providing priceless feedback. And I don't know where I'd be without CC Belle, my amazing personal assistant, who brings organization and so much joy into my life. Love you, ladies!

xoxo
Aimee

ABOUT
AIMEE NICOLE WALKER

Aimee Nicole Walker is an international bestselling author of Male/Male contemporary romance and romantic suspense novels. Her stories guarantee hunks with big…hearts, lots of humor and heat, and the occasional homicide. Aimee is a lifelong dreamer, an avid reader, and an off-key singer. Only two of those traits help her craft captivating characters and charming communities where everyone is welcome. She uses the other quirk to entertain her pets during writing breaks.

Aimee has loved the same guy for over thirty years. Her husband is the reason she can write romance novels, and he's possibly inspired a fictional murder plot a time or ten. They share three adult children, two adorable grandsons, and a menagerie of pets that don't include goats or donkeys…yet. Love inspires everything she does, books keep her sane, and coffee is the magic elixir that fuels her day.

Let's stay in touch!

Would you like to learn more about my work, sign up for my newsletter, or follow my social media accounts? Here's your fast pass to all things Aimee: aimeenicolewalker.com/links

www.ingramcontent.com/pod-product-compliance
Lightning Source LLC
LaVergne TN
LVHW091049080826
845145LV00002B/675
9781948273510